The Gift of Christmas

ROSEWOOD PRESS

979-8-9904728-3-9

The Gift of Christmas

Copyright © 2024 by Megan Leavell

All rights reserved. No part of this book may be reproduced in any form or by any electronic or mechanical means, including information storage and retrieval systems, without written permission from the author, except for the use of brief quotations in a book review.

This is a work of fiction. Names, characters, businesses, places, events and incidents are either the products of the author's imagination or used in a fictitious manner. Any resemblance to actual persons, living or dead, or actual events is purely coincidental.

Cover design by Evelyne Labelle

Praise for Olivia Miles

"Olivia Miles is an expert at creating a sweet romantic plot and setting endearing characters within it, which ultimately results in a delightful read." ~ *RT Book Reviews*

"A charming holiday tale of fresh starts, friendship and love with a heroine even Scrooge couldn't resist." ~ Sheila Roberts, *New York Times* bestselling author, for THE WINTER WEDDING PLAN

"Sweet, tender, and burgeoning with Christmas spirit and New England appeal, this engaging reunion tale sees one couple blissfully together, artfully setting the stage for the next book in the series."
~*Library Journal* for MISTLETOE ON MAIN STREET

"Hope Springs on Main Street is a sweet and worthy addition to your romance collection." ~ *USA Today*

"Olivia Miles weaves a beautiful story of healing and second chances."
~ RaeAnne Thayne, *New York Times* bestselling author, for HOPE SPRINGS ON MAIN STREET

"Readers seeking a peppermint-filled, cozy Christmas contemporary will be satisfied..." ~ *Publishers Weekly* for CHRISTMAS COMES TO MAIN STREET

Also by Olivia Miles

Stand Alone Titles

The Starlight Sisters

A Wedding in Driftwood Cove

The Heirloom Inn

Christmas in Winter Lake

Sunrise Sisters

A Memory So Sweet

A Promise to Keep

A Wish Come True

Evening Island

Meet Me at Sunset

Summer's End

The Lake House

The Blue Harbor Series

A Place for Us

Second Chance Summer

Because of You

Small Town Christmas

Return to Me

Then Comes Love

Finding Christmas

A New Beginning

Summer of Us

A Chance on Me

The Oyster Bay Series

Feels Like Home

Along Came You

Maybe This Time

This Thing Called Love

Those Summer Nights

Christmas at the Cottage

Still the One

One Fine Day

Had to Be You

The Misty Point Series

One Week to the Wedding

The Winter Wedding Plan

The Sweeter in the City Series

Sweeter in the Summer

Sweeter Than Sunshine

No Sweeter Love

One Sweet Christmas

The Briar Creek Series

Mistletoe on Main Street

A Match Made on Main Street

Hope Springs on Main Street

Love Blooms on Main Street

Christmas Comes to Main Street

Harlequin Special Edition

'Twas the Week Before Christmas

Recipe for Romance

For Faith, who will always have a home in my heart.

The Gift of Christmas

OLIVIA MILES

Chapter One
Melody

It was the most wonderful time of the year—usually. Melody Hart had always loved the holiday season, mostly because it gave her an excuse to sing all her favorite carols wherever she went, and without apology. Her singing often earned her smiles of passersby, and even the occasional role in an off-off-off-Broadway musical, but today it was only earning her a scowl from Santa.

With a heavy sigh, Melody adjusted her elf hat, stopped her cheerful tune mid-verse, and picked up a fresh roll of red tartan wrapping paper as another child wearing far too much winter clothing ran full force up the steps to Santa's throne and hurled himself onto the so-called jolly man's sturdy lap. She heard Frank (aka Santa for the young believers) struggle to suppress a grunt and smiled to herself. Served him right for forgetting his Christmas spirit, and not just because he was quite literally getting paid to feign some, but because this was Christmas. The most wonderful time of the year.

Granted, her gift-wrapping job at the Midtown department store wasn't exactly wonderful, but it was festive, and it was a great opportunity to be discovered by a Broadway casting director—that was if Santa here would ever allow her to get through an entire song without clearing his throat or shooting her dark looks from behind his fake wire spectacles.

"You're not tying the bows correctly," Dorothy, the head gift-wrapping elf, informed her in a clipped tone.

Melody didn't agree. "No," she explained, gesturing to her lopsided effort. "It's not meant to be perfect. It's meant to be whimsical." She'd even tried to make sure that no two bows were the same, so each person would feel like they received something special, created just for them.

Dorothy continued to peer at her with pinched lips. In the three weeks they'd worked together, Dorothy was yet to show her teeth, and in her twenty-five prided seasons of wrapping gifts, she had admittedly perfected everything from seamlessly lining up intricate patterns to shaping the perfect bow.

"Redo it, please."

Now Melody really was fighting to maintain her holiday spirit, and she had half a mind to tell Dorothy exactly where she could put her perfect velvet bows, but then she remembered that she hadn't been called for an audition in over a month, and she was losing hope of a callback for that last one by the hour.

It hadn't been a dream role—but she'd given up on those the day she hit thirty (even if her résumé did list her at a firm twenty-eight). Still, she'd rehearsed for days, delivering the three lines with just the right tone she'd settled on for a woman who had been let down by love yet again. She'd had plenty of practice in that department, and she thought she had struck just the right blend of disappointment, scorn, and a healthy sprinkle of cynicism.

Melody in real life was no fool, even if she was dressed like an elf, in public, right down to the striped stockings, and even if she did still share a cramped walk-up apartment with her ex-boyfriend, because as two struggling actors in New York City, neither of them could afford to move out, and Melody still couldn't bring herself to accept her sister's offer to move into her spare room. Commuting to Brooklyn would be bad enough, but she couldn't imagine confirming her sister's opinion that she was a screw-up.

"Oh!" Melody exclaimed when the cuckoo clock that had been set up as part of Santa's Village chimed the hour. "It's my break."

She gave Dorothy a smile that wasn't returned and hurried to the small employee room at the back of the toy department, where she fetched her worn leather handbag from its locker, made herself a strong cup of coffee, and then settled onto the lumpy couch that had never sold up in the furniture department.

She checked her phone for messages first, her heart sinking when she saw that she still hadn't received a callback for the last audition, and dropping further when there were no requests for more. Christmas was ten days away, she reminded herself as she sipped the hot drink, needing that extra caffeine boost to get through the second half of her four-hour shift. Surely things would pick up after the holidays.

Still, her stomach felt uneasy as she set her paper cup down on the scuffed coffee table and pulled a stack of mail she'd been avoiding from her bag. Bill, bill, bill. Her last gig had lasted six weeks, and that was back in the summer, at one of the playhouses on Long Island, and since then, her bills had just continued to pile up, and some of the envelopes were stamped with those scary "final notice" signs in red ink. The only reason she had heat in her apartment was because Guy paid the utilities —the least he could do, considering he'd cheated on her with a castmate while she was away doing summer stock.

She set the bills aside for another day and continued through the pile, frowning when she saw one from an attorney's office. Oh no, she thought, her heart starting to thud in her chest. Had it reached this point? Were the credit card collectors taking legal action? She wasn't even sure if they could, but she assumed it was a possibility.

With shaking hands, she ripped the envelope open, her eyes scanning the letter so quickly that she had to slow down and start from the beginning, not once but twice, her heart breaking with each word.

She glanced at the clock as she quickly shoved her mail back into her bag and stood, clutching the letter, her coffee all but forgotten. Nora was working in the holiday department today —Melody had spotted her creating a New Year's Eve display when she'd started her shift. As usual, when she saw her older sister on the floor, Melody had waved excitedly, but Nora just gave her a tight-lipped smile in return.

It was all business for Nora, even during the holidays. Especially at the holidays, as Nora would say. Her job was to decorate the giant department store for every special event and holiday, and Christmas was the biggest responsibility of the year. Each year, she had to outdo herself, something that caused her great stress when Melody thought it should probably bring joy instead. But even Melody knew when to keep her mouth shut sometimes, and convincing Nora that the holidays were anything but a time of stress was an argument she'd lost many times in recent years.

"Where do you think you're going?" Dorothy cried out as

Melody hurried past the gift-wrapping table in search of her sister.

"I'll be right back," Melody explained distractedly. From the corner of her eye, she saw Dorothy throw up her hands and shake her head.

"Um, Elf Melody, I believe that the line for gift wrapping is backing up," Frank said when Melody cut past Santa's chair. He scooted a toddler off his lap and gave her a death glare from behind his fake bushy eyebrows.

"I just need two minutes to find my sister," Melody explained. If she didn't stop her now, Nora would be rushing to catch her evening train, and she didn't want this to wait until later tonight in a phone call. No, this was news that deserved to be delivered face-to-face and it couldn't wait until the weekend, which was the only time that Nora was ever willing to relax—if you called running endless errands and cleaning her already spotless apartment from top to bottom relaxing. Melody certainly didn't.

"Elf Melody!" Santa's voice boomed, catching the attention of the line of children who were running out of patience. Their little faces now turned, all eyes on her, and they smiled at her in expectation as if asking, what was Elf Melody going to do?

Melody stared blankly at them, and then, not wanting to disappoint, she lifted her chin before she broke into song, holding nothing back.

From across "the village," she saw Dorothy's hands freeze mid-bow, and she didn't even dare look at Santa as she belted out the tune. The delight in the faces of the children was enough to encourage her to continue, and she did just that, as she plucked a handful of candy canes from Mrs. Claus's apron, whose jaw had now noticeably slacked. Melody distributed the candy as she walked through the line of children, singing merrily, careful not to lose her letter as she maneuvered her way out of the department and hurried to the last known place where she had spotted her sister.

Nora stood in the window display, carefully stacking champagne glasses into a tower. The look on her face was sterner than the one Dorothy made when she was working with ribbon, and Melody had mixed feelings about springing this news on her even though she saw no other choice.

"Nora!"

Melody had been careful not to be too loud, but all the same, Nora jumped, and nearly toppled two of the glasses. She visibly heaved as she straightened them and then threw Melody a scolding look.

"Can't you see I'm in the middle of something?" she asked tersely. "Besides, aren't you supposed to be in the North Pole?"

It was technically Santa's Village, but Melody wasn't about to correct her sister, not when she'd pulled quite a few strings to get Melody the job.

"I'm on my break," she explained, glancing over her shoulder to where Santa now gave her a thunderous stare through a forest of plastic, yet beautifully decorated by Nora herself, Christmas trees. "But I received this letter. And...I think you need to see it."

Maybe it was cowardly, but Melody couldn't bring herself to share the news. It was easier for Nora to read the letter and process the information on her own.

Nora frowned as she carefully stepped away from the display and took the letter from Melody's hand. She read it slowly and then closed her eyes for a moment.

"Nana passed away last month and this is the first we're

hearing of it?" Her voice was barely above a whisper, but it was strained with confusion and sadness.

"The letter said that they had a difficult time tracking me down." Melody didn't mention that she hadn't checked her mail in weeks. "The same probably goes for you."

It wasn't like Nora was on social media. It wasn't like Nora had any social life at all.

"I can't believe she's gone." Nora hugged her arms to her waist as her gaze softened. "It's been so long since we've seen her."

Melody's chest ached in a way that it hadn't in a very long time. Eighteen years. She knew that Nora had calculated this too—it was impossible to forget their father's death or the impact it had on everything afterward. It was as if their childhood was divided in half—before and after the loss of their parent. They hadn't just lost a father, they'd also lost all the family events that they'd treasured so much, including the biannual trips to Vermont to visit their paternal grandmother.

But Melody knew that Nora didn't like to talk about that time in their lives. They'd eventually gotten used to their new normal, and they certainly knew better than to pine for the way things used to be, even if Melody, being only twelve at the time, often did until Nora, being three years older in age and about ten years older in maturity, told her that it wasn't fair to their mother, who had taken the loss hard. Now, both adults (or at least one of them, to hear Nora say it), that time felt so distant, it was almost difficult to believe it was really them—that they'd once spent summers in the clear mountain air and their winters baking cookies in Nana's kitchen.

"After Dad died, Mom and Nana had that falling out," Melody mused. They'd never been supplied details—their mother told them it was "adult business"—but now they were adults and Melody still didn't know what had caused the family rift. "Did Mom ever tell you?"

She wouldn't put it past her sister to keep this information from her, but now there was no point in holding on to it.

Their mother had been gone for three years now, and Nora's expression grew even sadder at the mention of her. "No. I never wanted to upset her by asking. It was why I never reached out to Nana once I grew up, too. But what was our excuse for the last three years?"

Melody didn't have an answer for that. They'd lost touch. Moved on with their lives. Embraced all the struggles and routines of adulthood, engrossed themselves in their daily problems, big and small.

"Nana must have understood," Melody said quietly, "or she wouldn't have given us the inn."

That was the part of the letter she was most worried about; Nora's reaction to Nana was to be expected. It was a loss, even if they hadn't seen her since they were twelve and fifteen. But the inn—Melody knew better than to think that Nora would be excited about it.

Sure enough, Nora blew out a sigh. "Well, we'll have to do something about the property. Have it appraised—"

"You don't mean sell it?" Melody cried, even though she knew that Nora would do this. Her sister didn't have a sentimental bone in her body. Not anymore, at least.

"And what do you propose?" Nora stared at her, looking very no-nonsense in her crisp black pantsuit and tightly pulled ponytail. "You want to run it yourself? You won't even cross the bridge to visit me in Brooklyn!"

Well. When she put it that way, Nora had a point, not that Melody would admit it.

"I didn't say I wanted to run it. I just...I don't want to lose it." Her voice shook on the final words and her eyes welled with hot tears as the emotions hit her full force. They'd already lost their father, mother, and now Nana. What else was left of their happy memories but their ancestral home, the one that their grandmother had left to them?

Nora's face folded in sympathy but she wasn't demonstrative with her affection by nature, and so the most she managed was to stiffly set a hand on Melody's shaking shoulder.

"Look, we'll talk about this later. I have to finish this display and you'd better get back to the North Pole—" She glanced over Melody's shoulder, her lips thinning.

"It's Santa's Village," Melody said flatly.

Nora dropped her hand. "What?"

"It's Santa's Village," Melody insisted. "And the inn isn't a property. It's Nana's home. And once, it was our favorite place in the world."

A single tear slipped down her cheek, and she didn't bother to brush it away.

Nora opened her mouth to say something, but she closed it again as her eyes flashed at something in the distance.

"Elf Melody!" Santa's voice boomed louder than when he forced himself to say "Ho, ho, ho!"

Melody turned, holding up the letter. "I'll be back in a moment, Santa. I've had a bad day."

"There's no crying in Santa's Village. Or complaining," Frank said without a glimmer of irony.

Says the man who grumbled over my caroling since the first of

December, Melody thought. Only from the raise of Frank's crooked fake eyebrows, she hadn't just thought it.

She felt her cheeks burn as Frank stared her down. Behind her, Nora gasped, and for good reason. The problem was that Frank wasn't just Santa, he was also their boss. The big man in every sense of the word.

Frank Castle was the owner of this department store, one that was cherished by New Yorkers and had been passed down through generations, finally landing with him, because there was no one else left. He preferred to sit on the twelfth floor, behind closed doors, in what was apparently a corner office overlooking the skyline, but by unfortunate circumstances this year, the sweet man who had been hired to play Santa had broken his hip after slipping on a patch of ice, and by then all the other Santas in the state had been hired.

"Nora," Frank said, disregarding Melody. "You know how highly I think of you."

It was a warning, and one that made Nora gulp and then lick her bottom lip. "Of course, sir. It won't happen again."

No, it wouldn't happen again! It couldn't! Grandmothers didn't go around dying twice, did they? Melody felt her anger build. The stress of the day and her sister's reaction to the news was only making matters worse.

"We've just learned our grandmother died," Melody informed Frank.

"I'm sorry to hear that," he replied without a hint of sincerity. "Were you close?"

Something in his steely gaze told her that he knew the answer to that, if only because Nora had never taken a vacation day in the ten years that she'd worked for him.

"We just needed a moment to discuss a family matter," Melody replied.

"And you can discuss it all you want. After your shift," Frank replied. "This is the second busiest shopping week of the year, and the line is backing up. If we're going to get all those gifts wrapped before closing, we'll need you back at your station. Now."

Melody glanced at Nora, who gave her a subtle jut of her chin, her eyes wide.

"Fine," Melody said, clenching her teeth. She went to snatch the letter from Nora's hand, but at that moment, Nora turned to go back to her task, causing Melody's hand to swipe the edge of one of the champagne flutes instead.

For one horrible moment, the world seemed to hold still. She held her breath, daring to think that maybe it wouldn't matter. Maybe everything would be all right.

But how could it? Her grandmother had died. She had no family left but her sister. A sister who wanted to sell what remained of their family out from under her.

Melody watched in horror as—as if in slow motion—the tower of champagne glasses slowly tipped and shattered, one by one, like some twisted game of dominos. Nora let out a cry of despair and Melody could only clasp her hands to her mouth to stifle her own scream. She didn't know who she was afraid to look at more—Nora or her boss. Sometimes, it felt like they were one and the same, anyway.

With a pounding heart, she stole a glance at the big man.

"Two words," Santa said firmly.

Melody looked up at him with a weak smile. "Merry Christmas?"

"You're fired," Santa said.

Chapter Two
Nora

The four-hour drive from Manhattan to the small Vermont town where their grandmother had lived was a familiar route, even if Nora had never personally driven it until now. She'd always sat in the back seat, staring out the window as the buildings turned to trees, counting the miles until they finally arrived.

Now, she checked the time on the dashboard, only to realize that Melody had managed to keep quiet for exactly one hour and twenty minutes.

She glanced at her sister to make sure that she was still breathing.

"Are you ever going to forgive me?" Melody asked meekly from the passenger seat, where she'd sat squeezing her hands together since she'd climbed into the car Nora had rented and paid for, of course.

Nora should have known better than to jinx herself. She tightened her grip on the steering wheel and kept her eyes focused on the road. It had been a little over twelve hours since the debacle at the store, and she'd been up half the night replaying it, like some bad holiday movie, in her mind.

"At least you got to keep your job," Melody continued, her tone brightening.

Nora, however, was unable to see the bright side of this situation.

"Only because I have a long history there," Nora reminded her. She could no longer exactly say she had an upstanding reputation. And she could probably kiss that promotion she'd been hoping for in January goodbye. "Besides, I was asked to take a leave of absence."

"Only for two weeks!" Melody brushed a hand through the air. "I go for months without employment."

Nora glanced at her sister sidelong. Melody didn't take the hint, but then, Melody lived in a different world than Nora, and always had, partially because Nora had always protected her, always been there to pick up the pieces of the mess Melody inevitably made.

"I got you that job at the store. I put my name on the line for you," Nora said firmly.

"It was an accident," Melody said. "And I was the merriest gift wrapper in that place. If they had a problem with Elf Melody, then they should really take a hard look at Santa Frank. I've never met a bigger Scrooge!"

"He owns the store!" Nora had been working for the privately owned department store since graduating from NYU, slowly moving up from the accessories counter to overseeing the seasonal displays and special events. She had been hoping to transition into the executive offices soon, where she could sit at a desk instead of stand on her feet, where she wouldn't have to worry about one hundred crystal glasses toppling over and shattering. "And he had a right to be mad! Do you have any idea what our little mess cost him?"

"Well. You could have secured those glasses," Melody said with a huff.

It was true, and Nora should have. And Frank Castle had said the same thing when he told her to take some time off to deal with family matters. It was an oversight—and an expensive one. And now Lucy Rollins from marketing was spending the day re-creating Nora's New Year's Eve vision while Nora was driving to Vermont to settle Nana's estate. By the time she returned, Lucy would probably already be settled into a corner office on the twelfth floor, the Director of Special Projects title on her new business cards.

"I know what would make you feel better," Melody said brightly as her hand went to the dashboard and she flicked on the radio. Immediately, a festive carol filled the vehicle, and Nora struggled to bite back a scowl. She had to listen to these songs all day in the store for two months every year—another reason why she longed for an office position, where the only sounds to be heard would be the ringing of a phone or the clacking of a keyboard, business conversations, and lighthearted banter around the coffee machine.

Not surprisingly, it didn't take long for Melody to start singing the holiday tune—of course, she knew every word by heart. Nora released one hand from the wheel to press a finger to her temple. She then reached for the now cold cup of coffee that sat in the console, hoping it might ward off a headache.

But then the song had changed to one of Melody's all-time favorites, and Nora knew that there was no hope. Another glance at the dashboard confirmed they still had over two hours before they reached Juniper Falls. She stepped a little harder on the gas pedal as Melody cheerfully sang along with the radio, occasionally trying to cajole Nora to join in, even though they both knew that she wouldn't.

Nora didn't sing, and Melody really shouldn't, either.

No one had ever dared to tell Melody that she didn't exactly have the best singing voice, and Nora wasn't about to say it now, even though someone should probably save her from herself. There had been auditions that hadn't gone well, but Melody had always chalked those up to the usual criticisms, taking it in stride even when Nora heard the hurt in her sister's voice when she was turned down for yet another part.

Their mother had always drowned out Melody's singing with the television or radio, and Nora with a closed door, thankful that their prewar apartment building had thick walls. But Nana, bless her, had always encouraged Melody to keep going, often joining her with great enthusiasm as they rolled out sugar cookie dough or hung more tinsel on the tree.

Nora swallowed the lump in her throat. She hadn't thought of those days in a long time—at first because it was easier not to, and later because she'd cast it from her mind for so long that she'd almost forgotten.

But now it was all there. The memories, the music, the laughter. The love. Coming at her as quickly as the falling snow was hitting her windshield. She flicked on her wipers, hoping to push it away, but as the miles ticked by, the mountains grew bigger, and Vermont grew closer, she knew that the odds of that happening were about as poor as the ones of Melody being quiet for the remainder of the drive.

❄

The town of Juniper Falls looked like something out of a storybook, and even Melody fell quiet as they turned onto Main Street, past shops with front windows edged in lights, the sidewalks filled with families huddled in their winter coats, carrying shopping bags as they walked under the garland-wrapped lampposts. Despite it being a gray and snowy day, there was a glow to the town and a hush that made the world seem to be still for a moment.

It was so different from the rush of traffic in New York that even Nora fell under its spell, and she didn't realize that she'd been sitting at a traffic light, taking in the scene for too long, until the car behind her honked.

"Well, so much for small-town hospitality!"

Beside her, Melody's grin was wry. "They gave you a solid thirty seconds."

"Why didn't you tell me?" Nora asked, embarrassed.

"Because I could tell that you were taking in the scene, and I didn't want to rush you," Melody replied.

Oh no. None of this. Nora may have given her sister false hope about her voice, but she wasn't about to let Melody think she would even consider not selling that inn.

"You know that we're here to organize Nana's paperwork and put the house on the market," she reminded her sister. When Melody didn't reply, she said, "We've been over this. We both live in New York. Neither of us has any experience running an inn—"

"Yes, but there's staff at the inn," Melody pointed out.

"Staff costs money, and so does the business. So does the property!" Nora fought back her exasperation and took a breath before she launched into the same speech she'd given Melody last night, once Melody had handed over her employee badge.

"Nana left us the house, but a house is not a gift. There are property taxes. Repairs. Things that I can't afford and that I know you can't, either."

"But the letter mentioned that there was some money..."

Nora glanced at her sister. "Which is being used to pay the staff until they can be let go." Thinking of the old cook who had been at the Hart Inn for longer than Nora had been alive, she softened her tone. "Whatever is left will not be enough to pay for the annual upkeep of that house. I know it's tough to hear, but the money we can make from the sale of the house can really help us both, Melody. I can finally pay off my student loans and you can get out of that apartment you still share with Guy the cheater. You can have a nest egg. You won't have to worry so much."

"More like you won't have to worry so much," Melody replied. "You're the one that is always worrying."

Well, one of them had to, Nora thought but didn't say. And right now, she was very worried. Worried about what she was walking into, what fresh mess she had to pick up and make right.

Worried about how she would feel when she saw the house again, knowing that it would be for the last time.

She focused on the road as the snow picked up and she struggled to remember the way to Nana's house. The inn was just around the corner from town, technically within walking distance, but not too close as to interfere with its serenity. She was just about to stop and check her phone for directions when she saw the bookstore on the corner, the landmark that she'd forgotten about over the years. Through the window display of Christmas books, she could see the warm glow of lamplights and oversize chairs where people sat taking their time to browse back covers. It used to be one of her favorite pastimes, especially during the holidays, and it also meant that Nana's house was close. Just down the next street, in fact.

Nora didn't know what she'd been expecting to see, but the sight of the old sign planted firmly at the base of the road came as a strange sort of relief, and not just because it meant she could finally get out of this car and away from Melody's caroling. She longed to see this house again nearly as much as she feared it.

Slowly, she turned onto the winding driveway, the house drawing near as she pulled up the hill.

"Someone shoveled the driveway," she remarked.

"The letter from the attorney did say that the staff was still on site," Melody reminded her.

Yes, and it also said that they would only continue to be paid until Nora and Melody took control of the house and business, meaning that a decision would need to be made about the fate of the property by January, right on time for Nora to get back to her job in New York—if she still had a job by then.

She pushed that thought from her head as the snow-covered pine trees parted and the house came fully into view. She stopped the car and stared at the large Victorian, with its wraparound porch and gabled windows, struggling to believe that Nana wasn't going to greet them with a long, tight hug, and a tray of cookies waiting in the kitchen.

"It all looks the same," she finally said.

Melody could only nod and unbuckle her seat belt. "But it won't be the same inside. Not without Nana."

"No, it won't be," Nora agreed sadly, and that was why it would be easier to part with, even for her sister. They may have come all the way up here, but nothing was the same and it never would be. And it hadn't been for a very long time.

She stepped out of the car, immediately hit by a blast of cold winter air. Nora felt it sting her cheeks and settle in her lungs, and she wasted no time in popping the trunk and unloading her luggage. Together, she and Melody trudged up the salted cobblestoned path to the front porch, and it was only then that Nora hesitated.

"Well?" Melody said impatiently. She was shuffling her feet, trying to stay warm. "What are you waiting for?"

"It feels weird to just walk in," Nora said, even though they'd once done exactly that. Burst in was more like it.

"It's an inn," Melody reminded her. "People walk in all the time."

"But...they aren't expecting us." Nora now realized that they should have called and talked to someone on staff, to let them know that they would be arriving. But she hadn't gotten home from the department store until after nine, and that was only after having to listen to Melody convince her that they should come to Vermont. Then a rental car had to be secured and bags had to be packed and, well, wine had to be drunk.

It had been a crazy and unexpected day, but Nora couldn't completely fault that as the reason for her oversight. She'd forgotten that things weren't the same. She, of all people, had forgotten that.

"The staff must know we've inherited the inn," Melody pointed out. "I mean, this is all ours now. We can walk in if we want!"

That was true, but it did little to reassure Nora as she tentatively reached for the brass knob of the glass-paned door. Inside, she could see the front desk tucked under the curved staircase, where Nana kept a large guestbook. There was no one at the desk now, but the crystal chandelier overhead was on, and there was a light coming from the lounge just through the open French doors to the right.

She gave the door a push, heard the jingle of bells announce their arrival, and stepped inside.

The snow on their shoes melted on the faded area rug as Nora and Melody quietly looked around, both waiting, Nora supposed, for something to happen. Waiting, she thought, for Nana to come around the corner, wiping her hands on her apron, picking up the pace when she saw that it was them.

But there was no grandmother to welcome them today. And one glance into the lounge proved that there wasn't anyone sitting by the crackling fire, either. But someone had lit that fire. And someone had kept this house looking just like she remembered it—almost.

Probably Mr. Higgins, the cook.

"There aren't any decorations!" Melody cried. "There's no tree! No garland! No lights!"

"That's because I haven't gotten around to it yet," a deep voice said as a man appeared on the staircase and then paused. "Melody? *Nora?*"

Nora looked up at the familiar face, aged now by nearly twenty years. He was still recognizable, though, she could see it in the eyes, as clear and blue as the winter sky, Nana always liked to say. He'd been sixteen the last time she'd seen him. A year older than her—an older man, and an irresistible one, too. His once tall and lanky frame now filled his flannel work shirt, and a stubble graced his once smooth face. His floppy brown hair was cut shorter now, but the smile he gave her was all the same.

"Toby," she said on a breath, hardly believing what she was

seeing as he came down the rest of the stairs and stood awkwardly at the base, staring at them. What did one do in these situations? Hug? Shake hands?

It was finally Melody who rushed forward and hugged their old neighbor. Nora noticed a jolt of something pass through her when she watched Toby's strong arms embrace her sister. Something that felt a lot like jealousy, which was silly, truly. Toby Phelps had been a childhood crush, nothing more. A thing of her past, forgotten, like so many others.

Melody, however, had only ever thought of Toby as a surrogate big brother, and from the way she playfully punched his shoulder and chided him on his manly physique, it was clear that nothing had changed.

And that was just the problem. Nora set a hand to her stomach, willed her heart to calm down, and stepped forward with a smile as she then nervously opened her arms. It wasn't natural for her to reach for anyone anymore, but it wouldn't be right to stand back or simply shake his hand, not when it would only confirm what she already felt—that time had passed, and their bond had been broken, or at least neglected.

Even, she knew, forgotten. Pushed aside so she didn't have to think about it or remember.

Toby's gaze locked with hers for a moment before he leaned down and hugged her, something they'd only ever done, awkwardly, as teens, when it was time for them to return to the city.

But this hug was different. It was warm and firm, and she felt like she was being wrapped in a flannel blanket as her chest pressed against his. She closed her eyes when her chin rested on his shoulder, taking in the woodsy smell he still carried on his clothes and in his hair.

"I wasn't sure you girls would come back," Toby said when they pulled back.

Nora was a little shaky from the physical affection, but Melody just bounced on her heels. "How could we not? I can't believe that no one called to tell us that Nana had died!"

Toby's jaw set as the light left his eyes. "Well, it's not like you've stayed in touch over the years."

Nora felt her back stiffen and she glanced at Melody. "Our mother had a falling out with our grandmother after our father died. But you must know that."

It was a small town and people talked. And Nana had always treated the Phelpses like family.

Now, Nora realized, even more than she'd once thought.

"I didn't know that you were watching over the place," she said. She didn't know a lot about Toby in recent years, or anything for that matter, and her gaze immediately dropped to his hands, looking for a ring, and feeling strangely relieved when she didn't see one.

"I've been watching over the inn since before Gloria passed away," Toby replied.

Nora wasn't sure why she was so surprised. Toby had been as close to his grandmother as his own, who was Nana's best friend.

Her mind went to the woman next door, but she decided that now wasn't the time to inquire about her well-being. It had been a long day, and they were still in their coats and wet boots, luggage at their feet.

"I've been the caretaker here for years," Toby went on.

"Caretaker?" Nora tried to make sense of this as everything she'd ever known about this man came rushing back. She had the strange feeling that she didn't know him as well as she'd once thought. "What about law school?"

"I went," Toby said, and Nora was relieved to hear it. To know that he hadn't changed too much. "It's a long story for another day."

"Well, I can't think of a better caretaker for this place!" Melody beamed.

Nora met Toby's unreadable expression and gave a little smile, hoping it was convincing.

If Toby was running this place, chances were he wouldn't be too happy about her decision to sell it.

She decided that was another topic of conversation that could wait.

"Let me take your coats," Toby said.

Nora nodded. She'd forgotten she was still wearing a coat, and she looked around now, trying to come out of her fog. She felt unbalanced and out of sorts, but Toby stood patiently. He was at an advantage, technically, knowing that they could arrive at some point, even if he hadn't thought they would.

He hung both of their coats on the rack near the front door, where Nora spotted several others.

"Are there guests?" she asked, feeling alarmed.

"Just two." Toby shrugged. "It didn't seem fair to cancel their holiday plans. Besides, the place could use the money."

And there it was. Nora gave her sister a sharp look, one that Melody ignored with a purse of her lips.

"I can go over a few things with you if you'd like," Toby said, looking at Nora. "Seeing as you're now the new owners."

New owners. More like the sellers. Nora shifted uneasily but then nodded.

For the second time in her life, she had to shelve her emotions and step up to the task. And the more information she had, the easier it would be to sell the place and leave it in her past for good.

Even if one look at Toby made that suddenly feel impossible.

Chapter Three
Melody

Melody left Nora and Toby in the lobby to reconnect, happy for the chance to slip upstairs by herself—or rather to lug two suitcases after refusing Toby's offer of help.

While Nana's suite was downstairs, the second floor of the house was devoted to guests, with six rooms each decorated in a different color scheme. Nana had been sure to always set aside the pink room for Nora and Melody, furnishing it with two double beds, one for each of them, while their parents slept in the green room beside it, with a bigger, king-size bed and their own fireplace. Looking back, Melody supposed that Nana had forgone the business, prioritizing their visit instead, even during the busy summer and holiday months.

Standing on the landing, Melody scanned the hallway, taking in the closed doors, clutching the key that Toby had put in her hand. He'd spent enough time with them during their visits over the years to know the room they thought of as their own, and now she walked to the door and turned the key, not realizing that she was holding her breath until it released in a long sigh when she flicked on the light.

It was all the same, from the two double beds to the antique dresser. She bet the top drawer was still stuck, too. The walls were a dusty rose color, the duvets a marshmallow white, and the lampshades on the desk and table that separated the two beds were made of a sweet floral pattern. Large windows looked out onto the front lawn, interrupted only by a few tree branches that were covered in a thin layer of snow.

How many times would Melody and her sister look out this very window—in the summer to see if Toby was on his way over to play, and in the winter, to see if they might spot Santa on his sleigh after making his rounds on Main Street?

Melody turned around and looked at the beds, wondering how Nora was going to feel about sharing a room again, not just after all this time, but because of what had happened yesterday.

It wasn't like Melody had meant for it to happen. She'd been grateful for the work. She'd struggled to find a part-time job that would allow her to go on auditions, not that she'd ever admit so much. Still, Nora sensed it, of course. Silently judged, too. And Nora didn't forgive easily. Or forget.

And it was that part that Melody was counting on. She had one week until Christmas to make her sister remember how wonderful their holidays were here in this house. And two weeks to convince her not to sell the inn.

It wouldn't be easy, but she could strong-arm Toby into helping her case—that was if he didn't influence Nora all on his own.

With a little smile, Melody sprawled out on the bed that had always been hers and stared up at the ceiling. Nana might not be here anymore to tuck her in at night, but somehow her presence was everywhere. And just like when she was a little girl, a little uncertain, but always longing for something just out of reach, she felt her grandmother's silent support, and she knew that somehow, some way, everything was going to work out.

❋

After an hour, Melody had finished unpacking, thoughtfully leaving the best drawers empty for Nora in the hope of buttering her up. Every gesture that could help her cause to save the inn was a worthy one, however small. Nora hadn't come upstairs, meaning that she was either still talking to Toby or hiding out from Melody in the kitchen. Melody didn't mind. She could use a little space from her sister after that car ride, and she was eager to reacquaint herself with the house, too.

She walked into the hall, nearly forgetting to lock her room behind her with the brass key before sliding it into the pocket of her jeans, and then went back downstairs. The front desk was empty and one glance into the dining room with its three round tables and long buffet table didn't show any sight of Toby or Nora. Melody walked through it to the kitchen, drawn by the smell of something sweet.

"Mr. Higgins!" she exclaimed when she pushed through the swinging door.

She stared at the man, aged by nearly twenty years since she'd last seen him, trying not to show her shock at how much older he looked than in her memory until she saw the surprise register on his face and she realized that her own transformation was probably much bigger.

"Melody?" he asked in disbelief, stepping away from the center island where he was plating a tray of cookies. "What happened to the little girl with crooked teeth and two long braids?"

"Braces," she said with a grin. "And headgear. And a palate expander. And a lot of teasing from the kids at school." She chuckled and pulled her braided ponytail from behind her shoulder. "But I haven't changed that much."

"You haven't changed at all," he said warmly. "You've just grown into a beautiful young woman." He gave her a long hug, smelling like brown sugar and vanilla, and when he pulled back there were tears in his kind gray eyes. "If your grandmother could only see you."

Melody blinked to cover her own building emotions. It was all the same. The house. The smells. The people. But one person was missing. The heart of it all.

"How about a cookie?" Mr. Higgins went back to the island.

"Aren't those for the guests?" Melody asked.

"We only have two right now," Mr. Higgins said pleasantly.

"Are there more people coming before Christmas?" Melody asked. Toby hadn't implied if they'd be able to keep the pink room for that long—not that she'd told him how long they were staying. Nora and Toby were real friends, and she had no doubt that Nora had been quick to fill Toby in on their plans.

But would Nora tell him about her plans to sell the inn? She doubted Toby would take kindly to that news.

Or dear Mr. Higgins.

"I would *love* one of your cookies," she told the man who was the closest thing to a grandfather that she'd ever known. Nana's husband had died long before she was born, and her mother's parents had never been close to them and had passed away when she was little. "And coffee if you have it. Or tea."

"You're the lady of the house now!" Mr. Higgins opened his arms wide, displaying his portly belly that was only partly disguised by an apron. "You can have whatever you'd like. Not that it ever stopped you before," he added with a wink.

Melody laughed. "So you knew about all the times I'd sneak in here as a kid?"

"You weren't exactly discreet," he said, fighting off a smile at the memory. "You'd leave a trail of crumbs and the lid off the cookie jar."

"Well, I promise I have better manners now, not that my sister would agree." Melody reached for a cookie and took a bite, closing her eyes to enjoy it. It tasted like sugar and spice. It tasted like Christmas.

But more than anything, it tasted like home.

"Nora is here, too?" Mr. Higgins looked pleased by that. "Well, if this isn't a Christmas surprise!"

"Speaking of Christmas," Melody said, polishing off the cookie. "Why aren't the decorations up yet? Nana always had them up by the beginning of December!"

Mr. Higgins lowered his gaze and went back to his work, mixing a batter that he then started scooping onto a waiting baking sheet. "We're short-staffed. The housekeeper left after Nana..." He stopped to clear his throat. "It's just me and Toby these days. Toby would do anything for this place, but what with all the maintenance..."

Of course. This was an old house. It had always been creaky.

"There's only so much time," Mr. Higgins went on. He looked up from the mixing bowl. "And money."

Melody swallowed uneasily. "It's probably best not to worry Nora with that just yet. And as for the decorations, leave them to me. We'll get this place looking festive in no time!"

"We?" Mr. Higgins looked worried.

"Nora and me!" Melody smiled, but as she left the kitchen

with the tray of cookies for the lounge, it was she who felt worried.

Nora already saw no point in keeping this house. Once she found out that it was a money pit, there would be no way she'd entertain holding on to it.

Well. That just meant that Melody would have to get crafty. And quick.

She passed through the dining room, stopping when she saw a young woman with two suitcases standing at the front desk.

"Oh!" Melody smiled and set the tray of cookies on the desk. "Are you...checking in?"

And the role of Nana, the innkeeper, will now be played by her granddaughter, Melody.

Melody stood a little straighter, but her eyes glanced nervously at the desktop. There was a guest book and an iPad, which came as a surprise to her. Nana liked things done the old-fashioned way. The guest book was proof of that.

But then, she supposed that everyone had changed over time. Even Nana.

"If you have room," the woman said anxiously. "I don't have a reservation."

Remembering what Mr. Higgins had said about there only being two guests, Melody gave the woman a reassuring smile.

"We do have room." She pushed around some papers on the desk, looking for Nana's old reservation book, and not seeing it, she realized that it must have been replaced by the tablet. "How long were you planning to stay?"

The woman hesitated long enough for Melody to properly take her in. She'd peg her to be a few years younger than herself: late twenties, shoulder-length blond hair, big green eyes, and something else. Something that Melody couldn't quite put her finger on but that Nora would probably be able to catch.

She didn't miss a thing, that sister of hers.

"I don't have firm plans yet. I can pay through Christmas in advance, though. With cash." The young woman opened her bag to reveal several large bills.

Melody knew that Nora would find this suspicious, which was exactly why Nora didn't need to know about it. Money was money, and right now they needed it. Besides, Nana would never turn a guest out into the cold.

"It's a good thing that I was walking by as you came in!" Melody said brightly, and the woman matched her grin.

Well, Melody thought as she reached for the key to what she knew was the best room in the house, maybe their money problems weren't as dire as she'd feared. A third guest, and maybe more to follow—people in search of a cozy country Christmas or a romantic holiday weekend.

Anything was possible, that's what Nana always said. And right now, smiling at their newest guest, Melody downright believed it.

"Have a cookie," she said, motioning to the tray. "They're freshly baked. An old family recipe. My personal favorite."

The woman reached for a cookie but then looked back at her in something close to surprise. "Oh. Are you...the owner?"

Not exactly knowing how to answer that question given her current debate with her sister, Melody thought of a diplomatic response. "It's a family business."

"Oh." The woman stared at Melody for a moment, holding the uneaten cookie in her hand, as if she'd forgotten all about it.

"I saw on the website a woman named Gloria Hart owned the inn..." the woman said pleasantly.

"She recently passed away." Even now, Melody struggled to say that, and she quickly changed the topic when she saw sympathy register on the woman's face. "And her only son died years ago."

And she was officially the worst innkeeper ever. So much for winning an award for this role. Or even landing the part. She'd failed the audition. No doubt this poor woman would make up an excuse and find a cheerier option in town to celebrate Christmas, one where the proprietor didn't dump their personal drama as they counted the cash.

Cash. Her eyes went down to the stack of bills on the table. It was odd. But, hey, it saved her from having to figure out how to charge a credit card.

"Well, I should...get upstairs." The woman was backing away, but not to the front door.

"Don't forget your key!" Melody held out a key to the blue room, her personal favorite, other than the pink room. "I have you at the back of the house, overlooking the pond. There are plenty of skates in various sizes in the trunk near the door." At least, there were the last time she had been here. Surely Nana hadn't tossed them. The woman was nothing if not a holder of traditions, especially at Christmastime.

"Sounds lovely," the woman said a little breathlessly as she took the key and then moved back away from the desk. Her cheeks had lost a bit of their earlier color, and Melody wasn't entirely sure it was because she'd finally shed the winter chill.

Determined to make their new guest feel more welcome, Melody quickly said, "If you wouldn't mind signing the guest book?"

The woman froze with her hand on the banister and then slowly walked back toward Melody. Melody tucked the money into an envelope and scribbled the room number on it before sealing it and then sliding it into the top drawer. She'd talk to Toby about it the next time she saw him.

"Dinner is usually from six to eight. Or you can have a tray brought up to your room," Melody said, remembering what her grandmother used to say and hoping this was all still true. "And Main Street is just around the corner, and there are plenty of shops and restaurants."

The woman nodded and gave a tight smile. "Thank you."

Melody watched her disappear up the stairs, then kicked herself for not offering to help with the bags. She'd have to do better tomorrow, especially if Nora was watching.

But they had another guest. And a wad of fresh cash. Not bad for the first day, Melody thought. Not bad at all.

And it was all thanks to—she leaned forward to look at the guest book—Faith. No last name. Just Faith.

And maybe that was all she needed.

Chapter Four
Faith

Faith closed the door to her room behind her and firmly locked the door. Her heart was pounding as she walked past the big brass bed to the window seat and sat down to take in the view, still wearing her coat. The pond was frozen over, the mountains settled in the distance, but her mind was on anything but the breathtaking scenery right now.

She'd done it. She'd actually done it. Packed her bags, loaded up the car, and driven hundreds of miles, even in the snow, which had certainly been more than she'd bargained for.

She'd have to buy some snow boots if she was going to stick around Juniper Falls for a while. A better coat, too, or at least some warmer gloves. The knitted ones weren't going to cut it here—she could tell the moment she stepped out of the car and began walking up the steps to the inn she'd researched so thoroughly before embarking on this trip. The shops in town were within walking distance—even though that last stretch of the trip had seemed to take thirty minutes, what with the snow coming down and all.

Good. She liked walking. It cleared her head. And she needed a clear head right now.

Still shaky, she removed her weather-inappropriate shoes and draped her wool coat over the desk chair. The room was spacious and comfortable, painted a soft gray blue that felt soothing. The windows were large, letting in the waning light of the day.

She opened the drawers of the end tables and dresser before moving onto the desk—not sure exactly what she was looking for or why she felt disappointed when they all proved empty.

She'd have better luck downstairs, she supposed, in that lounge she'd spotted just off the front entranceway, or the rooms that were no doubt tucked behind it. It was a large home. A large family home, not just an inn.

A family business, too.

She hadn't seen that coming. All her research had pointed her to one woman, one owner—Gloria Hart—deceased on the fifth of November, just a week before Faith's mother.

The timing felt especially cruel, and not just because it was Christmastime.

Not that it felt like the holidays were happening here in this old house. Unlike the other businesses and homes in town, this one didn't even have so much as a wreath on the door.

Faith's stomach grumbled, and she set a hand to it, hoping to settle it. She glanced at the phone on the nightstand, remembering the offer of room service, but she didn't know who would answer the phone when she called down, and she didn't want to speak to the woman at the front desk again. She hadn't even caught her name. She'd been too rattled from the drive, from the mere fact that she'd arrived at all, much less in one piece.

And then there was the other part, of course. The part that she still couldn't shake, despite shivering from the cold. Somehow, that woman downstairs was related to Gloria Hart. It was too much to process, not when it didn't match the facts that she'd gathered before coming here. The obituary hadn't listed any living relatives.

Faith shook the cobwebs from her head. She was hungry and running on low energy, and she needed to address some basic needs so she could think properly. Her mind went to the tray of cookies. Maybe they'd been placed in the lounge, for the other guests. She could go downstairs, grab a few, and while she was there, take a look around and get a proper feel for the place instead of relying on what she'd gleaned from the internet.

They were very good cookies. Easily the best she'd ever had. And fresh, too. Homemade. She tried to think of the last time she'd had a homemade cookie and came up with nothing. Her mother had never been the type to bake treats, even around the holidays, and Faith rarely had time to make much more than a quick dinner most days.

Her stomach grumbled again, and this time Faith listened to it. She slipped into her damp shoes and all but tiptoed to the door, pressing her ear to it before slowly opening it and determining that the coast was clear. She was safe.

※

The lounge was empty, and a crackling fire warmed the room, inviting her in and immediately making her feel welcome. Still, she glanced over her shoulder to make sure she was alone before taking two of the cookies from the tray and then wrapping two more in a napkin, which she stuffed in her pocket for later.

Exhaustion was setting in, and she wasn't sure she'd make it until dinnertime. A hot bath might be just what she needed before a long rest in that cozy-looking bed. She'd be energized and clear-headed tomorrow morning.

But first, she needed to look around. The room was set up with a long couch facing the fireplace, flanked by two pairs of chairs. It was a family room as much as it catered to guests, with brass-framed photos grouped on a console table, and a few more on the bookshelves in the adjacent library.

She moved to the small console first, leaning down to get a good look at the photos, which were discolored from time. There was one of some people grouped outside the inn, smiling in the sunshine, maybe taken on opening day from the looks of it. She stared at the faces carefully, but the photo had been taken from a distance to get the full scope of the property, and the expressions were blurry at best. Another one was of a young man in an army uniform, another of an older couple, no doubt from generations ago.

Faith turned to the table behind the sofa, where a more recent photo caught her eye, but just as she reached for the frame, a light flicked on in the room, and she all but jumped.

"Didn't mean to startle to you," a woman said cheerfully. "It's already getting dark out there so I thought I should turn on some lamps."

Faith stared at the woman cautiously, unsure of her role here at the inn, all too aware that she was still holding the frame that didn't belong to her—something that she had no business keeping.

Faith carefully returned the frame to the table, noticing the sad smile that came over the woman's face as she looked at the photograph. She estimated her to be about five years older than herself. Pretty, with auburn hair that fell in soft waves at her shoulders, and curious eyes.

"I was just looking around," Faith explained. "I only got in a little bit ago."

"The lounge is a good place to make yourself at home," the woman agreed. Then, noticing the tray of cookies on the coffee table, her eyes widened. "I see Mr. Higgins has come through for us." She seemed to hesitate before reaching for a cookie but then went for it.

Feeling more relaxed, Faith inched forward and did the same.

"Oh, these are so good," the woman said, closing her eyes at the first bite. "I could probably eat the entire platter but that wouldn't be fair to everyone else. Or my waistline," she added wryly.

Faith chewed her cookie happily. Her own waistline was the least of her concerns at the moment, but she didn't immediately reach for another cookie, not when there were other guests to consider, and she did have two in her pocket.

"This is the first thing I've eaten in hours," the woman went on, as she did reach for another cookie, and then Faith did the same. "I just got in today."

"Where'd you come from?" Faith was happy to keep the conversation off herself.

"New York. City," the woman clarified. "I'd nearly forgotten how to drive," she added with a small laugh.

Faith immediately felt a kinship with this woman.

"A city girl, then," she said with a smile.

The woman's brow pinched on that but then she nodded. "Born and raised, but...well, there is something to be said for the peace of the country, isn't there?"

Faith nodded vaguely. She hadn't had a chance to soak in the feel of the place, and peaceful was the very last thing she felt at the moment.

She glanced over at the photo again, wondering how many other guests were staying under this roof and when she'd have another chance to explore.

"It's certainly colder here than I'm used to," she said.

"Oh? Where are you from?" the woman asked as she started to reach for a third cookie and then shook her head as if scolding herself.

Faith felt her heart begin to pound again. She'd slipped, but only because this woman was so easy to talk to, and because it had been a long, stressful day, and let's face it, a stressful few months, too.

"Down south," she answered, hoping that would suffice, her eyes darting to the lobby, which remained empty.

"What brings you all the way to Vermont?" the woman inquired.

Wasn't that the million-dollar question? One that Faith wasn't exactly prepared to answer, at least not yet. She thought of the excuse she'd come up with on her long drive here, hoping that it was somewhat acceptable for a single woman in her late twenties to show up at a remote New England inn a week before Christmas.

"Bad breakup," she said.

Sure enough, the woman's face turned to one of sympathy. "That must be tough. Especially around the holidays."

"The holidays are a lonely time," Faith agreed with a sigh. She couldn't even blame it on her mother's death. The holidays had been lonely long before her mother left this world.

"How long are you in town for?" the woman asked.

Faith was growing uncomfortable by all the questions, especially when she didn't have a good answer to this particular one, not when she wasn't sure of her plans beyond actually getting here in one piece. The woman seemed to sense the shift in the room because she said, "Sorry if I'm being too nosy, it's really not my way at all. That's more my sister's job."

They shared a smile, even though Faith, growing up as an only child to a single mother, couldn't relate.

The woman shrugged. "I sort of own the place..."

"Oh!" Faith hadn't realized that the inn had been purchased, but she supposed that it made sense. How else could it have remained open after the passing of its original owner? "I didn't realize. A different woman checked me in."

A member of the Hart family, she didn't mention. A distant cousin, perhaps? She could feel the blood rushing in her ears as she waited for the woman to explain the relationship.

The woman raised an eyebrow and then said, "That must have been my sister, Melody."

Sister. Now Faith stared at the woman with fresh scrutiny, taking in every angle of her face, the slant of her mouth, the slope of her nose. There were similarities, especially in the jawline, and maybe a little in the smile, too. Older sister, she'd wager. But not by more than a few years.

"I hope she got you squared away," the woman said a little nervously. "Neither one of us has much experience with running an inn. The most we have was from watching Nana on our visits."

Nana. Faith felt like she could barely breathe, and she reached out to set a hand on the back of the couch to steady herself.

"I heard about her passing," Faith managed to say. "I'm sorry for your loss."

The woman just gave a little nod. "Well, it's just us now with this big old house. No other family to help."

No other family. Faith let that sink in for a moment.

"Well, I'd better go before I really do eat all these cookies," the woman said. She extended her hand. "I'm Nora, by the way."

"Faith," Faith replied with a quick shake, feeling a little breathless by the physical contact.

"Well, let me know if you need anything, Faith," Nora said with a friendly wave as she walked away.

Nora. And Melody. Nora and Melody *Hart*.

Her research hadn't uncovered this.

Faith turned and looked back at the picture once more, the one she'd been holding when Nora came into the lounge, understanding now what she was seeing.

The photo was of her grandmother. Her father. His wife.

And her two sisters.

Chapter Five
Nora

Nora came downstairs the next morning to the smell of sweet cinnamon rolls and fresh coffee, and despite the stress of the past couple of days, she couldn't help but smile.

The dining room buffet was set up with a plate of baked goods, a tray of fruit, and chafing dishes of eggs and bacon. The three tables in the dining room were occupied by what Nora assumed were the inn's three current guests. An older woman, already dressed for the day right down to her red lipstick, sat closest to the kitchen, her back to the big windows at the front of the house. In the middle was a man around Nora's age. Handsome, reading a paper. Maybe here on business? And nearest the window was the nice young woman Nora had spoken with last evening.

"Good morning, Faith!" she greeted her as she walked over to the buffet and helped herself to a plate. She'd eaten a quick dinner in the kitchen last night while catching up with sweet Mr. Higgins, fighting back nostalgia that came in waves when she least expected them, like when she'd walked into the pink guest room and crawled into the very bed she'd slept in as a child.

Faith looked up from her coffee with surprise in her large green eyes, but she quickly relaxed into a smile. "Good morning!"

"Anything fun planned for the day?" Nora asked. She was just about to suggest a few activities that she'd once enjoyed when she saw Melody come in through the lobby.

Bracing herself, Nora watched as Melody entered the room with a broad smile and greeted each guest with a cheerful "Good morning!" before finally coming to stand beside Nora at the buffet.

"And good morning to you, dear sister!" Melody had mischief in her eyes this morning, Nora was quick to note.

"It is a good morning. I'd forgotten how good the breakfasts are here," Nora admitted as she added a blueberry muffin to her plate.

"Seems to me that you've forgotten how good things are here in general," Melody replied pertly as she grabbed a plate from the small stack.

Nora couldn't contain her sigh as she reached for a warm, gooey cinnamon roll. It wasn't like her to eat like this—breakfast was normally a banana on the go if she'd had a chance to buy any at the store, but this was technically a vacation. And it was the holidays, even if she didn't embrace them.

Besides, she needed some sustenance to get through this day. Or even this morning with her sister's energy. She intended to spend the day going over Nana's paperwork and calling on the local real estate office unless Toby happened to be around.

Nora pulled in a breath on that thought and released it.

Seeing Toby again had been a surprise, to say the least, and not an unwelcome one, but it also complicated things.

"Is this how we're going to start the day?" she asked wearily. She'd been so hopeful when Melody had turned off her bedside light last night without any more talk of keeping the inn.

She should have known better, that her sister was saving her attack for better timing.

"With me fighting to hold on to the last piece of our family? I don't see a better way to ring in the morning!"

"If you're so eager to keep this inn, perhaps you could start the day by cleaning the guest rooms," Nora replied, watching as alarm widened Melody's eyes. They both knew that Melody was a bit of a slob, one who cleaned only when it suited her, which wasn't often.

"I would..." Melody said slowly. "But I think Toby already beat me to it."

With that, Melody finished stacking her plate, poured a mug of coffee to which she added a comical amount of sugar, and then broke into a Christmas carol, pulling the attention of all three guests and Mr. Higgins, who had just come in through the kitchen door, holding a fresh plate of breakfast potatoes.

Melody sang with unsuppressed joy, and with a smile on her face, which caused every person in the room to smile back, except for Nora, who could only clench her teeth, and as she left the room, still regaling them with her tune, they clapped upon her exit.

From relief? Melody wouldn't see it that way, and Nora didn't have the heart to make her face reality.

She never did, and that was probably why she was stuck in the position she was in now, standing firm against her sister's desire to hold on to a property they could never afford.

Only after she could hear the sound of Melody's voice (now hitting a particularly high pitch) fading farther into the distant rooms of the house, Nora walked into the lobby, stopping short when she saw Toby standing on a ladder, changing a light bulb in the chandelier that Nora always thought felt so fancy when she was little and now saw was rather old and shabby, but charming and comfortable, like the rest of the house.

In the light of day, it was obvious that the floorboards had been scuffed over the years, and even the faded area rug couldn't disguise that fact. The walls were still the same shade of beige they'd been for as far back as Nora could remember and the baseboards could use a fresh layer of paint.

Not that she intended to improve the place. Just sell it.

Toby looked down at her when she entered the room. "She's still singing, huh?"

Nora caught the glimmer in his eyes and tried to smother a smile. "Melody hasn't changed."

"But you have," Toby said, his earlier amusement suddenly gone. His task complete, he climbed down the ladder. "When were you going to tell me that you plan to sell the inn?"

"Who told you I was?" she bristled, feeling the need to fold her arms across her chest in defense, but the plate and mug of coffee made that impossible.

She should have known that Melody would have pulled on Toby's sympathy. No wonder she'd come into the dining room looking so satisfied.

"Melody and I had a little chat this morning," Toby confirmed.

"About me?"

"About the newest guest, actually," Toby replied as he folded up the ladder. "And about your plans."

Her plans. The truth was that Nora didn't have a plan, and that was what made her so uneasy. She took comfort in routine, in knowing what came next in her day. But this...this had thrown her, and now she was presented with a problem that she didn't quite know how to solve.

Make that two problems, she thought, looking at Toby.

"I've only been in town for less than a day," she replied, but it was a lame excuse, and from the look he gave her, he thought so, too.

She stared up at him, still adjusting to the fact that he was now a solid six inches taller than her, and the only hint of that boy she'd once known remained in those sky-blue eyes and the smile that he wasn't wearing this morning.

It was just as well, she told herself. Each grin he gave her yesterday in their brief exchange just made her stomach turn over with nerves and memories and something else. Something she couldn't help but recognize as attraction. It was still there. After all these years. As sure as the old chandelier hanging above their heads.

"Melody just announced this?" Not that she needed to ask. Melody had no doubt started a campaign to get the staff on her side.

"She made a passing comment about how much she was going to miss this place and it didn't take long for me to figure out what she meant." He gave her a hard stare, all friendliness now gone. "And you've just proved my hunch was right."

Nora blew out a breath. "Look. This is a big house. A business. And it's not like I'm rolling in cash. My career is in New York—" Or at least it was. She still wasn't sure what would be waiting for her when she returned.

"I get it." Toby nodded, looking resigned. "You have a life."

Did she, though? Nora thought of how she usually spent her time and it certainly wasn't like this, and she wasn't talking about the delicious food, either. Her weekdays were busy—a scramble to work each morning, a long day on her feet, and a tired trek home to a lonely and tiny apartment. She hadn't admitted to herself that she was lonely, but now, standing here, with an old friend, as familiar as a favorite sweater, she knew that she was just that. Alone, yes. And...lonely.

"The problem is, this inn is my home in many ways, Nora. And Mr. Higgins's, too. Did you stop to think about him?"

Nora felt the heat rise in her cheeks. "Surely he'll want to retire soon. Especially with Nana gone. And you." She stared at him, struggling to keep eye contact when she saw the depth of emotion in his eyes, willing her to change her mind, to say something else. "Why don't you buy the inn?"

There. That seemed like a perfect solution. He was as attached to this place as she'd once been—more, given that he was still here, years after she'd left, not by choice at first, but later, just that.

He shook his head. "Believe me, if I could, I would. But this place... It's not cheap."

She raised an eyebrow. "My point exactly."

He pushed out a long sigh and combed a hand through his dark hair, resigned to the situation if not entirely happy about it.

"Well, so long as there are paying guests, we have a responsibility," he said.

"Of course." Nora wasn't going to argue with that. It was the least she could do while she was here, and it was what her grandmother would have wanted.

She didn't want to think about what else Nana would have

wanted. What her intention had been when she left the inn to her granddaughters. What had she been hoping would happen?

Nora set down her plate of food on the check-in desk, her appetite lost. She knew what her grandmother had been hoping. It was exactly what Toby had wanted. For Nora or Melody or both of them to run the inn.

Nora didn't know anything about running an inn but the man in front of her did.

"What do you suggest?" she asked.

Toby looked surprised to be asked for an opinion and he rolled back on his heels, sizing her up. "Well, for starters, we need some decorations. Christmas is next week."

Like she needed the reminder. But Nora nodded. Decorations. The guests would be expecting them.

"Did someone say decorations?" Melody asked, all but bouncing into the hall.

Nora narrowed her eyes on her sister, knowing that they'd have a little chat later. "Toby has suggested that we decorate the inn."

"Count me in!" Melody said happily, choosing to ignore Nora's warning look. "I used to love helping Nana with her Christmas decorations!"

Toby glanced at Nora, a single raised eyebrow proving that he didn't think he could count on her. And that stung. Bad. Because once, there was a time when she and Toby could count on each other for anything and everything.

"The more hands the better," he said.

Decorating the house might help generate interest from prospective buyers, Nora considered. She could feel the heat of her sister's eyes on her, and despite not wanting to send Melody the wrong message or give her false hope, she forced a smile and nodded.

If there was one thing she knew how to do it was decorate.

But she wasn't about to admit that she'd learned the skill right here, in this house. With these people.

And Nana.

Chapter Six
Melody

Haul out the holly! Melody sang along to the antique radio that Nana always kept on the console table in the lounge as she did just that, draping the mantel with fresh evergreen garland that Toby had brought in from the tree stand in town just before lunch, along with enough to wrap the rails of the porch, too. He knew just what Nana liked, but then, Melody supposed that he had been around for more holidays than she had, at least lately.

Toby had always been an honorary member of the family. Nana liked to joke that he was her only grandson, even though Toby had a grandmother of his own, who was Nana's best friend. The two women would bake shortbread every season, package them in cellophane bags, and tie each one with a cheerful red ribbon. When Melody and Nora arrived on their school break, their job was to distribute the homemade gifts to all the shops in town, with Toby in charge of pulling the sleigh that held the box of treats.

Melody wondered if Toby still remembered those snowy afternoons, which were often interrupted by warm mugs of hot chocolate from all of Nana's friends who invited them to stay for a while before moving onto the next house or shop. Or if Nora remembered, for that matter. Melody made a mental note to bring it up the next time she got those two together—which wouldn't be difficult. Nora and Toby had always been close.

But years had passed, and they weren't kids anymore.

And Toby... Well. Toby was like a brother to her. A cousin, at least. But there was no denying that the same sparkle that once lit Nora's eyes around Toby still shone through yesterday when they'd arrived and found him here.

Melody paused to take in the room. The fire was crackling in the hearth, Christmas music was playing softly over the speakers, and already this house was coming alive with festive spirit.

Now, to only make sure that Nora caught a little of it, too. It wouldn't be easy, Melody knew, especially given that Nora hadn't enjoyed Christmas since the last time they'd spent it here —but that was all the more reason to hope that by being here, at the inn, at Christmastime, Nora might just find that piece of herself that she'd lost somewhere along the way.

Before they both lost this inn and the last of their family memories.

Melody belted out the next verse, wishing her Nana could be here to join her, as she fluffed the garland and then stooped down to gather one of the fresh wreaths from the box, also compliments of Toby, but she stopped when she saw a man standing in the doorway, his hands stuffed in the front pockets of his jeans, an amused smile gracing his pleasant face.

"Please," he said with a deep, pleasant voice. He held up a hand. "Don't stop on account of me. I was enjoying listening to you sing."

Melody felt her cheeks flush, even though she'd always loved performing for an audience. "How long have you been standing there?"

His mouth twitched into a grin. "Was there a line about the brightest lights?"

"Lights!" Melody held up a finger to remind herself to get to those next. Then, realizing she might have said that a little too enthusiastically, she said, "Sorry. I tend to get a little excited when it comes to Christmas."

"You have a lovely voice," the man continued as he walked into the room. He extended his hand. "I'm James."

"Melody Hart." Melody remembered him from breakfast this morning. She also remembered that he was sitting alone. At Christmastime. In a romantic country inn.

But she didn't remember noticing how his hazel eyes crinkled at the corners, or how his smile made something in her heart smile back.

"And thank you," she added as she reluctantly dropped his warm hand. "For tolerating my caroling. It's more than I can say for my sister."

"I meant what I said. I enjoyed it."

Melody glanced at him as she found the ball of lights in one of the other boxes Toby had left for her, trying to decide if James was flirting with her or just being friendly, and hoping that it was a little of both.

She grinned. "Well, good. If you stick around until Christmas, you'll be hearing more of it."

"I am planning to stay for Christmas, actually," he surprised her by saying. Without asking, he reached out and took the lights from her, starting to untangle them.

"Oh." Melody hoped she didn't sound as pleased as she felt

as she went back to fluffing the wreath she planned to hang over the mantel. "Family in town?"

James shook his head. "Nope. It's just me this year."

Single, then. Not that she should get too excited about that—even if she already was, a little.

"Well, nothing beats Christmas at the Hart Inn," Melody promised him.

James hesitated for a moment and then nodded. "I'm counting on it."

Before she could ask him what he meant by that, he handed her the string of lights, no longer tangled into a ball.

"I can help with the decorations," he offered.

"Oh, but you're a guest!" And the last thing she needed was to have any of the guests complain to Nora about the service here. Awkwardly, she moved the ladder toward the fireplace, trying not to bump any furniture, even if it would all be sold or donated if her sister had her way.

"Yeah, but I've already read the morning paper," James said with a bashful shrug.

"The riveting *Juniper Falls Gazette*?" Melody made a mental note to grab a copy from the stack on the front desk. "Do they still have a 'Comings and Goings' column?"

James's eyebrows lifted. "You mean a gossip column? Yes."

Melody laughed and James joined in. It was a nice laugh, Melody noted, and she always paid attention to laughs. Actors tended to have great ones, at least the ones who were cast. It made her question her own laugh, nearly as much as she questioned her singing voice, given that her roles had always been fewer and farther between than she would have liked, more so with each passing year and new fine line.

"So tell me, what's your connection to this place?" James

asked as they started to wrap the lights over the garland that covered the mantel.

"My grandmother used to own it," Melody told him, hoping that she could say it without getting teary-eyed. "She recently passed away."

"I heard." James's gaze was sympathetic when their eyes met. "I'm sorry to hear that. I remember her very clearly."

"You've been here before then?" Melody thought he looked vaguely familiar, but then, she'd thought the same thing about the other guest—Faith. It was probably just part of the nostalgia of being back at the inn after all this time. Everything felt familiar. Everyone felt like family. And everything felt like home.

"Once." James nodded as he focused on his task. "A very long time ago. I came at Christmastime. Your grandmother had stockings for each of the guests."

Melody gasped. "I remember that now!" But she struggled not to frown, wondering how she could have forgotten such a cherished tradition in the first place—or the special stocking that Nana had made just for her.

"She made me feel so special," James went on. "*She* was really special. Seeing her again was one of the reasons I decided to come here for Christmas."

"I hope you aren't too disappointed, then," Melody said apologetically. "Unfortunately, the best you've got is her granddaughter."

James's eyes met hers over the garland. "That's pretty hard to beat."

Now Melody did blush, and she quickly turned on the lights, hoping that their glow would cover the pink in her cheeks, not highlight it.

"Looks pretty good," James remarked, stepping back to take

in their work.

Melody did the same, but she wasn't as satisfied as him. "Oh, I'm just getting started! I have to hang the wreath over the mantel, and then the candles have to go in all the windows. The tree will go in the corner, near the fireplace, and—" She looked at James. "I think a stocking for every guest is in order."

He looked at her in surprise. "Really? I mean—don't do it on account of me."

"I'm doing it *thanks* to you," she told him. "I mean it. Thank you. It's been a long time since I've been here for Christmas, and you brought back a memory that I'd somehow managed to forget. And I don't want to forget anything about my happiest holidays here."

"Me, neither," James said. Then, breaking eye contact, he cleared his throat and said, "So, put me to work."

Melody loved his enthusiasm, and she certainly didn't mind his looks, either. "Seriously. Aren't you on vacation or something? We have a library through the parlor doors if you want to choose a book."

"I am on vacation, but I'm here for Christmas. And I have a stack of books that I'm happy to read when I'm in my room. And besides, I don't call this work."

Melody couldn't agree more, and she didn't argue when James set a steadying hand on the stepladder as she took the first rung. "What is work, exactly?"

"Oh...boring. Finance. Just an office job." James was clearly being modest. His sweater was made of cashmere, an ashy beige, similar to his hair, his shoes were soft, cognac-colored leather, and he had time and money to spend over a week here in this inn, and Nana's rates weren't exactly low, especially at Christmastime.

"And where is work?" Melody asked as she carefully removed the mirror that usually hung over the mantel and passed it to James. She stole another look at him as he swapped the mirror for the wreath. He lacked Toby's rustic appearance and practical clothes. Boston, she assumed, since it was the closest major city to Juniper Falls.

But James surprised her when he said, "New York."

She whipped around, causing the ladder to teeter as she nearly whipped James in the head with the wreath she was holding.

"I live in New York! Greatest city in the world!"

Now James looked at her with surprise but he gripped the ladder with both hands. "Really? What do you do there?"

Melody had grown to loathe this question over the years. When she was younger, she'd proudly tell people exactly what she did—or aspired to do, if she was being perfectly honest. But contrary to what Nora thought, Melody wasn't completely checked out from reality. She saw the doubt cloud their eyes when she told them she was an actress. She saw the little pinch of disbelief when they asked if they'd seen her in anything, and she rattled off a few unknown stage productions. She'd spent years waiting for her big break. It still hadn't come. And with each passing month, she was starting to lose hope that it ever would. Most days, she could rally and be her own cheerleader, the way Nana had once been for her. Tell herself that it took only one opportunity. Just one!

But the other days she wondered why it was so hard to find.

"Oh, I was recently working at Castle's department store?" She didn't bother mentioning that it was a seasonal job, one her sister had managed to secure for her through a few calls and favors, and one she had blown within three weeks along with her sister's already dwindling trust.

"The store on Seventh?" He nodded. "I've been in a few times. Maybe I saw you there."

"Oh..." Melody wasn't sure how to respond to that, but she decided that she might as well just be upfront. "I'm not sure if you would have recognized me. Unless you were looking for an elf."

James laughed again, a deep rumble that swept through the room. Melody smiled as she secured the wreath to its hook.

"Do they make the staff dress up?" he asked, seemingly almost delighted by the possibility.

"Only those who work in Santa's Village," Melody replied. She knew she'd have to explain, but how could she? She was unemployed, and even her seasonal job had been a bust. "I... sang carols to the children."

That was true, at least, even if Santa had probably added her to the naughty list because of it.

"What got you into singing?" James asked.

"Oh..." Melody pulled another string of lights from a box, wondering if he really wanted to hear the story, but it was clear from the patient way he was watching her that he was sincere. "It was my Nana, actually. She said with a name like Melody, I was born to sing. Whenever we'd visit, she'd have me give a little concert to the guests here in this very room. The Christmas carols were my favorite." She smiled at the memory now even as tears filled her eyes. She quickly brushed them off with the back of her hand and went back to her task—and her story. "I started auditioning for school plays, and I always got a part. Admittedly, I was one of the only kids in middle school willing to belt out a solo on stage in front of my peers."

They both laughed again.

"So it was your grandmother who inspired you," James commented softly.

"She didn't just inspire me," Melody said as she finished adding lights to the remaining garland, with James's help. "She encouraged me. Not just to sing. Or perform. I don't think she cared what I did or where I ended up, so long as I was happy. She just...wanted me to be me. My best self."

"And are you...happy, I mean?" James asked thoughtfully.

"I'm happy here," she replied honestly. Then, because she was curious what would bring a successful, handsome, seemingly unattached man in his early thirties to this country inn for a week at Christmastime, she said, "And what about you? Are you happy?"

"I'm happy here," he said with a slow smile.

Now Melody realized that they were both grinning like a pair of those middle-school kids she'd just complained about. Maybe she hadn't imagined the attraction. And maybe it wasn't even one-sided.

Or maybe this man was lonely. And maybe she was a little lonely herself, even if she didn't like to admit it.

But there was work to be done if she wanted to try to save this house, meaning that she couldn't linger in the lounge any longer. Even if she wanted to do just that.

"I suppose I'd better go find Toby and see where else I can be of use today," Melody said with great reluctance.

"I'll see you around?" James looked at her hopefully.

"Just follow the sound of my singing," Melody told him, and with that, she left the room, humming one of her favorite carols, feeling even better than she had half an hour ago. Feeling like somehow, this might be her best Christmas ever.

Chapter Seven
Faith

Faith had slipped out the front door of the inn while Melody— her sister!—was decorating the lounge with one of the other guests. He was handsome, and idly, she wondered if they were flirting. If he was Melody's type. Or if Melody had a boyfriend.

She wondered where Melody lived. What she did for a living. What Nora did and where Nora lived and if Nora had a boyfriend, too. Did Faith have any nieces or nephews?

She wondered if the sisters were close. Nora's offhanded comment last night had made Faith wonder, and this morning there had been noticeable friction at breakfast between the two.

But then, wasn't that how it was with sisters? She wouldn't know. She was an only child—or so she'd always thought. But she had friends with sisters, and they were always squabbling and then making up. Growing up, Faith had envied that, longed for it even, not knowing that it already existed for her. That the family she craved was out there all along.

And from what she gathered, they didn't know about her any more than she'd known about them.

Faith sighed heavily as she carefully maneuvered the sidewalk in her weather-inappropriate shoes, grateful that the shops were already in sight. Juniper Falls was as pretty as a postcard, and she made a note to buy a few to send to her friends back home.

It was a true New England Christmas town, and she stopped as she approached Main Street for a proper look, unlike the cursory glance she allowed herself yesterday when she finally pulled into town, stressed and tired, questioning what she was doing here, wondering what she would find.

Well, now she knew. She'd found her sisters.

Only now, she had to decide what to do with that information. And she was at a total loss.

The shops and restaurants on Main Street were housed in brick buildings with crisp white trim lined with pine garland and twinkling lights, and there, in the center of it all, was a town square complete with a large white gazebo, decorated with red ribbons, housing a large Christmas tree.

It was like something she had dreamed up as a child, long before she knew that she had any connection to this place or that she even had any family at all beyond the mother who had raised her. She wondered, as she often did these past few weeks, what she would have done if her mother had shared Faith's father's name sooner. If she would have come here to search for a link to that side of the family like she did now, or if she would have had a chance to meet her grandmother before she was gone.

Tears stung her eyes, and she blinked them away. It seemed wrong, somehow, to grieve a woman she'd never known when Melody and Nora had lost someone special. Nana. That's what they called her. It seemed like such a pet name, something so personal, different from the standard "Grandma" that she'd used for her mother's mother. Faith had a visual image of her father's mother but now she longed to know more, to hear stories, to bring this vision to life, if only in her mind.

And, she supposed, in her heart.

Right now, it felt like it was breaking again, and Faith took a big intake of the cold winter air to bring herself back to the present. She had no plans for the day, and she wasn't ready to go back to the inn just yet, not when she was feeling so overwhelmed and confused.

Coffee was in order. Then shopping. And luckily, both options were close enough that she wouldn't have to worry about slipping and falling before she was safely tucked inside.

All the same, she gingerly pushed through the door of the nearest coffee shop, feeling instantly better when the warm room and rich aroma of a fresh brew and sweet baked goods hit her. She peeled off her thin gloves and walked to the wooden counter, scanning the menu on the chalkboard that hung on the back wall.

"Let me guess," a man said, interrupting her thoughts. "Peppermint mocha? Extra whip? Crushed candy canes?"

Faith looked at him with interest. His deep brown eyes were sparkling, his grin bore a hint of mischief, and his dark hair was slightly curled.

Perking up, she replied, "Do I look like I work in the North Pole?"

He laughed, and she smiled broadly. It had been a long time since she'd bantered with a cute guy, even longer since she'd wanted to. The past few years since her mother's diagnosis hadn't been easy, but then, none of her years had been exactly easy. Some were just easier than others, relatively speaking.

"What'll it be then?" he asked, tipping his head.

She noticed the way his gaze never left her as she walked across the counter to stand closer to him, studying the display case as she did so. "Vanilla latte. No whip. Definitely no candy canes. And...what's that delicious smell?"

Now his eyebrows shot up, and he looked pleased when he said, "Cranberry spice muffins. We only sell them at this time of year. And only because my daughter insists."

Daughter. Immediately Faith felt her spirit wilt, and not just because he was spoken for and handsome.

She should have known by now that not everyone walked this earth alone as she did, but all the same, it just reminded her of her current situation and made her feel lonelier.

"I'm also not from the North Pole," he said with a wink.

Now Faith frowned. A wink from a married man? Maybe that's just how people were in small towns such as these.

"You're from Scroogeville!" a little voice called out, and Faith turned to see a girl of about five or six kneeling on a stool at the counter, clutching a pink crayon in her hand.

"See?" The man grinned boyishly, and Faith felt her shoulders relax. "I don't lie."

Faith wished she could say the same for herself, and she felt a familiar surge of anxiety swoop through her stomach when she thought of what would happen when she told Nora and Melody who she was—if she even told them at all.

"This is my daughter, Star," the man told her. "I'm Aiden."

"Faith." She smiled at the little girl as Aiden started her order. "What are you working on?"

"My Christmas wish list," Star said as she continued scribbling on the paper.

"Yeah?" Faith leaned in, trying to make out the words

written in thick crayon. "And what's at the very top of your wish list? A dollhouse? A bike?"

"A new wife for my dad," the little girl replied.

Faith felt her eyes widen and when she looked up, she saw that Aiden's face was as red as the Santa mugs lining the back counter.

"We've talked about this, Star..." he warned, giving Faith a look of apology.

But Faith just grinned, showing she wasn't bothered. If anything, she was amused. And more than a little curious. So, the friendly coffee shop guy was single, after all—and maybe he was being more than friendly, too. Maybe he *was* flirting.

She'd been out of the game for so long she wasn't even sure she remembered how.

As she took her drink from him, their fingers grazed, sending a flutter through her stomach.

"But if you had a new wife, you'd be happy again!" Star insisted.

"Kids," Aiden muttered to her, clearly flustered. "They say the darndest things." To his daughter, he said, "How could I not be happy when I have the best daughter in all of Vermont?"

"Well, you're pretty grumpy," Star pointed out, sounding rather grumpy herself.

Aiden laughed, a rich, booming sound as warm as the drink in Faith's hands.

"Are you?" Faith asked, enjoying the banter. "Grumpy?"

"Let's just say that the holidays aren't my favorite time of year," he replied, his expression sobering.

"Mine, either," Faith confided, and this time, they shared a small smile until she was the one blushing. "But you've decorated the place very nicely," she felt the need to point out.

"Star's doing." Aiden shrugged. "It's not easy to say no to that face."

"I'm a Daddy's girl," Star announced proudly, sharing a chubby-cheeked smile with her father.

Faith felt something inside her break all over again, like it had so many times in her life, only this time it was worse. As a little girl around Star's age, she'd always wondered who her father was, if he'd loved her, why he never visited, why he wasn't around. It hadn't been easy, especially when the annual father-daughter dance rolled around at school, or she and her mother went shopping around the holidays, surrounded by bigger families, people who were buying gifts for people on their long lists, or decorations and sweets for the parties they would have.

The closest thing Faith had ever gotten to a large and festive Christmas gathering like the ones all her friends and neighbors seemed to have was the class party at school, and those had stopped after her elementary years.

Their world had always been kept small; her mother preferred it that way. "If you don't let people in, they can't disappoint you," she liked to say.

Only now, she couldn't help thinking of her father's two other children. The ones he loved and spent time with. Had they been Daddy's girls? They'd at least been given the chance.

She hadn't even learned her father's name until two weeks ago.

"Here's a cranberry muffin on the house." Aiden interrupted her darkening thoughts and held out a plate. "Sorry, I forgot to ask you if you wanted it to go."

"Thank you! And...I can stay," she said, even though she hadn't exactly planned on that. Still, it was warm inside the coffee shop and the smell was inviting and the company was, well, unexpected. And nice. And it wasn't like she was in a rush. She had nowhere to be. Not today. Not tomorrow.

She tried not to let that thought unsettle her too much. Her job had always been a means to an end, taken to help pay the mounting bills, a desk job at a large insurance company that offered good benefits. Her mother had been proud of her for taking that job, calling it sensible and stable, and Faith didn't bother to explain to her that it was also soulless.

She'd quit her job last week, without a plan in place other than to spend her holiday in Juniper Falls. She'd felt guilty, about all of it, until she remembered that she didn't have to explain her decision to anyone now.

Except maybe to her newfound sisters.

"I don't think I've seen you around before," Aiden remarked. "Are you in town for the holidays?"

Faith nodded. "I'm staying at the Hart Inn."

"Of course!" Aiden nodded. "Great place. Visiting family?"

Faith didn't want to lie, but she couldn't exactly tell the truth, either, could she? "Sort of reconnecting with family."

"No better time of year for it," he replied.

"I thought you weren't into the whole Christmas spirit thing," she chided, eager to get off the topic of herself.

He held his hands up. "Again. The things I do for my kid."

She gave him a knowing smile. Like her, Aiden might not love the holidays, but she sensed that he wished he could.

Like her.

Chapter Eight
Nora

After breakfast the next morning, Nora made the rounds of the house, cross-checking the list that she and Melody had made last night in their room with what still needed to be done. The lobby was now exactly how she remembered it from all those trips up here each December—if not a little better. Nora had spent most of yesterday rifling through boxes of decorations and coming up with a plan for how to best use what she found. There was now a big evergreen arrangement on the check-in desk and garland wrapping its way up the stair rail, secured by big red bows. The dining room's three tables had been covered in Nana's tartan cloths, and greenery anchored each end of the buffet table. There were red pillar candles on each table, lit for dinner, even though only two of their guests, James and Edith, had come down for dinner last night. Faith had ordered a tray up to her room, much like Nora and Melody had done.

There was still much to do, but already the house felt alive and—to use Melody's favorite word—*festive*.

One look on Toby's face as he came through the front door said otherwise.

"We need to get started on the porch," he grunted.

"Well, hello to you, too," Nora said with a forced smile, hating that there was tension between them, and fighting off the guilt that it was all her fault.

He gave her a look that said he wasn't amused, and as he came closer, she could still feel the cold coming off his thick wool coat. It was comforting, sensing his presence like this, even if it was a little unnerving, too. The Toby she knew was leaner, less rugged, and maybe even a little less handsome. Time had only enhanced his looks, and, it would seem, her attraction to them.

"How about a warm cup of coffee before we tackle the porch?" she suggested, hoping to make peace. The last thing she wanted to do was to hurt Toby. Or Melody. Or her grandmother, even if only in spirit.

Couldn't Toby see that Nora was no more in a position to take over this rambling old place than he was?

Toby's shoulders relaxed as he nodded. "A coffee would be great." He gave her a little smile as he shed his coat and hung it on the rack, and something in her stomach swooped and then soared.

Feeling suddenly flustered, she walked into the empty dining room, sensing him close at her heels, and nervously reached for a mug that rested beside the carafe. The tea and coffee station remained open throughout the day, and she knew that often Mr. Higgins liked to set out a surprise plate of cookies, especially around the holidays.

When their coffees were made, Toby pulled out a chair at the table closest to the windows and Nora took the seat across from him. There was so much that she wanted to say, but with so many years lost, she didn't know where to begin. Once, there would have been a time when they simply picked up where they'd left off—the gaps between summer and winter seemed to disappear within minutes of being in each other's company. They'd fall back into old conversations, run out to the pond for a swim in the summer or skate in the winter. It had been so easy to fall back on old habits.

But they weren't kids anymore. And eighteen years was hardly the same as a single autumn or spring.

"So, how long have you been working at the inn?" she asked, feeling uncomfortable that she didn't know the answer to this, not just because she now owned the property but because this was, as Melody kept pointing out—their family house. Their family business.

"About seven years," Toby surprised her by saying. Before she could ask whatever happened to his plans for law school, he added, "I was working for a big law firm before that."

"In New York?" Nora felt horrified at the thought that they could have lived in the same city and never knew it.

"No, Boston." He gave her an incredulous look. "You think I would have lived in New York and not looked you up?"

"I've heard I'm not exactly easy to find," she admitted, giving him a little smile over the rim of her mug.

"Is that on purpose?" he asked.

Nora hesitated and then shook her head. There were plenty of reasons that she kept her world small and contained, and he was one of them. It had broken her heart to know that she'd never see him again, that the boy she'd dared to get close to, open up to, and love had been taken from her like so much else.

"We're talking about you right now," she said. "Not me."

She was eager to hear the rest of his story, to fill in the blanks from where they'd left off when she was fifteen and he was just a year older. They were so young but they both already had plans for the future. Ones that they'd both followed, at least in part.

She'd never thought she'd stop making her biannual trips to this town, for starters. Or that her parents would both die much too young.

Or that the last summer they'd said goodbye would be the last time she'd see Toby.

Until now.

Toby took a sip of his coffee. "Law wasn't for me in the end. The hours were too long, making it difficult to find time for anything else, especially when I was working my way up to partner. And then I found out that my grandmother passed away."

"Oh no!" Nora set a hand to her chest. She had been just about to ask about Franny Phelps, and now an image of the kind and fun-loving woman who lived for her monthly ladies' poker nights filled her heart with longing for times gone by. "Oh, Toby. I...didn't know. I'm so sorry."

He nodded along. "It was a long time ago." Still, she could see the pain in his eyes. His grandmother had been like a mother to him, more than his actual mother, who never could settle down, stopping into town once a year at best after she'd dropped Toby off when he was only seven. When they were young, Nora and Melody had asked Nana about Toby's parents, but Nana had just shaken her head and told them not to ask about such things. Still, Nora could sense a sadness come over Toby at times, especially around the holidays, when her parents were passing out gifts in the lounge and his were nowhere to be found.

It wasn't until they were older that Toby opened up about his childhood. By then, his mother was visiting only every few years. They barely had a relationship, and Toby didn't seem to want one, either. He always said that he had found his family right here. That he had everyone he needed.

Nora grew quiet when she realized what he had meant by that. That Nana had been his family. This house was his home.

She had been a part of it all. And now she was taking it all away.

"I came back to figure out what to do with my grandmother's house...and your grandmother sort of took me in," Toby continued.

Nora smiled. "She always did consider you to be a part of the family."

"She *was* family," Toby said firmly. A shadow passed over his face for a moment and then he sipped his coffee.

Nora opened her mouth to say something—anything—that would take away the pain she was causing him. Unlike Melody, Toby was sensible. Surely he could understand her position. That it wasn't about what she wanted, it was about what had to be done.

It was a lesson she'd learned as just a teenager. One that Toby had learned long before she had.

"We should get back to the decorations if we want them finished any time before Christmas," Toby said, suddenly standing.

Deciding that now wasn't the time to make things worse by talking about the fate of the inn, Nora scrambled to her feet.

"I made a list." Nora followed him into the lobby and snatched it from the desk.

Toby scanned the paper. "You thought of everything."

"That's sort of my role," she said. Not wanting to get into her personal struggles since she'd last seen him, she said, "I'm in charge of decorations at a department store."

"That explains the checklist." Toby's expression softened. "And why you did such a good job with the decorations in the house."

"Well, Melody helped," Nora admitted. It was her sister who had remembered to add the stockings for each of the guests. Nora could only hope that Toby would remember where they were stored.

"Eagerly," Toby agreed. "She roped in one of the guests, too."

"Faith?" Nora asked.

Toby shook his head. "James."

Nora nodded, letting that sink in. She'd noticed James, of course. He was friendly. Handsome, too. She could only hope that her sister was being careful.

"I can help with the porch if you'd like," Nora offered. She waited, nervous that he'd turn her down, that he wouldn't want to spend time with her. That he'd confirm what she feared most —that their friendship wasn't just a part of the past, but that it was also something that they'd lost. Along with so much else.

"Well, we still don't have a tree."

She stared at him, wondering if this was just an excuse to not work together. "Melody volunteered to pick one up today."

Toby looked doubtful. "Melody plans to haul a tree all the way up the hill and get it set up in the lounge? All on her own?"

Nora could only toss up her hands. "You know Melody. She's tenacious. That's one thing I have to say about my sister. She's not a quitter." Even if sometimes, she probably should be.

Nora sighed. Melody was yet again unemployed, or "between gigs" as she preferred to tell people. It was all fine and good when she was twenty, but now she was thirty, and though Nora wasn't keeping score, Melody had been cast in only two plays in the past year, and one had lasted for only two weeks before closing down production due to low ticket sales.

Nora went and saw all of her sister's performances, of course, and she couldn't help but note that they seemed to be in increasingly obscure locations, with less seating, and even fewer audience members. She always made sure to clap extra loudly to make up for the lack of energy in the room, but she felt it. And even though Melody always came out smiling, she knew her sister. She saw the lack of shine in her eyes. She knew she felt it, too.

Still, she didn't give up. And Nora was beginning to worry that she never would. That she'd forever be bouncing around, holding out hope, waiting for something that would never happen.

Hadn't they done enough of that as kids? Nora had, that much was for sure—until she'd come to her senses. And that was why she prided herself on good, hard work and a guaranteed paycheck. A place to be every day. Responsibility that she could both depend on and handle.

"The tree will be up by tonight," Nora said firmly. She'd haul it up the hill by herself if she had to, if only to prove to herself that she didn't need this man and that she was perfectly fine on her own.

Even if she wasn't exactly...happy.

"If you say so," he said, the doubt evident in his tone.

"I do," she said pertly. "Since when did you lose faith in me?"

"You really want the answer to that?" He stared at her, and she realized that she wasn't so sure that she wanted the answer. That she'd rather remember Toby the way he used to be. And the way she used to feel when she was around him. How every graze of his touch would send a shiver through her, how the light in his eyes was enough to make her heart feel like it might burst, how his grin was enough to bring out her biggest smile. How there was nowhere she wanted to be, other than right here. At this inn. With him.

Now, seeing the hard set of his jaw, she realized that somewhere in time, they'd lost that connection. But not the feelings. At least not for her. And oh, how she'd really thought they were lost forever—right along with him and any chance she ever had of being the girl she once was when she was with him.

She cleared her throat and went back to her list. "Melody mentioned stockings. Nana—"

"Had one for every guest," Toby finished for her. He managed a crack of a smile. "You're forgetting that I've been here day in and day out for years while you were down in New York."

"Fair enough," she replied but then, thinking of his words, shook her head. She stared straight into his soft blue eyes, which still had a way of pulling her in even after all this time. "Actually, no. That's not fair. It's not like I was avoiding Nana by choice. I hope—" She swallowed hard, pushing back the emotions that were starting to get the best of her as an uneasy thought took hold. "I hope that's not what Nana thought."

"Nana wasn't judgmental. And she certainly didn't assume the worst in people." Toby's voice turned softer when he said, "Look. I'm sorry. You know your grandmother loved you. And she knew that you and Melody loved her."

"So the judgment's just coming from you, then?" Nora eyed him closely, not sure if that was supposed to make her feel better, because it didn't. Not at all.

Toby turned away from her as one of the guests appeared on the landing of the staircase. "Edith! Good morning to you."

"And to you," the older woman said warmly.

Nora noticed that like yesterday, Edith was dressed elegantly in a cashmere sweater and gray slacks, not a silver strand of hair out of place, and her red lipstick carefully applied.

"Any plans for the day?" Toby asked as Edith took the remaining stairs and met them in the lobby.

"Oh... Oh! Mr. Higgins!" Edith's face lit up when the inn's longtime cook appeared through the dining room doorway. "I've been hoping to see you."

Mr. Higgins raised an eyebrow in surprise. "There's not a problem with the food, I hope?"

"Quite the contrary!" Edith rushed to tell him, putting a hand on his arm and letting it rest there. "I...I...just wanted to tell you how good your muffins were this morning!"

"Oh." Mr. Higgins looked noticeably chuffed, standing a little taller than his already sturdy frame. "Well, I'll be sure to put out extra for you tomorrow, that is if you'll be staying with us another night?"

"Oh, I'm here through Christmas," Edith assured him. Then, when she dropped her arm, the smile seemed to leave her face for a moment. "Same as every year."

Mr. Higgins smiled and gave them all a nod before pulling his heavy coat from the rack and heading out the front door, no doubt to run into town for some supplies, but hopefully to take a much-needed break from the kitchen. Nora hadn't thought of it the last time she'd been here, or all the times before that because she'd been too young, but the old cook was here by five every morning to get a start on breakfast and often didn't leave until after eight.

He was still spry, she noticed, watching him through the windows that framed the front door. And she wasn't the only one watching him, either.

"Well." Edith eventually turned back to them with a sad smile. "I think I'll go find a good book to read from the library."

Toby waited until Edith had disappeared from view before leaning in and whispering, "I think she's after more than that man's muffins."

"Stop it!" Nora swatted him but she was laughing, and it felt so good to laugh with Toby again. It was as if the past eighteen years—and all their troubles—were forgotten for a moment. "I never thought about it before, but is there a Mrs. Higgins?"

Toby shook his head. "Hasn't been for years. Mr. Higgins has been a widower for as long as I've known him."

"Children?" They would have been as old as her own parents, she figured.

"No," Toby said with another shake of the head. "He started working here after his wife died. This inn is home to him."

Nora dropped her gaze, unable to look Toby in the eyes for another second, even though she knew they were both thinking the same thing. If the inn closed, people would lose more than their jobs. Jobs could be replaced. But a home—and a family—couldn't.

Chapter Nine
Melody

Melody pushed out the door of the inn onto the porch and inhaled a big breath of frosty winter air. She smiled as she opened her eyes and took in the stretch of white snow that covered the front lawn like a sparkling blanket, remembering how, as a child, she and Nora were only allowed to build snowmen or make angels in the backyard, so every guest would have a picture-perfect first glance of the inn when they arrived.

The snow sparkled under the sunny sky, but the clouds were moving in, meaning snow was coming later that day. She didn't mind, so long as she had the tree picked out by then.

Tugging her mittens from the pocket of her coat, Melody walked down the steps to the salted pathway, happy to be on a mission, even happier that Nora had assigned her such an important and special task—even if it was only probably because Nora didn't want to do it herself, being a Grinch and all.

Or maybe, Melody thought with a secret smile, it was because she wanted to stay back at the inn...with Toby.

"Melody!"

She stopped at the sound of a male voice and turned to see not Toby but another handsome face instead.

"James," she said in surprise as she saw him hurrying down the porch steps. He was bundled in a navy wool coat, brown leather gloves, and a designer plaid scarf. Melody was suddenly all too aware of her hand-knitted scarf, made last spring when she had too much time to kill backstage at show rehearsals, and which may or may not have a few holes where she'd dropped a stitch. "You heading into town?"

He nodded, his nose already turning a little pink as the wind picked up. "Thought I'd walk around for a bit until the snow hits. Where are you off to?"

She smiled broadly. "To pick out our Christmas tree for the lounge! We're inviting all the guests to decorate it tonight. There will be snacks and cider, per tradition." She, for one, couldn't wait to relive it.

"Perfect night for it." James's gaze locked with hers for a moment. "I could help you pick out the tree if you'd like."

"Sure!" She wasn't about to turn away some helping hands, and not just because, when reality set in, she was a tiny bit worried about getting the tree back up to the inn if it couldn't be delivered on short notice. James enjoyed Christmas—and right now, he seemed to be the only person in her world who did.

They began to walk in the direction of town, carefully avoiding slippery patches and icy puddles that had formed overnight. When they were finally on safe footing at the base of the hill, and the country road turned to one with sidewalks, lined with shops that sold everything from books to toys and from coffee to ice cream, the tree lot came into view at the edge of the town square.

"It's kind of hard to miss," she said. "I just hope that they aren't all picked over by now. Most people have probably had their trees up for a couple of weeks by now."

"I was a little surprised not to see the tree when I arrived last week," James admitted. Then, seeing the worry in her face, he grinned and said, "But this is better. Now I get to be a part of it all."

She felt herself blush and hoped that it would pass as her skin's natural response to the cold air.

"You said you've been to the inn before," she said, curious about what he'd mentioned yesterday.

James nodded as they crossed the street and approached the tree lot, where Melody relaxed when she saw there were still dozens of trees to consider.

"A long time ago. When I was a kid."

"Oh?" Melody stared at him more carefully, trying to imagine a younger version of his face, only to be reminded of what a handsome face it was indeed. "I spent every summer and Christmas break here when I was little. Maybe our paths crossed."

He looked at her in surprise. "I don't think I'd have forgotten a face like yours. Or a voice."

Now she blushed again, so fiercely that she had to look away, happy for an excuse to change the topic for a moment.

"They sell hot chocolate," she said, pointing to the sweet little wooden stand decorated with garland and colored lights. "I might need something to keep me warm while we consider our options."

"Ah, so this isn't going to be a quick errand?" He looked amused, but still, Melody felt a moment of doubt.

"I should have probably told you. I'm not just here for any tree. It has to be the right tree. It has to...speak to me."

"Here I thought you might say it has to sing to you." He grinned until his eyes crinkled.

"Wouldn't that be something? Most days, I'm singing alone." Melody felt her throat tighten when she thought of how it wasn't always that way, that once, the inn had been full of music and singing during the holidays. "My grandmother was the one who would always sing with me," she explained. "My parents were too busy to bother with that sort of thing, and my sister... Well, have you met my sister?"

He tipped his head for a moment as if considering this. "Not officially, but I've seen her around the inn with a clipboard."

Melody rolled her eyes. "That's Nora, all right. Everything she does is by the book. Not from the heart. If she were in charge of picking out a tree, she'd probably have measured out a space first, written down the exact dimensions she required, handed the paper to a worker here, and been content with what was delivered a few hours later."

"That would be efficient," James commented, but there was doubt in his voice.

"That would be taking the fun out of it," Melody corrected him.

"So...I take it that you didn't measure the space first?" There was amusement in James's voice now and Melody felt her mouth curl up into a guilty smile.

"Like I said. When I see it, I'll know." She stopped talking, realizing that this all may have been more than James, a paying guest at the inn she now owned, had thought he was agreeing to. That maybe, being a successful businessman from New York rather than a "starving artist" as Nora liked to call Melody, he was more in Nora's camp. That he would have approached this task with efficiency rather than emotion. That it was just one more thing to scratch off a list. "If you have to get going—"

"And let you haul what I assume will end up being the largest and fattest tree left on this lot back to the inn on your own? What kind of gentleman would that make me? Besides. There's nowhere I'd rather be," he said, giving her a smile that made her stomach turn over as he pulled out his wallet and ordered two hot chocolates with extra whipped cream and a candy cane garnish for one. "I took a guess," he said, handing it to her.

"Is it that obvious that I love Christmas?" she asked, taking a long sniff of the peppermint mixed with chocolate. A perfect combination if anyone were to ask her.

"Just a little," he said, and they both laughed. "But can I tell you that I'm grateful for it? I would have been more than a little disappointed if the inn wasn't the way I remembered it."

"So, when did you come visit the inn for the first time?" she asked as they walked toward the first row of trees.

"The Christmas I was fourteen," James replied. "So...seventeen years ago."

Melody nodded. "We wouldn't have met then. We stopped coming here when I was twelve. Eighteen years ago," she added.

He frowned a little as Melody stopped to consider and then quickly discard a tree. Too small. She needed something big and memorable, a tree that would make up for all the years that she hadn't been here to enjoy one.

"Why'd you stop coming to visit?" James asked.

"I don't know actually," Melody admitted with a sigh. "My father died and after that, my mother stopped taking us here.

Nana was my father's mother, you see. My sister told me that our mom and grandmother had an argument, but we didn't know what it was about. And now...well, now it's just me and my sister so we'll never know." She felt her voice catch on the last few words.

"I'm sorry," James said softly. "It's not easy to lose someone you love."

He frowned deeply, his gaze far away, across the town square, but his mind clearly even further than that.

She stared at him, wondering whom he had lost, and if that was the reason why he'd come here all by himself for Christmas this year. Why did he choose to spend the holiday with a bunch of strangers instead of family or someone he cared about?

And she decided that it was all the more reason to be sure that this Christmas was extra special, especially if she had anything to do with it. That's what Nana would have wanted. Even if Nora refused to see it that way.

They turned a corner, entering another row of trees, each one nearly more perfect than the next.

"You might be surprised to hear this, but they are all so beautiful that I think I'd be happy with just about any of them."

"Even this one?" James raised a playful eyebrow and reached out to grab a sad-looking tree that stood only about as high as his elbows. Its needles were sparse, and it was more than a little crooked.

Melody laughed. "Well, maybe not that one. Although I do feel sort of sorry for it."

"You feel sorry for a tree?" James studied it carefully. "I'm not exactly sure it has feelings."

"Well, I have feelings," Melody said. Too many, to hear

Nora tell it. Or maybe Nora didn't have enough; it was hard to tell. "And this little tree will probably not get chosen. Too much competition. Too hard for it to stand out."

She felt her emotions rise when she thought of her career, of how she was rarely chosen for a role anymore. The feeling, however, was fleeting, and quickly replaced by fear that she might not get chosen ever again.

"There's no rule against having two trees, is there?" James asked lightly. "I mean, it's sort of like a backup. Or...a little sister."

Or an understudy, Melody thought. Another part she was never given.

"We could put it in the dining room, in that corner near the front window?" Melody didn't know how Nora would feel about that and right now she frankly didn't care. That inn was just as much hers as it was Nora's, even if her sister didn't see it that way.

Decision made, she nodded.

"You're a bad influence on me, you know," she said, edging closer to him as he dragged the smaller tree along the row through the bigger, more impressive ones.

"And how's that?" James asked, glancing sidelong at her.

"You indulge me," she said simply.

"Maybe we're just alike, you and I," James said, his smile warming her up more than any cup of hot chocolate ever could.

Melody glanced at him while he stopped to study a tall, sturdy tree, wishing that this were true, but knowing that a man like James, with his expensive clothing and successful New York life, probably didn't have anything in common with her at all.

Even if she suddenly wished that he did.

Chapter Ten
Faith

Faith spent the day taking in the house, going from common room to room, picking up frames and studying their photos, opening books and reading the inscriptions, and walking the grounds and imagining who the people were who had once lived here. Each photo brought a clearer image. She now knew what her father looked like as a baby, and as a young boy, that he seemed to have liked to fish in the pond, and sled down the hill that led into town. She knew what he looked like on his wedding day. And later, when he was a new father. She saw the pride in his eyes. The joy when he held his two daughters. And she tried to imagine how she might have fit into this life. This wonderful, cozy world. Until she remembered that it couldn't have been as wonderful as it seemed. If it had been, then she never would have existed.

The afternoon snow had brought everyone inside by early evening, and over a dinner of roast chicken and potatoes, Melody entered the room and announced that dessert would be served in the lounge for the annual tree decorating. Faith watched her sister—her sister!—happily share the news, but while Faith was busy staring at Melody, Melody was busy staring at the only male guest of the inn.

Faith's gaze drifted to the man who had claimed the middle table of the dining room. With only three guests staying at the inn, it worked out perfectly that no one was forced to share. But now, Faith considered that someone could join them any day, at any moment really. And somehow that bothered her. She'd gotten used to this small mix of people that made the inn feel more like a house than a business. She'd grown familiar with their odd routines, like the way Edith always sat at the table closest to the entrance of the room, facing the kitchen door, and with her back to the windows, shutting out the view.

How Nora liked to frown over her clipboard and move about the inn with Toby, who watched her from afar and then looked away if she noticed, and how they seemed to know each other very well, but not quite like brother and sister. No, that was more Toby and Melody's dynamic—they jostled and joked in a familial way that Faith craved. It was how she'd always imagined a cousin might be, how a big family might come together for Christmas. And even though she was here, a part of it now, she still felt like an outsider, no different than the little girl who used to stare in the windows of other people's houses on Christmas Eve, watch through the warm glow as people embraced and gathered around the tree, wondering how it might feel to be invited. To have a full house.

A full heart.

Earlier in the lounge, the male guest had introduced himself to her as James when he and Melody had hauled not one but two Christmas trees into the house, the smaller of which was now set up in the dining room, adorned with a simple strand of lights. He was friendly enough but also fine with keeping his space and letting Faith have hers, which she appreciated.

The last thing she needed was for anyone here to start asking too many questions. At least until she figured out what she was going to do next.

With Melody and Nora.

With her life.

Everyone stood and filed into the lounge, where a large tree stood in the corner beside the fireplace. Even though most of the house had been decorated yesterday, seeing the tree made it feel like...well, Christmas. And not just any Christmas. A proper Christmas.

And a beautiful one, too.

Faith hesitated in the doorway. She didn't do proper Christmases, not like the ones her friends had or the ones she saw on television. There was the plastic table-topper-sized tree that she and her mother used to put on top of their small kitchen table. Faith would decorate it with paper ornaments she'd made at school. On Christmas morning, there would be a few wrapped gifts surrounding it—practical items like new sneakers or pajamas, along with a few sweets. There was no big meal. Certainly no cookies. Definitely no cider that now filled the lounge with the smell of warm and inviting spices.

"Here!" Melody was suddenly in front of her, wearing that bright, big smile of hers, holding out a box of ornaments.

Faith took them carefully. It was clear that they were old, and it dawned on her that they'd once belonged to her grandmother. To her father, when he was a boy.

Had he stood in this very room, holding this very box, walking toward the tree like she was doing now?

Melody bounced across the room to the old-fashioned radio

and switched it on. Soon, the sounds of holiday music filled the air, and Faith saw Nora flash Melody a warning glance from across the room.

"Don't worry, Nora," Melody said, shaking her head. "I won't start singing. Yet," she added with a wink in Toby's direction.

Toby struggled to hide his grin when Nora shot him a look of exasperation.

"Is Mr. Higgins going to be joining us this evening?" Edith asked pleasantly as she hung a glass ornament shaped like a dove on a branch. It was one of the prettiest ornaments that Faith had ever seen, like something in the windows of the department store she liked to stare into as a kid.

"Don't you worry, Edith," Nora assured her. "Mr. Higgins is just putting the finishing touches on the cookies for tonight. He should be in with the tray any minute."

Faith was happy to see that she wasn't the only one eager to enjoy those cookies. Tonight, she wouldn't pocket any, though. Staying up in her room no longer appealed to her as it did that first night. Now, she longed for every interaction she had with her sisters, every stolen glance and snippet of conversation.

Melody was the energetic sister of the two, the cheerful, friendly one. But Nora wasn't unfriendly, just reserved. And although Faith didn't know her any more than the other people in this room who had come to Hart Inn for their Christmas holiday, Faith couldn't help but sense that something was worrying Nora and keeping her from completely enjoying all the festivities. When she didn't think that anyone was watching her, she seemed to let her guard down, and the usual pleasant smile she gave was replaced with a frown that Faith recognized all too well as worry.

She'd seen it in her own mother's face too many times. Especially at Christmas.

Edith glanced at the hallway and then smoothed her red cashmere sweater as Mr. Higgins came into view, carrying a large tray of assorted cookies.

"Oh, that all looks wonderful!" Edith cried as the older man set the tray down on the coffee table.

"If you need more, just let me know. I'll be cleaning up for another hour or so," Mr. Higgins said to the room with a friendly smile.

"Oh. You won't—" Edith looked flustered. "You aren't going to be joining us?"

"Join us!" Melody called out, looking up from a box she'd been rummaging around in for the better part of a few minutes. "It won't be the same without you."

Mr. Higgins seemed to hesitate but then, after one long look at the tree, gave a single nod. "Okay, then. Can't pass up a Christmas tradition in this old inn. Wouldn't be fair to Nana."

"Does everyone call her Nana?" Faith asked, wishing she could take back the words as soon as she'd said them. She longed to know more about the woman who had once run this establishment, but by the way everyone looked at her, she felt rude and out of turn.

But when one by one, each of them started to smile, she felt her shoulders relax.

"Nana wouldn't have it any other way," Mr. Higgins replied. "And she was only five years older than me."

Edith laughed, louder than anyone else, and put a hand briefly on Mr. Higgins's arm. "You knew her the longest, Jim. She must have been like a sister to you."

Jim, was it? Faith felt a pull and looked over to see Melody staring at her with a raised eyebrow and a smothered smile. Faith gave a small one in return. It felt like a bonding moment. It felt...nice. Wonderful, even.

"Nana insisted that I call her Nana, too," Toby said, sounding wistful as, with Nora's help, he began untangling a string of lights. "Even though she knew I had a grandmother of my own, she made it clear that I was family whenever I was here."

His hands stilled for a moment when he glanced up, giving a quick sweep of the room, before returning to the task. It was Nora who stopped then, only for a moment, to study him. She looked like she wanted to say something but then thought the better of it.

"I, too, called Mrs. Hart Nana," Edith admitted, looking almost girlish as she and Mr. Higgins—Jim—sat side by side on the sofa and sorted through some old boxes of ornaments.

"I did, too, actually," James confided, looking a little embarrassed to say so.

"You've been to the inn before, then?" Nora looked at him with curiosity.

James helped himself to a sugar cookie. "Just once. Years ago. But...I always remembered it. And her."

"I thought you looked familiar," Toby said, tipping his head as his eyes narrowed. "You came with an older man, right?"

James nodded. "My grandfather." There was a whisper of a smile before it vanished. "You have a good memory."

"I know everything about this place," Toby said. "And about Nana Hart."

Faith busied herself by taking a mug of hot cider from the tray on the console table. Just how much did Toby know about the woman who was her grandmother? And just how much had Nana herself known?

"Nana was a grandmother to us all," Toby said fondly as the room lapsed into a moment of silence.

Only Faith had nothing to contribute to the conversation. She was the only person in this room who had never met Gloria Hart. The only one who hadn't had the privilege to call her Nana or to feel like a member of this family.

Even though that's exactly what she was.

※

The tree slowly came alive, filled with ornaments that each person took time deciding where to carefully hang, the lights wrapped by Toby. Even Nora had set aside her clipboard for the night and seemed to relax, sipping cider by the fire, laughing when Toby told a story about the time they'd all gone sledding down the front yard and he'd ended up in the street, nearly taking out poor Mr. Higgins, who was heading into town for groceries.

"My happiest Christmases were the ones spent in this house," Melody said a little sadly. She glanced at the guests and explained, "We used to come every single year, no matter how bad the weather, remember that, Nora?"

"The snow can't stop us. That's what we used to say," Nora said slowly.

"That's what Dad would say," Melody corrected her, and Faith jolted so hard that she almost knocked an ornament she'd been hanging from a branch.

Her cheeks felt as hot as the fire that Toby was stoking. "Sorry," she said, flustered.

It had been the first mention of her father in her entire life—outside of her mother finally handing over his name. How she'd longed for this moment, craved it and imagined it, and then given up all hope of it when she'd learned through her internet research that he was gone, and that his mother was, too.

But neither obituary had mentioned Melody or Nora or any other next of kin, and now here they were, two women who knew not just Nana Hart, but Faith's father. Their father.

She froze as Melody continued reminiscing with everyone. "Dad grew up in this house. He was used to the outdoors."

"Unlike Mom." Nora gave a little smile. "She was a city girl at heart. Like you, Melody."

"Dad always said the only thing he loved about the city was Mom," Melody mused. "He met her when he went to college there, and he couldn't bring himself to ever be apart from her again."

"Well, other than when he traveled for work," Nora pointed out. To the guests, she said, "He worked in sales, so he was on the road a lot."

Faith felt uncomfortable at the mention of her sisters' mother and used the opportunity to walk over to the tray of cookies that had been set beside the cider. She didn't know if her sisters knew of her existence, and if they didn't, how would they feel to know that their father had been unfaithful to their mother?

"Enough about us," Nora suddenly said. She stood and chose another ornament from a box. "What are all of your favorite Christmas traditions?"

She looked around the room, and Faith inwardly cringed when her gaze fell on her.

"Oh...the holidays weren't a big deal in my house growing up." Faith gave a little shrug, wanting to gloss over that time in her life so she didn't have to think about it anymore. "I was raised by a single mother, and she was always busy working. My mom wasn't close to her mother, and without any other extended family or siblings, we didn't make a big deal of the holidays."

Melody was looking at her with noticeable pity until she finally said, "Then Nora would have fit in perfectly with your family."

Faith swallowed hard. "How so?"

"Instead of celebrating the holidays, Nora has made a business out of them," Melody said, giving her sister a knowing look.

"It's known as the busiest time of the year," Nora replied with a hint of irritation.

"Which is why this is so special," Edith cut in, clearly picking up on the tension that was growing in the room. "I've made a tradition of coming here every Christmas for the last ten years."

"Has it been ten years?" Mr. Higgins looked surprised at this fact and then nodded along. "Time does have a way of moving along faster than we notice."

"It feels like just yesterday that we were here for Christmas," Melody agreed. "Even though it's been so many years."

Now Faith looked up in confusion. "You didn't come last year?"

The room seemed to go still as Toby exchanged a glance with Nora and Melody.

"We stopped coming here after our father died," Nora explained.

Melody stared into her mug. "We stopped doing a lot of things."

Silence hung in the room for a moment while Faith let this settle in. It was so easy to envy her sisters for the relationship that they'd had with their father that she hadn't stopped to consider how hard it must have been for them to lose him.

And who was she to mourn something she'd never had?

"Well, that's why this Christmas we're bringing back all of Nana's traditions," Melody said cheerfully, setting her mug on a coaster with a bang. She stood and crossed the room to another large box in the corner. "James reminded me of one of Nana's best traditions."

She reached into the box and pulled out a hand-knitted stocking in a beautiful Fair Isle pattern.

"Each guest will have a stocking to hang and keep up through Christmas," Melody told them as she brought out more and more stockings in shades of green, red, and ivory. They were each unique, some velvet, some made for children.

"And you never know," Toby said, stepping forward to claim one that Faith noticed bore his name in small letters. "There may even be a little gift tucked inside on Christmas morning. Something special, that was just waiting to be given on that day."

"From Nana?" Had it been one of her many traditions? Faith had to ask, she had to know, everything, anything; it was all a gift to her.

James gave Melody a little smile. "Or from a secret admirer."

Faith looked down at the dozens of stockings that had been made and collected over the years, now spread out on the seat of the couch, each one more beautiful than the next.

"Pick whichever one calls to you," Nora reassured her.

Faith studied them, wondering what the story was behind each one, if her grandmother had a favorite, or if she'd made them for specific people over time.

"I always do the turtle doves," Edith said, holding hers fondly.

"And I always have the one with the bells," Melody said, hanging hers on one of the holders that had been placed on the mantel.

Nora came to stand beside Faith, so close that Faith could feel her sister's arm brush against hers. Nora's hair was a rich nut brown compared to her lighter coloring, but still, Faith wondered if they looked at all alike, even though Melody and Nora didn't exactly closely resemble each other. She wondered if they noticed—if anyone did.

But everyone was busy chatting and talking about their stockings, sharing a memory of the first time they'd received it.

"I forgot," Nora whispered, her tone full of wonder when she reached for an especially pretty stocking with velvet trim and intricate gold embroidery. "Nana told me this was mine because I loved helping her make everything beautiful."

"You've certainly made this house look beautiful," Faith told her. "It's like a Christmas house from a movie."

Like the house of her dreams.

"Which one chose you, Faith?" Melody asked, looking at her brightly.

Her choice of words wasn't lost on Faith, and without giving it any more thought, Faith reached out and picked up the one that had stuck out, calling to her as soon as she saw it. It was all ivory, and soft, with three beaded snowflakes covering the front.

"Oh," Nora said, her voice thick with emotion. "Nana

made that one our last Christmas here. Three snowflakes. All different, but somehow, all the same."

Faith carefully hung her stocking beside Melody's and stood back to take a long look at it.

Three snowflakes. All different. But somehow, all the same.
Much like the three sisters.

Chapter Eleven
Nora

Nora could get used to the breakfasts at the inn, not that she'd be admitting that to Melody. Last night's storm had left a solid six inches of fresh powder outside, and Nora was content to be inside, wrapped in a warm cardigan, a cup of coffee in her hands, and a blueberry muffin on her plate.

She watched through the paned window of the door as Toby shoveled the path from the driveway, which had fortunately been cleared by a plowing service well before dawn. Just hearing the noise had pulled Nora from the good feelings she'd gone to bed with—all the cozy and nostalgic sentiments that had been brought on by decorating the tree and hanging the stockings were replaced by a cold slap of reality, as bitter as any New England cold snap.

Someone was paying for that plow service, and she doubted it was Toby. Toby himself was, technically, another bill, another check that would have to be written to keep this inn going. She'd studied all of Nana's paperwork, ledgers, and receipts, and even though Nora didn't exactly have an accounting degree, it was obvious that Nana had been bleeding money for years to keep the inn going. It may have lasted for her lifetime, but at this rate, it wouldn't last for another generation.

Nora sipped her coffee and checked the forecast on her phone, sighing when she saw that more snow was expected throughout the late morning, meaning it probably wasn't going to be the best day to head into town and have a talk with the real estate agency, but a phone call would hopefully get things moving.

She'd put it off, knowing that talk would fly, that she'd have to give sweet Mr. Higgins the courtesy of knowing first, even though he had to assume that selling the inn was a possibility now.

What was one more day, she thought with a sigh as she went back to the front desk to see if anyone had left a message overnight, hoping for a last-minute Christmas reservation. But the old but still functioning answering machine wasn't blinking, and one glance at the tablet proved empty. Business was slow, or slower than she remembered, or maybe this was how it had always been and she just hadn't noticed as a child. Back then, her world felt big and full. Complete.

She pinched her lips against the reminder of how small her world had become.

Through the dining room entrance, she saw Mr. Higgins setting a fresh batch of muffins on the buffet table. He stopped to chat a little with each guest, as content as he'd always been within these four walls. He'd spent a lifetime here, under this roof. Stayed on even after Nana had passed, in good faith, or maybe because he didn't want to be anywhere else.

A wave of guilt washed over Nora, and she had to look away. Maybe it would be for the best if she was already on her way back to New York when the listing was posted. If they could list by early January, with any luck, they'd have a buyer before March, someone in search of a summer country home, or maybe someone from town who'd been eyeing the place for years. There was no denying that it was the prettiest house in all of Juniper Falls.

Not that she'd be telling Melody that. It was time to put these notions of keeping the inn out of her sister's head once and for all.

Still, she smiled as her sister came down the stairs, halting when she saw Nora waiting for her. Her eyes narrowed in suspicion for a moment.

"You look chipper today," Melody said slowly.

"Oh, just going through my to-do list," Nora replied.

Melody rolled her eyes as she hopped down the remaining stairs. "You and your lists. I'll admit that they do seem to bring you a strange satisfaction."

They did. Because thanks to them, life, however chaotic, could feel contained and manageable. She may not be able to predict tomorrow, but she could control today with one sheet of paper.

"So, what's on your list for today?" Melody asked.

Nora smiled sweetly. "Cleaning the guest rooms. I know Toby has been handling it, but seeing as he's outside shoveling snow, I thought we might take that task off his hands."

Melody's face paled. "I've never been very good at cleaning."

"Oh, I know." Nora struggled not to laugh as she stared at her sister, who was giving her that wide-eyed pleading stare like she used to give when she was little and there was only one cookie left in the jar. Nora always caved and let her have it, but not today. "But you've made it so clear that you want to keep the inn. And running an inn involves guests. And cleaning up after those guests."

Melody's eyes went wide, but before she could get carried away with hope, Nora said, "There are cleaning supplies in the laundry room upstairs. I'll need you to tackle the bathrooms, especially the toilets. And be sure to give the tubs some elbow grease, we wouldn't want anyone complaining that there was mold. Oh, and you'll want to keep the mirrors streak-free, of course."

"Of course." Melody's voice was barely audible, but her eyes narrowed when she rallied. "And what are you going to be doing?"

"I'll be washing all the linens. Of course, you can never be too careful about bed bugs."

Melody could only stare at Nora, who had to bite the inside of her cheek to keep from laughing.

She let out a heavy sigh, no longer able to look at her younger sister, as she instead picked at her muffin. "But then, this is all just part of it. Waiting on other people. Making the house nice and tidy, just for them. Catering to their every need since they are paying for the experience. To think that Nana did this every single day. Day after day. After day." Her gaze skirted to her sister, whose eyes couldn't get any bigger.

"Well, Nana did have a housekeeper on staff," Melody suddenly said.

Nora had already prepared herself for this. "Yes, but of course she took time off. Vacation days. But an inn...it's never closed. Not if you want to keep the lights on."

"You don't think Nana ever got a single day off?" Melody looked aghast, especially considering that she spent most of her days not working.

Nora, however, was silenced for a moment. She thought of her grandmother, tending to guests, filling her home with strangers, and making sure that they had a wonderful stay. She probably never did take a day off—other than the few times she came to New York, but that was often just for a single night.

But something told Nora that she wouldn't have wanted to have this big old house to herself. She wanted to fill it.

Pushing back the lump in her throat, Nora said, "We'd better get cleaning while the guests are still at breakfast."

As she pushed passed Melody, she could no longer bask in the triumph of getting her point across. She could only think of how much pride her grandmother took in every aspect of this business. And this home.

❋

Nora had finally finished tidying the three guest rooms and helping Melody with the bathrooms, and it had taken the two of them a fair portion of the morning. Already exhausted and in dire need of coffee, she came downstairs just as Toby pushed through the door, his cheeks pink from the cold, snow starting to melt off his boots. He pulled them off, replacing them with a pair of shoes that he kept in a wooden box near the door, and walked up to her, rubbing his hands.

"Coffee?" she asked. "I was just about to get a cup." She checked the old clock that hung next to the watercolor a guest had painted of the inn years before Nora had been born. "Or a sandwich? The day is slipping away from me."

Toby shook his head. "We have to finish decorating the porch before the next round of snow hits."

We, was it? Nora didn't push his choice of words any more

than she planned to argue with it. Decorating was something she could do. It passed the time. It sometimes served a purpose. Only right now, she didn't see what that was.

"I think the guests are content with everything we've done," she said. And so was she. "Wreaths are on the doors, and the garland is wrapped around the porch. It's not like we're hoping to attract walk-ins this close to Christmas."

Or buyers, she thought to herself.

It was a sleepy time; people were busy with shopping and family. They'd made the house look festive and welcoming. Sure, Nana used to put out lanterns and lights, but the inn was closing at the end of the month. Any more decorations would be inefficient.

He stared at her for a moment, his eyes slightly narrowed. "Is that what Christmas has become for you? A business?"

She didn't want to point out that in many ways, Christmas, just like New Year's and Valentine's Day, was a business—and a big one. When she set up displays at the department store, she knew what to highlight for each holiday and what to skip. She didn't bother putting out lingerie and chocolates and perfume at New Year's and she certainly didn't make toys a focus for Valentine's Day.

"I'm just saying that maybe our time is better spent—" She stopped herself. She didn't dare mention that she'd hoped to clean out closets and cabinets so the house would show better.

He raised an eyebrow as if waiting for her to enlighten him. "Go on. What did you have in mind? Talking to the local real estate agent? Scheduling the demolition crew?"

"Toby." She frowned at him, but a flicker of panic made her pause. No one would buy this property just to tear it down, would they?

Only one look at the set of Toby's jaw told her that they just might. This was prime land, close to town. And this house was old and needed a lot of work.

"I was just pointing out that we don't have any more people checking in before Christmas. And what goes up must come down." In other words, more time. More work. More money to keep Toby on the payroll unless she wanted to do it all herself, and that wasn't possible, not when she was due back at work by the second of January.

"Sometimes, it's good to do nice things just for the people under this roof," he said, giving her a pointed look. "That was Nana's way."

"Of course," Nora rushed to say, hating the thought of letting her grandmother down in some way, even though she had, and she still would. "I mean, that's the point of hospitality—"

"No. That's the point of love. And Christmas. And you might be determined to cut corners and scale things back for the bottom line, but I, for one, am determined to have a nice Christmas this year, especially if it's my last one here. Now, do you want to come up to the attic with me to find the rest of the decorations?"

Nora gulped. "The…attic?"

Toby's expression softened to one of amusement. "Oh, that's right. You're afraid of the attic."

"No, I'm not," Nora replied quickly. She prided herself on not being afraid of anything—or at least not being affected by anything.

Toby's mouth twitched. "You mean that was Melody I heard screaming all the way from the pond that one summer morning? I could have sworn it was you I saw flying out the back door, brushing at your clothes and hair frantically."

"I walked into a cobweb," Nora explained with a sigh. "But the scream—"

Toby looked at her with interest as Nora thought back to that day. It had been Melody's idea to explore the attic, all because Nana had told her that she had an old record player up there and some vinyls that were practically antiques. Melody had wanted to sing along, no doubt, and Nana had begged Nora to go up with her so that Melody didn't break the machine or hurt herself trying to carry it back down the stairs.

Nora could never say no to her grandmother, not when she always looked at her with such soft, kind eyes, and so she'd gone up to the third floor, having no idea what to expect until she opened the door to the dimly lit room. Melody was thrilled to see the old mirror, the dollhouse that they'd played with as younger girls, and the wedding dress that Nana had worn when she was barely twenty. But all Nora saw was the possibility of spiders. Worse—mice. She stood perfectly still in the corner, urging Melody to come back down, bribing her with the promise of ice cream in town—her treat, from her allowance—but Melody had other ideas. And so, Nora dared to move, to walk over to the wedding dress, just to touch it, until her face hit something stringy and sticky and a scream filled the house.

Her scream.

Nora pinched her lips together as she stared at Toby. "It might have been me."

His eyebrows lifted a notch higher. "It might have been?"

"It was a long time ago," she said casually. "I don't really remember much about my time here."

Toby's smirk was replaced with a frown, and he looked at

her sadly for a moment. "That's too bad, Nora. But I remember everything."

Nora stared at him, wondering if he was referring to the day they'd almost kissed. If, like her, he'd thought about it for weeks and months afterward. Or if, like her, he'd finally let that memory go, because holding on to it was too difficult.

And holding on to each other wasn't possible. Then or now.

❋

The attic had been cleaned since the last time she'd been up here—no doubt by Toby. It was brighter, too, with more overhead lighting, and not a cobweb or dust bunny in sight.

Nora smiled at the old wedding dress, still hanging by the three-way mirror. It had yellowed with time, but it was still beautiful. She wondered what would happen to it when the house was sold. Would they move all of Nana's things into storage? She hadn't been able to bring herself to go into Nana's small living quarters between the kitchen and the library just yet. It would be too sentimental. Too...painful.

But at some point, they'd have to clear it out. Pack it up.

Maybe Melody would want to take some of Nana's special things—not that she exactly had space in her minuscule city apartment. Not that Nora did, either.

"See?" Toby said as the floorboards creaked and groaned under the weight of each of his steps. "Not so scary."

"Of course not. I'm an adult now."

"So I've noticed." Toby's reply was wry enough to indicate he wasn't flattering her grown-up figure.

"And what are you implying?" Nora crossed her arms and stared at him expectantly.

He gave her the once-over and then shrugged. "I'm just saying that you're all business now."

"Well, someone has to be. I can't exactly count on Melody to be responsible," she said.

Toby didn't look convinced as he moved to the back wall and started sorting boxes. "Melody might surprise you if you give her a chance."

"A chance to do what?" Nora stared at him in disbelief from her safe corner of the room. "Are you saying that I should let Melody run this place?"

It was a preposterous thought given their financial situation, not to mention the fact that Melody would never give up her beloved Manhattan for a small town in Vermont. She didn't even bother pointing out that to Toby because to do so would mean that she was defending her choices, and she shouldn't have to do that to anyone, including Toby.

Even if somehow, she felt she had to do just that.

"I'm just saying that the house is paid off, and you both own it."

"That doesn't mean there aren't bills and taxes. And an entire business that is the sole source of income." She shook her head. But then, because she was worried about what Toby had said downstairs, she took a deep breath and asked, "Do you really think someone will tear it down?"

Toby hesitated. "Not many people can afford to buy a house this size, especially with all the updates they'd probably want to do."

Nora frowned. The old charm of the house was what made it special. But Toby was right—there wouldn't be a huge pool of buyers in the market for this kind of investment. And it would only end up costing her money in the long run if it didn't sell. Money she didn't have, because she was barely able to pay her steep monthly rent as it was, not to mention her student loans.

"So," Toby said as he walked around boxes, stopping occasionally to peek into one. "What do you plan to do with all of this stuff when you sell the place?"

Nora sighed. "I don't know. Melody will probably want a few things. That wedding dress for starters."

Toby turned to look at her with interest. "You don't want it for yourself?"

Nora barked out a laugh. "Me? No," she said firmly.

"I sense a story behind that," he said, giving her his full attention.

Nora wasn't about to satisfy his curiosity by talking about her love life, or lack thereof. There had been a few dates over the years, mostly in college and right afterward, before she buried herself in her career, hoping to make it up to the corporate office.

So much for that.

"I'm not seeing anyone" was all she said.

"Me, neither," Toby said simply.

Nora looked away so he wouldn't see her blush. Really, why should she care if Toby was single or not? His life was here, in Juniper Falls, and in a short time, she'd be leaving this town for good, this time with no reason to ever return.

Heaviness filled her chest as she watched Toby move around the attic, stopping to peek into a box here and there.

Eventually, Nora did the same, but her heart wasn't in it. Looking at these old treasures felt as overwhelming as it was nostalgic, and both feelings made her want to run back to New York and her job there, where there was no emotion connected to any task.

No emotion connected to anything, really.

"Oh, look!" Nora cried out when she popped open a box. "These are the nutcrackers that Nana used to put out at her Christmas Eve Gala."

She picked one up and held it in her hands, carefully lifting the lever to watch the toy soldier's mouth open and close.

"I almost forgot about those," Toby said, coming to stand so close that she could smell that woodsmoke on his sweater, from a morning tending to the fire.

"I thought you didn't forget anything," she teased.

A shadow passed over Toby's face. "Nana stopped having those parties years ago," he said gruffly, moving on to the next box.

Nora frowned as she set the nutcracker back in the box with the others. "But Nana was all about traditions, especially at Christmastime. Why would she have stopped?"

Toby stopped rummaging to turn and look at her. "The parties ended when you and your family stopped visiting."

Nora fell silent as she took that news in, thinking of her grandmother grieving the loss of her only son—and then of her grandchildren.

"But she kept up with all the other decorations," Nora said, her eyes pleading with Toby to tell her what she wanted to hear. What she needed to believe. That Nana had been happy.

"Oh, well, she couldn't let the guests down," Toby said. "And Nana loved Christmas. She always said that if she made the house look beautiful, good things would come."

"You mean more guests?" Nora supposed there was some

truth to it. She'd seen the books. This year's December reservations were leaner than the previous years.

"I think she meant you," Toby replied. "She never gave up hope, even if she never said it."

Nora felt the emotions well in her throat and she struggled to swallow much less meet Toby's eyes.

"I should have come after my mother died. There was no good reason not to." She'd gotten caught up in her life, the small and not-so-small things that consumed every hour of each day. It had gotten her through the loss of her mother, just like keeping busy and focused had helped her when she lost her father. But there was more to it, she knew. She'd closed herself off from love because feeling led only to pain. And coming back here, seeing her grandmother, would have stirred up more wounds than being here now.

Now Toby's expression softened. "Hey. Don't be so hard on yourself."

"How can I not? She was our last living relative," Nora replied. And the only grandparent she'd ever been close to.

"The holidays are a busy time," Toby said gently. "For everyone."

Nora nodded. It was true, and they were busy, especially for her. She'd made them that way, not by design but by default. The busier she was, the less she had time to think about the season and what it had once meant to her. Decorating a tree was no longer a fun activity, it was a project. There was no joy in hanging ribbons and garlands at the department store, just strategy.

"Was she...mad at us?" Nora asked, dreading the answer as much as she needed to hear it.

Toby's eyebrows shot up in surprise. "Nora, she loved you. She could never be mad at you."

"But we stopped coming—" Nora swallowed; she couldn't say any more.

Toby stepped forward and put a hand on her arm. It felt solid and reassuring. And in that moment, despite all that she'd lost, she felt like she'd found something at least. His friendship.

"She understood," Toby said firmly.

"Did she? Because I don't even understand. At first, I thought it was because my dad had died. My mother and grandmother had a terrible argument after his funeral. I can still remember it, even though I never did know what it was about." She thought back—hard—to that awful night, when she and Melody had cried for so many hours that day that they were both exhausted, their eyes red and puffy, curled up in their beds in the room they shared in their Upper West Side apartment, trying to drown out their sorrow with a movie that played on the small television their father had given them for Christmas the year before. It wasn't long before the sound was overridden by raised voices coming from the other end of the apartment.

Nora, being the eldest, had snuck out into the hallway, alarmed at the sound of her mother so angry, even more alarmed that she was angry at Nana of all people. Nana with her warm hugs and Christmas carols and her crafts and homemade cookies. Surely she must have misunderstood?

But as she crept down the hall, the voices rose louder, and even Nana was shouting now. Only she wasn't shouting in anger, not like her daughter-in-law. She was pleading, insistent, as if she were trying to explain something.

Or, looking back, Nora thought, defend something.

"When my mother saw me eavesdropping, she closed the

pocket doors to the kitchen," Nora remembered. "The next morning when I woke up, Nana was gone. My mother said she had to leave, that she was needed back here at the inn. That summer, my mother enrolled us in camp instead of taking us here. At the time we assumed it was all just one more change. She was working more, so of course there wasn't going to be vacation time. A few months later, she said we were having Christmas in the city, like it would be new and special. She took us to Rockefeller Center to skate. And she took us to Radio City Music Hall to see the Rockettes. We had a proper New York City Christmas for the first time, even though we're New Yorkers. Melody loved it." She gave a sad smile at the memory.

"And you?" Toby asked.

Nora bit down on her lip. She'd hated it. She'd asked her mother repeatedly why they couldn't come to Vermont, why she couldn't spend her holiday in this beautifully decorated home instead of the apartment that didn't have any decorations other than a sad-looking tree with a few lights and ornaments Melody had made, since they'd never had a reason to collect any before, not when Christmas was always spent here, at this inn.

She'd hoped that the next Christmas they'd be able to return, that the city Christmas experience was a one-time thing, something that their mother had wanted to try, once. She'd held out hope all year until she'd worked up the courage to ask in the fall, when the leaves in Central Park turned golden and the air turned crisp and stores were starting to get an early start on their decorations.

And when their mother told her that they wouldn't be spending any more holidays at the inn and that life was different now, she'd felt like her father had died all over again, only this time, he took the best parts of their time together with him.

She'd cried that Christmas harder than the first year without him. But after the tree had come down and the holidays stretched into the long, snowy, dark days of winter, her heart seemed to freeze, too. She never cried again at Christmas. She never celebrated it, either.

"It was fine," she said briskly, turning away, hoping her casual tone was believable. That, just like that teenage girl she'd once been, if she told herself enough times that Christmas was just another day, another twenty-four hours that would come and go like all the rest, that it wouldn't matter. Or hurt.

"What's that smell?" Nora sniffed the air just as the shrill sound of the smoke alarm interrupted the quietness she'd become so accustomed to. Even in a house that was never empty, it was surprisingly peaceful.

Toby was quick to get on his feet and Nora scrambled to follow him down the attic stairs and through the upstairs hallway, past the guest rooms to the stairs, where down below she saw James and Melody had gathered into the lobby along with Faith.

"What's going on?" Melody looked up at Nora as if she had the answer.

But that was how their relationship had always worked, especially once their father died and their mother was working all the time—not only because she had to, but because it was easier for her to cope that way. Nora was well into her teens, old enough to stay home, but Melody had still been a kid. And she still was in so many ways.

Unlike Nora, she hadn't been forced to grow up too quickly. Unlike Nora, she'd had someone sheltering her from the pain as best Nora could.

It was Edith who emerged from the dining room, her face

flushed, brushing a hand through the air dismissively as the smoke alarm finally subsided.

"No cause for alarm," she told everyone. "Jim—Mr. Higgins—had an incident in the kitchen."

"Is he okay?" Melody asked, the alarm still evident in her voice.

"I'm fine!" Mr. Higgins walked in through the kitchen, looking more than a little flustered, his gray hair mussed and his cheeks pink. "I somehow set the temperature too high and I'm afraid, well, I'm afraid that there won't be a roast for dinner service tonight."

Nora saw Toby eyeing the cook, but he said nothing as the man returned to the kitchen and the guests—and Melody—wandered back into the lounge.

"Darn," Toby said with a shrug. "That's one of my favorite meals."

Nora's, too. Mr. Higgins cooked it low and slow all through the afternoon, filling the house with rich, warm smells until their stomachs grumbled. It was a winter treat each year that they visited.

Her father's favorite, too, she thought with a pang.

Nora stared up at Toby, wondering if he'd suggest dinner in town, or if he was waiting for her to—but instead, he just trekked over to the coatrack and began shrugging on his coat.

"We'd better finish decorating that porch," he said.

And because Nora didn't want to argue with him any more than she wanted to let anyone in this house down, she nodded.

A call to the real estate agent would have to wait. But Christmas could not.

Chapter Twelve
Melody

As much as Melody was enjoying James's assistance with a few more decorations in the library, she was also relieved when he mentioned he needed to make a few work calls before the office closed for the day. She glanced into the lobby, where Nora was alone and positioned behind the desk, sitting on the wooden chair and frowning at a stack of papers.

Typical Nora. They were in a house decorated with beautiful garlands and ribbons and lights and all Nora could do was look down and worry about her troubles. She was so capable of creating a beautiful atmosphere, but Melody couldn't remember the last time she'd stopped to enjoy the outcome of her hard work. She was always too busy making lists and scratching off tasks, treating life and everything and everyone in it like a giant to-do list.

Well, not tonight. Ever since they'd arrived, Nora had dodged her as best she could—turning off her bedside light when Melody was still in the shower or rising well before the sun and slipping out of the room when Melody was still toasty in her bed.

But unless they wanted to stick around and eat the sandwiches that Mr. Higgins promised to set out on a platter, they'd have to make a plan for dinner. And Melody knew just the place.

"Hey," Melody said, startling her sister. "Wow. Must be riveting reading material."

"I'm reviewing the inn's legers," Nora said flatly.

This was certainly not the conversation that Melody was looking to have tonight. Nora needed to be pulled out of her head. She needed to be reminded of her heart.

"Why don't you take a break and join me for dinner in town?" Melody suggested. "We could go to Birdie's. For old times' sake."

Nora's expression softened at the mere mention of their favorite bistro—just as Melody hoped it would.

"I forgot all about Birdie's."

Melody wasn't surprised to hear this, and it was all the more reason to go. She needed to remind her sister of how special this place was—not just the inn but the town. Juniper Falls wasn't just where they'd spent their summers and winters as children.

This was the last place they'd been a complete family.

The last place they'd been truly happy.

"It's settled, then." Melody wasn't going to take no for an answer. "I'll meet you back here in twenty minutes?"

Before Nora could protest, Melody shot up the stairs, taking them faster than Nana would have liked, only Nana wasn't here anymore, and Melody was too old to have someone telling her what to do—especially her sister.

She changed into a fresh sweater made of soft ivory wool, ran a brush through her hair, and then grabbed her hat, gloves, and coat, before moving back downstairs, more slowly this time.

The lobby was vacant now but Nora would know better than to try to dodge her—they both knew every nook and cranny of this house, from the storage door under the stairs where they used to hide from the staff or spy on the guests, especially the ones who had secrets to keep or troubles to share, to the upstairs attic, full of treasures of time gone by. Nora may have ventured up there one time and one time only, but on many rainy days, Melody loved to explore the old boxes, even going so far as to try on Nana's wedding dress and admire herself in the three-way mirror.

She'd dared to think she'd even wear it when her day came. Now, that idea seemed about as far-fetched as getting the lead in a Broadway show.

Or off-Broadway for that matter.

Or getting any role in a Broadway show.

Time had caught up with her. But she wouldn't let it sneak up on the inn. She wouldn't lose everything. She couldn't.

Melody ducked her head into the lounge just in case Nora had a sudden burst of Christmas spirit and decided to enjoy the tree for a bit, but the only person in the room was Faith, who was sitting in a chair, a book on her lap, but her attention on the flames dancing in the hearth.

"Hello!" Melody smiled as she walked deeper into the room.

Faith quickly closed the book, giving Melody her full attention. "Hi."

She seemed so pleased to see her that Melody didn't have the heart to turn and leave as quickly as she'd planned.

"I was just looking for my sister," Melody said.

A strange look seemed to shadow Faith's eyes for a moment, but then she smiled and said, "I saw her go into the dining room a few minutes ago. Maybe she's checking on Mr. Higgins?"

"Probably," Melody said. That would be a very Nora-like thing to do, and not just because she took running a business—any business—seriously.

Nora was nurturing like that, in her own way. She took on other people's problems. She took on more responsibility than she should have.

"Shame about dinner tonight," Faith said with a little smile.

Melody remembered that she was technically the co-owner of this fine establishment and that she probably shouldn't respond with her true feelings to a paying guest.

"It's a good excuse to get out and enjoy the town," she said. "Juniper Falls has some really cute shops and restaurants."

Faith nodded. "I like the coffee shop. And the boutiques are really nice. I bought this sweater the other day. My wardrobe wasn't exactly practical for a New England winter."

Melody realized that Faith had never mentioned where she was from, and she hoped, as an innkeeper at least for this week, she wouldn't be rude to ask. "And where is home?"

"Oh, I grew up down south." Faith seemed a little flustered by the comment, and Melody was about to apologize for prying when she heard her sister's voice in the distance.

"Well, don't hesitate to ask if you need anything. Nora and I are just heading into town for dinner," Melody said. She started to leave but something made her pause. Maybe it was thinking of what Nora had done—checking on Mr. Higgins. Or maybe it was the fact that Faith was a long way from home, sitting alone in this room days before Christmas, with no plans for dinner and no one to share it.

She knew the loneliness that Christmas could bring—the memories of happier times that it could stir up, for better or for worse. And she knew that there was more to Faith's story than she was telling. And she also knew what it felt like to hide heartache behind a bright smile—and twinkling lights.

"You can join us if you'd like," she offered.

Faith had gone back to reading but now looked up from her book in surprise. "Oh! Oh, I wouldn't want to intrude."

"Not at all," Melody replied, warming up to the idea. With Faith there, she and Nora couldn't exactly squabble in public as they might have done otherwise. And that wasn't what she wanted to come from this dinner, anyway. She wanted it to feel festive and fun, full of laughter and memories. A proper family dinner. Like old times.

"Come on," she said. "The best you'll probably get here is a ham sandwich, not that it wouldn't be delicious."

"Everything Mr. Higgins makes is delicious," Faith agreed with a little smile.

"The town will be all lit up and the snow is fresh. Everything will be sparkling and festive. The way Christmas should be."

Faith pulled in a breath and then gave a little nod as she set down her book. "The way Christmas should be. Okay, then."

"Yeah?" Melody was pleased as she turned to see Nora standing in the lobby, pulling her hat onto her head. "Faith's going to join us," she told her sister as they moved into the lobby.

Nora looked from Melody to Faith, her expression one of such obvious relief that Melody felt a little slighted. Was her company all that bad? Or was Nora that determined to sell this inn—and all their memories to boot?

One thing was for certain. If Nora thought she was off the hook for tonight, she had another think coming. Melody might not be in a position to have a direct conversation with her sister about the fate of Nana's inn, but she'd find a way to get her point across all the same.

She always did.

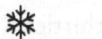

※

Birdie's sat on the corner of Main Street and Pine, directly across from the town square, where the large community tree sparkled in the moonlight. On the way there, they exchanged small talk, mostly about their various jobs, and Melody was pleased to hear that she wasn't the only one of their little trio who was out of work—even if it did seem that Faith's unemployment was by choice. Still, it did make her wonder why she chose to pay with cash, and if she was running from something.

But Faith was perfectly lovely and easy to talk to, so Melody didn't question it, instead enjoying the conversation and the sights, and the smell of fresh snow mixed with the pine trees. She was grateful when they were seated near the window—the more that Nora could be reminded of all the things she'd once enjoyed, the more difficult it would be for her to part with it forever.

Or so Melody hoped.

"So," Melody said as the three women studied their menus. "What's everyone thinking? We can share a bottle of wine?"

She glanced at Nora because they both knew that Nora would be the one footing this bill, not just because Faith was a guest and they'd invited her, but because Nora always paid when she and Melody went out—which wasn't often, and when they did it usually involved Nora giving gentle but unsolicited advice about Melody's career.

Melody always protested when the bill came, but Nora

always insisted on taking care of it, and so eventually Melody stopped agreeing to go out with her. Sure, Nora made more money because she had a more consistent income, but Melody suspected that there was more to it than that. Even now, when they were both in their thirties, Nora felt the need to take care of Melody.

Frustration grew in Melody's chest when she thought of how her sister still thought of her as a kid, not a responsible adult.

"My treat!" she blurted before she could calculate the consequences of such an offer. She scanned the menu again, relieved to see that the prices here were considerably lower than they were in Manhattan.

Nora must have done the math or decided that she didn't want to argue in front of a bystander, because she gave a serene smile and said, "That's very nice of you, Melody."

"Oh—I can't," Faith said as her cheeks flushed.

"Nonsense," Melody said. "You're doing me a favor by coming out with us tonight. You're keeping us from engaging in a sibling argument."

Faith swallowed hard and looked back at the menu before closing it and setting it on the table. "Do you do that often?"

Melody and Nora exchanged a knowing glance. "Oh, it's just how sisters can be, I suppose. That's the nice thing about being an only child. You missed out on all the rivalry."

"I can't help but feel like I missed out on a lot," Faith said a little sadly. Then, lifting her shoulders a bit, she said, "So you used to come here a lot when you were younger?"

Melody was so grateful to have the opportunity to visit memory lane without Nora accusing her of trying to guilt-trip her that when the waitress stopped at their table, she splurged on the second-to-worst bottle of wine rather than the absolute cheapest.

With their orders placed, and the wine promptly delivered and poured, Melody thought of some of their best moments here in this very spot. There were so many of them that they seemed to blur together, a big happy mess of laughter and conversation, and a feeling that she hadn't experienced in so many years that she'd almost forgotten it—but not completely. Not like Nora.

It was a feeling of completeness. Security. Comfort. And so much joy.

She looked at her sister now, picturing her as a ten-year-old girl with her crooked-toothed smile and her long French braids that would poke out from under her knitted hat. The way she'd chatter on and on about all their big plans days before they happened, not because it was work, but because it was fun. How her eyes would light up every time the waitress brought out a slice of their famous candy cane cake, and how they'd all shuffle home to the inn, their hearts as full as their stomachs, the wind and cold and snow somehow unnoticeable by the warmth of their spirits.

She took a sip of wine, feeling something in her shift and soften toward Nora. All this time, she'd thought she alone had missed so much, but now she saw that Nora had lost more.

She'd lost her spirit. Her ability to believe that tomorrow would be a good day. That everything would work out in the end.

But more than anything, she'd lost love for Christmas. And she'd once loved it most of all.

"When we were really little, our dad used to pull us into town on a sled," Melody started, sparking a hint of a smile from Nora. "That's something we'd never be able to do in New York because the sidewalks are too crowded. But here, everything slowed down, and everything always felt..."

"Magical," Nora finished for her. She cleared her throat and took a sip of her own wine.

Melody glanced at Faith, to be sure she wasn't boring her, but Faith looked riveted, her gaze never straying from Melody.

"Of course, the real work for him came with dragging us back home. That hill could be a bit steep, especially when we did little to assist in the effort."

Nora shook her head even though she laughed. "He never complained, though. He said that his dad used to do it with him, and he liked being able to pass down the tradition."

"Dad was all about traditions," Melody agreed, smiling sadly. "Especially here. He loved it here. We all did."

She eyed Nora firmly, and Nora pinched her lips and looked down at her hands.

"Did you ever know your grandfather?" Faith asked.

Melody sighed. "No. He died before we were born. That's why Nana started the inn. It started as a way to make ends meet. But it turned into a labor of love."

"It had to have been, given how little money she was making by the end," Nora commented as she reached for her wineglass.

Not to be deterred, Melody turned back to Faith and pressed on. "I think it gave Nana that sense of always having family. Even when she was alone, she never really was."

"Did she ever visit you in New York?" Faith asked, sipping her wine.

"A few times," Nora said. "She liked to make it down for Melody's school performances."

"Well, she *did* encourage me," Melody said, waggling her eyebrows dramatically until Faith grinned.

"Don't I know it!" Nora laughed. "But I suppose she encouraged me, too. I probably wouldn't have gone into my profession if it weren't for our grandmother. She had a way of seeing through to our true selves, helping us to be our best."

"That's why she never minded that Dad moved to New York," Melody agreed. "She was happy to see him going off, having a family of his own, living a full life."

Faith chewed at her lip, saying nothing as the waitress returned with their orders: pot pie for Melody and Nora, and a creamy pasta for Faith. Comfort food, and it was comforting.

One glance at Nora, who was already tucking in, proved that. Maybe even her heart could thaw a little tonight.

"I have to wonder what Dad would think," Melody sighed and stole another glance at her sister, who was stubbornly fixated on her food. "Thinking of his childhood home going to the highest bidder."

Nora shot her a glare but said nothing.

"You're going to sell the inn?" Faith sounded so shocked that immediately Nora's face turned pink.

"Oh, it's all up for discussion," Melody was quick to say, because it was, if she had anything to do with it.

But the silence from Nora did little to comfort her concerns, and Melody struggled to think of another tactic, another way to break through to her sister, or to her heart.

"Actually, I found time to call the real estate agency this afternoon. They're coming by tomorrow to take photos with the house all decorated," Nora replied.

"But—but you haven't even told Mr. Higgins that you're planning to sell!" Melody cried, all too aware that she'd lost her manners along with any hope that Faith might be a buffer tonight.

"I'm surprised you didn't beat me to it," Nora said flatly. Then, after another bite of food—food that was supposed to make her remember all those cold winter nights when she'd order this very dish before hopping on the sled to go back to the inn or walking through town to admire the lights—she said, "I'll talk to him in the morning. I'm sure he'll understand."

"I am sure he will not," Melody said. "He's spent his entire adult life working for Nana. He wasn't just her employee; he was her friend. Nana took care of him, provided for him, and gave him more than a job. She gave him a home. I can't imagine what Nana would say to know that you want to turn him out onto the streets!"

Nora's shoulders dropped as she heaved a sigh. She looked at Melody and said softly, "No one is going to be out on the streets, other than us if we have to carry the overhead of that place. Pushing things off won't change the inevitable."

Melody could feel Faith's eyes on her, but she couldn't look at the guest who had been shamelessly brought along to witness this family drama rather than prevent it.

She forced herself to take another bite of food. Hot tears threatened to spill, but she blinked them back as she stared at her sister, knowing better than to make a scene in front of their dinner guest.

But she knew that even if Faith hadn't joined them tonight, she'd be at a loss for words for right now. And maybe a loss of hope, too.

Because no matter what she'd done or said these past few

days to make Nora change her mind about the inn, none of it had made a difference.

And as the waitress reappeared with three plates of dessert and a coffeepot, she suspected that even a slice of Birdie's famous candy cane cake couldn't bring out Nora's truest self, or the happy girl she used to be.

Chapter Thirteen
Faith

The breakfast service had just been cleared when a middle-aged man with a professional-looking camera walked into the lobby and straight to the desk, where Nora greeted him in hushed tones.

Faith knew that this was coming; Nora had told them as much last night at dinner. But somehow, like so many other things in life, she'd hoped it wasn't true. That somehow, she'd wake up this morning in her beautiful room, no doubt decorated by her grandmother, and all of last night would have been nothing more than a bad dream.

Only all of last night hadn't been terrible, had it? It had been a surprise, to be invited like that by Melody. At first, she wondered if Melody knew, or at least suspected, but the more she sat and listened to the women tell story after story of their family time here in Juniper Falls, Faith was convinced that they had no idea of her existence. Their childhoods had been as rosy as their holidays here at the inn.

Faith hovered in the doorway to the dining room, watching as Nora and the photographer moved into the lounge, where the man was setting up a tripod. The tree in the corner sparkled, and the entire room glowed from the crackling fire in the hearth. When it started to get too low, Toby would come along to add another log or two.

Melody appeared on the stair landing, her eyes narrowed on Nora's back, and for a moment, Faith felt a kinship to her sister. A connection that went beyond biology. A desire to hold on to the past. To re-create it. Or at least not part with what remained of it.

"She's really going through with it?" Faith couldn't help but whisper as she moved into the lobby.

Melody looked miserably at her as she descended the rest of the stairs. "When Nora sets her mind to something, there's little to be done to stop her."

"But you could stop her?" Faith pressed. She'd wondered why Melody had shut down last night, eating her dessert in silence and then trekking up the hill to the inn without another word.

"I tried," Melody said with a sigh. "And not just last night. I hoped that coming back here again after all these years would help Nora remember how wonderful it was. And still can be."

"But she didn't?" Faith struggled to believe that. She'd seen the way Nora lit up when they recalled special moments from when they were younger.

But then, she supposed that Melody knew Nora better than Faith ever would.

Melody hesitated and then shook her head. "Nora's not the sentimental type. I should have known."

"Was she always like that?" Faith didn't think of Nora as cold. If anything, she saw her as kind and helpful. But there was no denying that there was something else there, too. A wall. A sense of stoicism. A brave face.

But what did she know of her oldest sister? She saw only glimpses, reserved for guests. Nora at her best, or at least on her best behavior.

But Melody—Melody knew the real Nora. And unlike Nora, Melody didn't hold back. She wore every emotion on her face. And, Faith thought, her heart on her sleeve.

Melody smiled. "When she was little, she was such a dreamer. No one loved Christmas as much as Nora."

"Even you?" Faith had heard Melody's singing enough to know that she was bursting with holiday spirit.

"She loved Christmas first," Melody said thoughtfully. "She was the one who would tell me all about Santa, every Christmas Eve when she let me crawl into bed with her. She'd tell me to listen for the thumping on the roof because that meant that the reindeer had landed. And she told me to always dig to the bottom of my stocking, even if I thought it was empty, because even when you least expected it, you were sure to find something wonderful there."

Faith's mouth felt dry as she pictured the two sisters, looking just like they did in the photograph in the lounge, snuggled together in flannel nightgowns, enjoying their Christmas right here, in this very house.

"What changed?" Faith couldn't help but ask.

"Everything changed when our father died," Melody said somberly.

Faith stared into her sister's dark eyes, hoping her face didn't give anything away, but every mention of the man she knew only by name made her eager for more.

"After that, we stopped visiting here," Melody continued. "And Nora stopped believing in the magic of Christmas."

Faith swallowed hard. "That's sad."

"Without my big sister, I don't know who I'd be." Melody's face clouded over, and she blinked quickly. "Anyway. Enough of my boring stories! Are you heading out for the day?"

Faith nodded, even though she would have preferred to stand here listening to Melody's stories for hours. None of them were boring to her.

"I thought I'd walk around town." Faith pulled her new hat onto her head as Melody went up the stairs, quicker than most adults would move, and no doubt eager to get away from the clicking of the camera nearby.

Outside, the sun was bright, but it did little to lift Faith's mood. She took her time walking into town, past the restaurant where she and her sisters had dined last night, and the little bookshop that Nora had mentioned she was so fond of.

Even though the breakfast Mr. Higgins had made was delicious, Faith hadn't had much of an appetite this morning, and she perked up at the thought of coffee—and, admittedly, running into Aiden again.

Pushing into the coffee shop, she was greeted by the smell of fresh gingerbread, but it was the man behind the counter who caught her attention.

"You're back!" Aiden's eyes seemed to sparkle from across the room and the grin on his face made her stomach do a funny little dance.

"Well, you do make the best coffee in town," she said with a smile as she approached the counter.

"I happen to be the only coffee shop in town," Aiden replied, not taking any offense.

He seemed genuinely pleased to have her here, and the feeling, Faith realized, was mutual. Contrary to the excuse she'd given Nora her first night at the inn, Faith hadn't been in a relationship in a while, or even in the company of an attractive man. Between caring for her mother and working full-time to cover the bills, it hadn't left much time for a social life.

"What will be it? Your usual?"

Faith didn't think a second visit warranted her having a routine just yet, but she did plan to order the same drink as last time, and she did like the way it felt to belong somewhere. Even if it was in a coffee shop.

"That would be nice," she said, hiding her smile as he started to prepare it.

She turned and looked around the room, at the people who called this town home, mothers with young children, women leaning across the table, spilling secrets, and out onto the snow-covered sidewalk to the tree lot where Melody and James must have purchased the trees for the inn.

"What's all the commotion in the town square?" Faith asked, motioning through the big windows to the activity that seemed to occupy dozens of people across the street.

Aiden looked up from the espresso machine. "They're setting up for the holiday market," he replied wryly. "They do it every year."

"It must be good for business?" Faith asked. "With so many people visiting just across the street?"

"You'd think, but most people who go prefer to sip mulled wine." He gave a mock shudder, and she laughed in appreciation.

"I prefer not to mess with good wine," she agreed.

"A girl after my own heart," he said. "We'll have to split a bottle sometime." Then, perhaps seeing the surprise in her face, he added quickly, "To ring in the new year. If you're still in town."

Would she still be in town? She hadn't thought that far ahead, but now the thought of leaving or staying brought her panic for different reasons.

She focused on the window, on today. On the celebrations across the street. But her cheeks were flushed with heat and her heart was pounding. The thought of sharing a bottle of wine with Aiden did sound nice. About as nice as the thought of staying in this charming town for a while.

And right now, both felt downright impossible. Like a dream, just out of reach. Like what might have been.

"What else do they sell there?" she asked, curious about the small wooden stands she saw being set up.

"Oh, ornaments. Stockings. Snow globes. More ornaments. If it has something to do with Christmas, you can assume there will be a stand dedicated to it."

"Ah, so you've attended this holiday market?" She gave him a knowing look.

"Not by choice," he argued. He jabbed his thumb at his daughter, whom Faith hadn't noticed was sitting at a table near the counter, coloring in a book. "But Star loves it."

"You should come with us!" Star cried out, giving them both a hopeful look.

Aiden's cheeks looked ruddy. "What did I say about eavesdropping, Star?"

"I was just coloring," Star replied. Then, going back to the task, she grumbled, "I can't help that I have ears."

Faith let out a laugh but smothered it with her hand.

Aiden shook his head fondly before saying, "You're welcome to come with us."

Faith felt herself blush as she pulled her hand away from her face. "Oh." She struggled to think of what to say, or what she even wanted to say. She liked talking to Aiden, and Star was adorable. But there was no denying the fact that her stay here was temporary.

Maybe even shorter than she'd expected, she thought, thinking of the potential sale of the inn.

"I'm sure you have plans with your family," Aiden said quickly and went back to making her drink.

She wasn't sure if what she was doing here constituted plans or a lack thereof, but she did know that she enjoyed Aiden's company, and visiting the holiday market did sound fun. Like a real, festive tradition.

"I've never been to a holiday market before," she said slowly. "And the family members I'm visiting have a lot going on."

Like photographing the house and getting it ready to list. Her heart sank just thinking about it.

Aiden looked up at her and grinned. "You've never been to a Christmas market?"

She shook her head. "Nope. My town never did anything like that."

"And where is that town?" Aiden asked, still smiling, but now Faith wasn't so amused.

"South Carolina," she said, her mouth dry. Quickly, she said, "So...it does sound like fun."

Star clapped and Aiden just shook his head. "Why do I feel like I'm being ganged up on?"

"When are you planning to go?" Faith asked, taking the hot paper cup from his hand.

"We're going tomorrow night," Star informed her. Then, sliding a glance at her father, she said firmly, "Daddy promised."

"And I always keep a promise," Aiden said with a nod.

A man with integrity, Faith thought. But she wasn't surprised. There was something about him, about the way he looked at his daughter with such doting affection that made something in her feel tight and shaky all at once.

Was this how her father had looked at Nora and Melody?

"Here," Star said, handing Faith a piece of paper with colorful writing on it in thick letters. "This is all the information you need. You can meet us right here at the coffee shop, at seven sharp. That's when Daddy's finished closing up for the day. Be sure to dress warmly, too. We like to take our time and see everything."

"Do we?" Faith flashed a look of amusement Aiden's way. "No rushing through?"

Aiden lifted his palms. "I wouldn't want to disappoint a little girl at Christmastime."

"Oh, is that your excuse?" she chided. "Or is it that you secretly want a cup of that mulled wine?"

She'd never had mulled wine, or attended a holiday market, and she found herself more than a little curious. And more than a little caught up in the way that Star's eyes shone when she described all the stands and snacks and the carolers that roamed the crowd, dressed in Colonial costumes.

"It sounds really special," Faith commented. She wondered if Melody and Nora had gone as kids. She wondered if it was one of the many Hart family traditions that had made their winters so warm instead of cold.

She wondered if her father took them and if he dragged them back to the inn by a sled.

"It is really special. That's why I always make Daddy promise to take me," Star explained. "And when Daddy makes a promise, he always makes sure it's a good one."

"Your dad sounds like a really great guy," Faith said in a mock whisper.

Star grinned. "So, will you come? Please? I can be your tour guide. I know all the best stands."

Faith gave Aiden a little smile. "Well, I wouldn't want to disappoint a little girl at Christmastime..."

And from the bashful grin Aiden gave her before the customer behind her in line got restless, she suspected that he knew as well as her that no excuse was needed.

Chapter Fourteen
Nora

Nora folded her arms across her chest as the cold winter wind cut through her wool sweater, watching from the porch as the photographer studied his camera.

"I think we have what we need," he told her. He took a long look up at the house from the base of the stairs where he stood on the driveway. "This house sure is something special. Like something right out of a Christmas story."

Nora shifted on her feet uncomfortably. There was no denying that the house was beautiful—even more so from the decorations. It looked like a scene from a movie, like an idyllic greeting card setting. Normally, she'd pat herself on the back for a job well done. Christmas captured, buyers intrigued. But this wasn't the department store. Or a product. Even if the real estate agent she'd spoken to made it feel like just that.

"Well, thank you again for coming out so quickly," she said.

"I'll send these over to your agent quickly, too," the man promised. He gave her a wave. "Merry Christmas!"

"Merry Christmas," Nora managed as she turned to go inside, stopping at the sound of a horse's hooves approaching.

She turned in surprise to see a horse-drawn sleigh gliding across the field that divided the inn from Toby's grandmother's house—now Toby's house, she supposed. She frowned as it drew near. It couldn't be. Not—

"Toby?" The cold temperature all but forgotten, she stepped down off the porch as he pulled to a stop at the driveway. She laughed, taking in the sight of the large chestnut-colored horse and the gleaming red sleigh, Toby sitting on its bench holding the reins. "What in the world?"

"I'm offering sleigh rides at the holiday market," he told her. "Thought I'd give the old boy here a little test drive."

Nora walked over to the horse and smiled into his dark brown eyes, giving him a gentle stroke on the neck. She hadn't been around horses in years, not since she'd visited the stables about a mile down the road that last summer here. She'd never been much of a rider, but over the years she'd gotten comfortable enough to trot, and now she could remember the feel of the wind in her face, her hair blowing behind her, the thrill of the speed as she felt the horse move confidently through the forest paths.

"I have a bit of time if you'd like the first ride." Toby raised his eyebrows at her.

"I don't know," she said hesitantly. The sleigh looked old but freshly painted in a deep shade of red with gold trim. "How do you even know how to steer one of these things?"

"Did anyone ever tell you that you worry too much?" he told her. "What happened to the girl who used to hop up on a horse and tear off through the woods?"

"She grew up and realized that some risks aren't worth taking," she replied wryly.

He stared at her for a moment. The only sound around

them was the clopping of the horse's impatient hooves, and Nora wondered if he was thinking about that last summer like she was, when they'd torn off into the forest, stopping at a clearing, and how he'd almost kissed her under the shade of a maple tree, until the sound of Melody catching up to them stopped him.

For months afterward, she'd thought about that day, wondering what might have happened—until she'd stopped playing the "what if" game in life. Some things just were what they were, and it was easier to accept reality than to fight it.

"Besides," she said, "the last thing I need is for us to end up at the bottom of the frozen pond."

"Oh, we used to skate on that pond without a second thought," Toby said with a grin.

But those were the days before fear set in. Before Nora's world came crashing down and she learned to guard herself. Before she couldn't look at a frozen pond without thinking of how easy it would be for the thin layer of ice to crack, and for a moment of joy to give way to the dangerous icy water underneath.

"You loved skating on that pond," Toby said fondly.

Nora couldn't help but smile remembering the winter afternoons when she and Melody would hurry over to the pond with the skates that Nana kept on hand in all different sizes for her guests. Toby would meet them there, in his hockey skates, always up for a race. Two laps would turn into five, and no matter how many times Nora asked for a rematch, she never did beat him. Melody would tire of the competition after one round, opting to practice her spins in the middle of the frozen pond instead.

"Tell you what," Toby said. "You go get your coat, and I'll

let Prancer here know that he can't go within ten yards of that pond."

"Prancer?" She raised an eyebrow.

"His name's actually Pete, but at Christmastime, he's Prancer." Toby laughed. "Just don't tell the kids."

Nora pulled in a breath and looked out toward the old pond, almost hearing the squeals of joy that once accompanied those days gone by.

"All right," she said, turning to fetch her coat. She was grumbling to herself as she pulled it from the coatrack inside, but she also couldn't fight the bubble of anticipation as she pulled her gloves from her pockets, slid them on her hands, and went back outside.

Toby held out a hand to help her into the sleigh. His hand was warm and steady, sending a flutter straight through to her stomach. She gripped it tightly, and not just because she didn't want to fall. Because she didn't want to let go. Not then. Not ever.

It had been a long time since she'd let someone get close enough to hold her hand, even longer since she'd wanted someone to. Her heart pounded at the closeness, at the longing in her heart, battling with her head.

Just as quickly as he squeezed her hand, he dropped it again, lifting the other rein instead. She felt the tension leave her shoulders, but she didn't feel safe by the distance between them. Instead, she wished for more. And she'd promised herself that she'd stop wishing a long time ago.

Nora sat on the bench, waiting for the ride to start, but Toby was giving her a funny look.

"What?" she asked.

The corners of his lips curled. "You can get a little closer, you know. I don't bite. Can't say for sure that Prancer doesn't, though."

Nora matched his smile as a flutter went through her stomach. He lifted the blanket on his lap, an invitation for her to share it, and she moved a little closer, and then, a little closer still, until he dropped the wool blanket over her legs and signaled for the horse to go.

They took off like a shot, and Nora let out a whoop of delight and then laughed. "You didn't tell me this was a racehorse."

"He'll settle down soon enough," Toby assured her as the horse slowed his pace. "See? You can still trust me, Nora."

She stared into those clear blue eyes and then looked away out onto the snow-covered fields. Trust was something that came with letting people in, and she hadn't done that in so long that she had forgotten how. Leave it to Toby to notice.

They circled the property, all the way out to the back forest line, avoiding the pond, because as Toby had said, she could trust him, and maybe she should. But letting him back in was different—and that was something she couldn't do.

Even if a part of her wanted to.

She wondered if he knew about the photographer who had been to the house this morning. She should tell him, and she would, but she didn't want to ruin this moment.

"You know, you never told me what you overheard, that night that your grandmother and your mother had their argument," Toby said as they went for another lap.

Nora frowned, thinking of that awful night. She tried not to think about it, and she and Melody never discussed it anymore. What more was there to say? But Toby didn't know the story, and he deserved to hear it if only to understand why she'd never come back.

"It was the last time I ever saw my grandmother, and I didn't even know it would be. It was the last time I'd hear her voice." Tears prickled the backs of her eyes and she blinked against the cold wind.

"Do you remember anything about what they were saying?" Toby asked.

Nora thought back, trying to remember the details of a night she'd tried so hard to forget. One that her mother never spoke of again, and one that she knew better than to mention.

"They were arguing about my father," she said, thinking of the few words she caught, even though she couldn't make out a complete sentence from her hiding spot, and never could figure out what was so upsetting to both women. "And...faith. They kept mentioning faith."

"Faith?" Toby glanced at her, his expression intense.

Nora shrugged as she adjusted the blanket on her lap, careful to leave enough for the man beside her. "That's all I heard. Maybe it was a disagreement over my father's service. Nana was much more religious than my mother ever was." She sighed and looked out over the snow-covered fields and the mountains that were visible in the distance. "Whatever it was, it was bad enough to divide our family forever."

Toby looked pensive as he guided the horse over one of the town's covered bridges adorned with a large wreath that hung from its very top. The house appeared in the distance once they cleared to the other side, and before Nora could comment on how well their decorations had turned out, her phone started ringing in her pocket. She ignored it, and a moment later, it beeped with a text message alert.

Reality beckoned. New York? She didn't even want to think of that world right now, not when she'd be right back in it all too soon, never to be here again. Melody? She could wait.

"You'd better check that," Toby told her. "It might be a problem with a guest."

"Oh." Nora hadn't even considered that possibility.

But when she pulled her phone free, she wished it had been Frank, or her sister, or any of the guests with any number of issues, save a flood or a fire.

"It's from the real estate agent," Nora said, staring at the phone. She read the message and then pulled in a breath, bracing herself for Toby's reaction. "She sent someone to take a few photos this morning. Just of the outside and the common rooms."

Toby nodded but kept his gaze straight ahead.

Things were moving more quickly than Nora had expected. She couldn't keep this from Toby, even if she knew he probably didn't want to hear it. "She already sent the photos to a few prospective buyers on her list. One couple might be interested."

Nora bit her lip as she waited to hear what Toby would say to that. Would he be surprised or angry? Or just sad?

She couldn't read his expression any more than she could understand her own conflicting emotions. She should be relieved. Thrilled even. It was a Christmas miracle! She could go back to New York without this hanging over her. She could make a fresh start for the New Year. Maybe she'd even get ahead on some of her bills with a little cushion in the bank.

She certainly wouldn't have to worry about Melody as much.

But instead of the satisfaction that usually came when she

checked a problem off her list, she felt panicked. Rushed. And something else—something that felt a lot like heartbroken.

"Do you know anything about these people?" Toby finally asked.

Nora looked back at her phone as another message came in. "They're a young couple. Tech money. Looking for a vacation home."

"A vacation home," Toby said flatly. "A young couple. Meaning that they're probably going to gut the entire place."

"You don't know that!" Nora bristled.

"Are you kidding me?" Toby was incredulous. "That house is over one hundred years old, and the only modern improvements that have been made in the last fifty years were the installation of central air and updated kitchen appliances."

Nora fell silent. Toby had a point. The house was old, the woodwork original, as well as the floors and windows. That was all part of its appeal. And its charm.

"Is this really what you want?" Toby asked. "To sell to just anyone?"

"Of course not!" Nora hadn't considered that she'd be faced with this possibility. "I want whoever buys it to love it. To take care of it."

"The way you would have?" he asked. "If you had the funds?"

Nora tightened her mouth before she could say something she'd regret. There was no sense in thinking about what it might have been like to keep the inn. To imagine that this was an option would only make selling it that much more difficult. That was Melody's way. They couldn't both afford to wish for life to be different than it was.

"The way Nana did," she replied. Fighting back her rising

defenses, she started to climb off the sleigh. "Look, I'll call the real estate agent. I'll let her know that whoever buys the property has to appreciate it for what it is. Not just be after a piece of land."

Toby hesitated for a moment and then gave a quick nod. "Good."

Nora stood at the base of the sleigh. The bonding moment they'd just shared seemed like half a lifetime ago now, and she was reminded once again of how quickly things could go from good to bad. How quickly life could change.

"Well, I should get back inside, then. I'm sure Prancer needs a rest, and maybe a carrot, too." She patted the horse, and a rush of memories consumed her when she thought of how easily she'd once saddled the horses, how she'd loved to ride through the fields with the wind in her hair, Toby leading the way.

He looked at her for a moment and then nodded. "I'll see you later, Nora."

"See ya," she said, realizing it was the same thing she used to say to him all those years ago, casually, with the comfort that there would always be another day. Another moment to share.

Only now, as she trudged in her boots up to the house, she had the sinking realization that time was running out.

For the inn. And for her and Toby.

❄

Mr. Higgins was in the kitchen when Nora went in search of some cookies after finishing her call with the real estate agent.

She stopped in the doorway when she saw him, but his kind smile invited her to enter.

"I was worried you were mad at me," she admitted, even

though their talk this morning had gone well enough. Mr. Higgins had been understanding about her decision to sell the inn and not in the least surprised. And he'd admitted that he'd been tipped off—by Toby this time, not Melody.

It seemed that Melody couldn't bring herself to break the elderly cook's heart any more than Nora could.

"I told you this morning what I'll tell you now," he said. "This place had a good run, just like Nana. There can never be any hard feelings associated with the Hart Inn."

No, there couldn't be. But Nora felt shaky as she approached the counter where a tray of sprinkle cookies was waiting to be brought out to the lounge. She couldn't shake the conversation she'd had just now, and she needed to tell someone. Melody was not an option, and Toby was too upset about the potential sale to further discuss it.

But Mr. Higgins was patient, and he'd known Nana longer than the rest of them.

Because that's who Nora realized she really wanted to talk to right now. Nana. For her wisdom. Maybe for her blessing.

"There might be some interest in the house," Nora said carefully.

"You don't look very happy about it," Mr. Higgins remarked.

"It's not the kind of buyer I was hoping for." Nora sighed, and Mr. Higgins slid the tray of cookies across the counter, a quiet invitation to share. Sure enough, it worked. Nora took a bite of the cookie and chewed thoughtfully, replaying what she'd learned from the real estate agent. "It's clear that the people who are interested in the property are also planning to make significant changes to it. I guess I was hoping that someone would come along and love it for what it is, not what it could be."

"In other words, you want this old house to stay the same," Mr. Higgins surmised.

Nora nodded. It was just like Melody said. This was the last piece of their family they had left other than each other.

"But Nana's not here anymore," Mr. Higgins said gently. He had the same kind of understanding in his eyes that he'd had this morning when she'd asked him to talk, struggling to work up the nerve to break the news.

"But Nana trusted me with this house." And Melody, not that she was in a position to ensure it stayed in the family, either. "I don't know what she wanted us to do. She must have known we'd have jobs in New York. Responsibilities. That we couldn't just pack up and move here. That we wouldn't have the financial resources to keep this place going even if we wanted to."

"And do you want to?" the cook asked.

Toby had asked the same question, and she hadn't been able to bring herself to answer him, but to Mr. Higgins, she gave a silent nod.

"But please don't tell Melody," she pleaded. "It would get her hopes up, and I'm trying to protect her from disappointment."

"You're forgetting something," Mr. Higgins said with a slow smile. "Christmas is the season of hope."

Nora wished that this were true, but her magical Christmases had ended a very long time ago. "I just hate the thought of letting Nana down."

"She didn't give you this house as a burden, Nora."

Nora nodded. "I know."

She'd given it as a gift.

Only now, it was a problem. "I have to be back at my job by the second of January or I'll be out of work. It's easier to entertain a possible offer now, while I'm in town, but..." She searched his gaze, begging him to tell her what to do, what Nana would want. "But it doesn't sound like the right buyer."

"It won't be easy to find a buyer like the one you're describing," Mr. Higgins said with a sigh. "To find people like that, you'd have to showcase the place, draw attention to the upside of keeping the inn the way it is. And you'd have to bring in as many people as possible to have any chance of finding a person who would be willing to do that."

Nora considered Mr. Higgins's last thought. Bring in people. Show off the house at its very best. There was a way she could do that.

She thought back to the Christmas Eve Gala that Nana used to throw every year—it was famous in town. People stopped by for a drink and ended up staying for hours.

"I think I have an idea for how we could get a lot of people in here quickly," Nora said excitedly.

But she couldn't do it alone.

Chapter Fifteen
Melody

Melody had waited upstairs until the photographer left, only then deciding that it was safe to enter the common areas of the inn. Her heart sank with each step down the stairs, her hand dragging along the garland-wrapped banister, but she couldn't fight the warmth that rose in her chest when she saw James sitting in the lounge, reading a book near the fireplace.

"Good day!" she said cheerfully as she entered the room.

"It's impossible not to have a good day in a room as festive as this." James motioned to the decorations, which Melody had to admit looked just as good as the ones she held in her memory. "Your grandmother would be proud."

Melody stiffened, thinking of what was going on under this roof, what she couldn't stop, no matter how badly she wished she could. "Oh, how I wish that were true."

That and so many other things. She'd wished to spend more Christmases in this house, and summers, too, until she'd abandoned all thought and hope for that. She'd wished for roles she hadn't been given. Every time, she managed to lift herself back from the disappointment, but this wasn't the same.

Selling this house was permanent. It wouldn't be a disappointment, but a loss.

James set the book he'd been reading on the coffee table and picked up his coffee mug. "Why wouldn't Nana be proud? Her granddaughters transformed this entire house in a matter of days, just like she would have done it herself if she could. This Christmas tree looks like something out of a magazine. And if I don't say so myself, we did a pretty good job selecting the right one, even if it did make for a workout getting it back to the house."

Melody smiled. James had done most of the grunt work getting the tree back up to the inn, and he hadn't complained once. She knew he was feeling the burn when he had to stop and take off his hat and unbutton his coat halfway back, despite the windchill.

He was a good guy. Someone Nana would have liked.

And did, considering she had met him once.

Somehow, knowing that James had known her grandmother made her like him even more.

Nora, however, would not approve. Not one bit. But then, when did Nora ever like any of the guys that Melody dated? Her mouth would pinch the moment Melody would start talking about them, however wonderful she described them. Though, in fairness, Nora had been right about her most recent boyfriend, who had cheated on her with a stagehand, and for that, Melody knew that she should probably give her sister some credit.

"The way I see it, there's not much more you and Nora could have done with the place," James said. "It doesn't get more picturesque than this."

Melody did a quick sweep of the room, from the crackling

fireplace to the stockings that hung above it, all mismatched but somehow coordinated, like they were all meant to be together. Was that what Nana had intended when she'd given her inn—her home—to Melody and her sister? That they would all find their way to be together again, under this roof, where they belonged?

"I suppose you saw the photographer," Melody said, dropping onto a worn leather chair across the coffee table. She didn't want to be presumptuous and sit on the sofa, too close to James, but she also had the impression that he didn't mind her company.

That maybe he even enjoyed it as much as she enjoyed his.

"New photos for the website?" he asked.

"If only." Melody's heart felt so heavy that she almost didn't trust herself not to cry. It was probably unprofessional of her to blurt out all of her problems to a paying guest, but James didn't treat her like a member of the staff, and technically she wasn't one, either. "My sister's listing the house."

James's eyebrows shot up in surprise. "Wow. I didn't see that coming. I'm guessing from the look on your face that you don't agree with her."

"My sister and I rarely agree on anything, and this is not one of those things." Melody sighed. "But I'm also not in a position to stop her. It's not like I have the money to keep this place."

James looked thoughtfully around the room. "What will come of it?" he asked. "Do you think it will still be an inn?"

"I don't know," Melody answered honestly. "I'd like to believe that whoever buys this house will be someone who cherishes it as much as my grandmother did. Someone who doesn't see a reason to strip the creaky floors or replace the vintage charm. Someone who will make as many happy memories here as we once did."

James was quiet for a moment and then he sat forward and rested his elbows on his knees.

"You're upset about this," he observed.

"Is it that obvious?" she asked with a brittle laugh. She couldn't muster her usual joy for the holiday right now, even if she was sitting in a picture-perfect room with wreaths on the windows, a tree that put any other to shame, and a handsome man, giving her a funny smile from across the room.

"Well, you didn't come down the stairs singing, so that was my first hint."

Despite her gloom, Melody laughed. Then, deciding she really should rally herself, she shook her head and stood.

"I should let you get back to your book," she said, even though she was reluctant to leave. The day stretched ahead of her, but at the same time, each minute that passed brought her that much closer to letting go of this house. She wanted to hold on to it, to savor it, to relive every moment that made it so special.

"What do you have going on today?" James asked conversationally. He hadn't picked up his book again yet, and he tilted his head with interest.

Melody thought back to all the things she and Nora used to do in the days leading up to Christmas, and her mind rested firmly on the one that brought her the most joy. Standing in the kitchen with Nana, singing carols, and baking cookies. Even if they were too ugly to put out for the guests, Nana still did, always with a flourish, saying that these were special cookies, because her granddaughters had made them. Anyone who was staying at the inn that year would make a big fuss, taking a cookie and showering Melody and Nora with praise, whether it was deserved or not.

It always made Melody feel special. It made her feel loved, faults and all.

"I think I'm going to bake cookies," Melody said decisively.

"Mr. Higgins will be willing to share the kitchen?" James asked.

"Oh, he's probably taking a break until the dinner hour," Melody said. "But I don't mind if he's there. The more the merrier."

"In that case," James said, "would you mind if I joined you?"

Melody's heart skipped a beat, and she felt her cheeks flush. She knew she should say no, that she should make up an excuse to keep this man at a safe distance. But he was a guest. And he was so friendly. And he loved Christmas just as much as she did.

And who was she kidding? She was struggling to resist his charm. Or his good company.

"Only if you promise not to eat them all when we're finished," she warned.

James grinned. "That's going to be a difficult promise to keep, but I'm a man of my word and you have it."

Melody fought back a smile as she turned and walked toward the kitchen, James right behind her.

The day had started with heavy disappointment, but thanks to James, things had suddenly gotten a little brighter.

❄

The kitchen was empty, and Melody was both happy and nervous to share the space with James. She busied herself by digging through the old recipe books on the shelf above the spice rack, her wariness about being alone with a handsome man completely forgotten when her fingers grazed an old binder.

"It's Nana's recipe book!" She clutched it in her hands, in disbelief that she had found it when she hadn't even been searching for it.

When, truth be told, she'd all but forgotten it, just like the handmade stockings. Slowly, memories she'd buried were resurfacing. She just wished the same could be said for Nora.

She opened it carefully as James came to stand beside her, turning the pages as recipe after recipe in Nana's handwriting revealed itself. Everything from her famous pot pie to—

"Nana's jam thumbprints!" she cried out, then looked at James excitedly. "We have to make these."

"I'll start getting the ingredients," he said, reaching for some of the canisters that Mr. Higgins kept on the counter near the mixing bowls. The kitchen wasn't just organized for strategy, it was thought through with love. It was more than where Mr. Higgins worked. It was where he'd spent years of his life, making food and feeding the people who walked through the doors of this house.

"I'm not usually a baker," Melody admitted as she carefully set the recipe to the side where she couldn't spill anything on it. "My kitchen in New York is about as big as the shoe closet in the lobby of this house."

James's smile was knowing. "But it's a great city."

"The best," Melody said with a sigh. She preheated one of the ovens to the temperature Nana had noted and then walked back to the counter, where James had found the measuring spoons and cups. "Something tells me that you have a bigger kitchen than me."

"I like to cook" was all he said. "Takeout most nights is tempting, but cooking relaxes me after a long day in the office."

"And you haven't told me what a long day is," she said as she started to measure out the dry ingredients. "Finance is a broad description."

"Oh, mostly I spend my days listening to my clients complain and finding a way to make them happy," he said with a wry smile. "But I love it. I work in personal finance, so I get to know all of my clients and what their goals are, and sometimes their setbacks, too. I like solving problems. I like making life easier for people if I can."

She gave him a sidelong glance. "You're what my Nana would call a good egg, James."

His grin turned bashful.

"So, what do you do at the department store?" he asked. "When you're not on elf duty, that is."

He was chiding her, and his eyes were as warm and inviting as his smile, but Melody hesitated as she began measuring out the ingredients for the cookies. It was one thing to gloss over the details of her life when she first met James, but they'd spent time together now, and she'd come to see him as more than a guest. He was more like...a friend.

"Actually, I was working as one of Santa's elves. In the toy department," she clarified, darting her eyes nervously while she waited for his reaction.

James wore a suit to work every day, not shoes with bells on the toes.

"They must have hired you for your Christmas spirit!" he said with an easy smile. "And your beautiful voice, of course."

Melody flushed at the compliment, even though she knew she shouldn't read into it. Maybe this was how James talked to all the girls back in New York. Maybe it was just his way.

Or maybe...

"I'm not so sure that Santa liked the singing. The man was more of a Grinch than a jolly old Saint Nick." She shrugged. "I'm an actress. This was just a gig between gigs, you could say."

"An actress?" He looked impressed, bless him.

"Now don't get too excited," she said quickly. "Like I said, I'm between gigs."

And they were further and farther between.

"Have I seen you in anything?" he asked.

She highly doubted it. "Not unless you're into the off-off-off-off-Broadway scene."

"What better scene is there?" he asked without a hint of malice. "I love the local stuff. Grabbing a pizza and then stopping at an off-the-beaten-path theater that I never noticed. Some of them do their own writing. Some of it's quite interesting."

Some of it was, but even those little holes-in-the-wall weren't calling these days.

"Have you always wanted to be an actress?" James asked as they worked to put together the cookie dough, each adding the ingredients in two separate bowls, one for the dry ingredients, one for the wet.

Melody found the beaters in the last place she remembered seeing them, comforted that nothing in this kitchen had changed, even though it would, and all too soon.

"Always," she said with a smile. "But it was Nana who encouraged me. She came to all my school plays growing up. Well, until..."

There was silence while she beat the eggs and sugar, but James was watching her when she turned off the machine.

"My mother and Nana had a falling out after my father died," she felt the need to explain. "We stopped coming here after that and Nana stopped visiting, too. But I always thought of her when I went up on that stage. I still do," she said sadly.

"I think of my grandfather a lot, too," James said with a wistful smile. "He's the one that brought me here that one winter. I've been thinking of him more than usual since I've arrived."

"Christmas has a way of bringing back the best memories," Melody said.

"And creating new ones," James said, giving her a little smile.

"Melody?" Nora burst through the door, her expression changing from surprise to confusion to displeasure in a matter of seconds. "I've been looking all over for you."

Melody held her breath, waiting for bad news because she couldn't imagine Nora would seek her out for any other reason right now.

"We're just baking cookies," Melody said defensively. She was grateful to have James at her side, even though she was sure that Nora was not. She wasn't going to let her sister dismiss him, though she was sure that Nora was trying to figure out how to do just that without being rude. James didn't share her plight, but the inn meant something to him, and he understood why it was important to her. Why Christmas was, too.

Nora glanced at James as if deciding whether she could speak freely in front of him. Melody waited, knowing that if there was an offer for the house, Nora would ask to speak to her alone. But instead, Nora smiled and said, "I was talking to Mr.

Higgins a bit ago. We decided to bring back Nana's biggest holiday tradition this year."

Melody stared at her sister, waiting to see if she was joking. But Nora didn't joke. Or even laugh, at least not much. Heck, she rarely even cracked a smile.

But she was smiling now. And she definitely wouldn't joke about something like this.

Nora might be practical to a fault, but she was never mean.

"The Christmas Eve Gala?" Melody could barely believe it, and all at once a flood of images filled her mind of parties from the past, and all that this year's event could be.

She pictured the dancing in the dining room, the guests mingling near the open fire in the lounge, helping themselves to punch and snacks in the library. The lobby would be filled with excited people, all eager to shed their winter coats and show off their holiday dresses.

"It was the best night of the year!" Melody said excitedly, pulling James into the conversation.

"It was," Nora agreed. "And I'm hoping it can be huge again."

"Christmas Eve is three days away!" Melody stared at her sister, wondering just what had gotten into her. But if Nora thought she could pull this together in such a short timeframe, who was Melody to stop her? Who was Melody to say no to anything when it came to Christmas? "Oh, this is exciting. Does Toby know yet?"

"Not yet." For the first time since she'd come into the room, the little pinch returned between Nora's eyebrows. "He's giving sleigh rides at the Christmas Market."

"How perfect that Christmas Eve falls on the day after the market closes," Melody gushed. "It will be the perfect way to round out the festivities for Juniper Falls. We might even get some people from out of town."

Nora licked her bottom lip but said nothing. Melody reminded herself that she was getting carried away, but she couldn't help it. The Christmas Eve Gala could only be topped by the magic of Christmas morning itself.

"Well, I have to go get organized and then I'll head down to the market this evening to tell Toby," Nora said.

"Do you think she's changed her mind about selling the hotel?" James asked once Nora had left.

Chances were that Mr. Higgins had talked Nora into having the party one last time—as a tribute to Nana, or a final goodbye to this inn and all its wonderful traditions.

"I wish," Melody said. But then, she'd wished for a lot of things in her life, and she was still waiting for most of them to come true. There'd been the wish for her dad to come back, even though she knew that was impossible. Then the wish for her mother to be home more. The wish for Nora to laugh again.

She smiled, and James caught her eye.

"What is it?" he asked.

"It's funny," she said. "I was just thinking of how many wishes I made over the years that never came true. But one did. And that was to come back here for Christmas. I guess I just never thought it would be like this."

"And what is your Christmas wish this year?" he asked.

She gave him a pointed look. As if he needed to ask. "Another wish that won't be coming true. But still, I have to try. Every way I can."

"This place is special. To a lot of people," James added. "Who knows? Maybe Nora will get caught up in the party and change her mind."

Melody doubted it, but she could at least wish for it.

"When I was little, my favorite part of the party was getting to dance to the Christmas music," she said, picturing it now. "I'd tire myself out so much that I was always sure to get a good night's sleep, despite the anticipation of presents the next morning."

"Maybe we can enjoy the party together," James said. "Unless your dance card is already full."

Melody's heart started to hammer but she fought back her smile, lest she appear too eager, which, according to Nora, she was known to do.

"I think I can make room for one more," she said coyly.

Because wasn't that always Nana's motto? There was always room for one more in their family, and in this house, especially at Christmastime.

James gave her a long, intense stare, and something in Melody's stomach fluttered and then rolled over.

They were interrupted by the swinging of the kitchen door. Melody turned to see not Mr. Higgins, but one of the other guests standing in the doorway.

"Oh!" Edith looked surprised at seeing them in the kitchen, but her expression turned to one of disappointment when her gaze flicked over the rest of the room. "I was looking for Mr. Higgins."

"He'll be back to start prepping for the dinner service soon," Melody assured her, but this seemed to do little to ease Edith's worry. "Is there something I can get for you in the meantime?"

"Oh, no. No." Edith started to back away but paused at the door to give a coy smile over her shoulder. "There's nothing like romance at Christmastime, is there?"

Melody's cheeks flamed and she couldn't even look at James, but from her periphery, she caught a flash of his smile. Did he think this was funny? She waited to see if he'd protest because frankly, she, for once, was at a loss for words.

"It's certainly the most magical time of the year," he said with a smile.

Melody stiffened as Edith went on her way, and only once the door swung shut did she turn and stare at the man beside her, who was now continuing to scoop out the batter as if that entire exchange had never occurred.

"The most magical time of the year?" she asked, raising an eyebrow.

He gave a little shrug. "What can I say? It's true, isn't it?"

It was true. And what Edith had said was true, too.

There was nothing like romance at Christmastime. And there was nothing like Christmas at this inn.

Chapter Sixteen
Faith

Downtown Juniper Falls was filled with people wrapped up in their warmest coats and hats, but somehow, despite the softly falling snow, Faith had never felt warmer. There was a glow that seemed to shine over the town square, which was filled with wooden kiosks wrapped in garland and twinkling lights. The songs from the carolers could be heard from a distance, and the smell of mulled wine was as inviting as the sparkling crafts that the locals were offering.

"This is amazing!" Faith marveled as she took in the scene. Star ran ahead to look at another stand selling homemade ornaments. "You can't tell me that you'd rather skip this every year?" she said to Aiden.

He gave a guilty shrug underneath his heavy parka. "Christmas memories aren't happy ones for everyone."

Faith nodded. She understood. More than he knew. But she was curious to know his story—if he was willing to share it.

"Star's mom left us late on Christmas Eve, three years ago," he said. "We knew it was coming. She'd been sick for a long time. Star was too young to understand, and she'd been so excited about Christmas that year. I knew that her mother wouldn't have wanted it to be ruined for her. So for her—and for Star—I rallied myself. Gave Star a happy Christmas morning, even though I felt like a part of me had died overnight, too. It was one of the hardest things I've ever done."

Aiden had stopped walking so they remained out of Star's earshot, and Faith set a hand on his wrist, looking into his eyes, which still bore the pain of that memory.

"You're a really, really good father," she said, meaning it.

"Just doing what any dad would do," he said gruffly.

"No." Faith's voice came out firmer than she intended it, but she wasn't going to walk it back. She meant it. Aiden was a good father. The best, really. And certainly better than any she'd known before.

Now he was looking at her quizzically.

Faith sighed. "I never knew my father. He was a married man. He had an affair. I was the result."

Aiden's eyebrows shot up. "Did he know..."

"Did he know I existed?" Faith nodded when she thought of the letters she'd found, the ones that were tucked away in her suitcase. They'd given her a name. A starting point.

But not much more than that. The letters themselves were brief. Some mentioned money, checks that she wasn't sure her mother had ever cashed. In each one her father had asked how she was. But he never asked to see her, and why, she didn't know.

And never would. Not for sure, anyway.

"I'm sorry. I can't imagine," Aiden said.

"It was okay," Faith said, even though it wasn't always, not really. "My mother tried her best, but money was always tight, and she worked more than one part-time job to get by.

Christmas was just another workday and one she liked to get through. We didn't make a big deal out of it. I knew not to ask for anything too big or expensive. I knew not to believe in Santa," she added, lowering her voice further as a group of children dashed past her, the pom-poms on their hats bouncing. "So what you did, keeping Christmas magical for Star, that's pretty special, Aiden."

"She's all I have," Aiden said gruffly, and they both looked over to where Star was happily chatting with a woman selling ornaments made out of clay. "Star's a nickname, you know. For Stella. Her mother..." He trailed off for a moment. "Her mother always told her that she was her star. When she passed, I told Stella that her mom was a real star now, that she could always search for her in the night sky, and that she'd be up there, shining bright, and looking down. After a while, calling her Star just felt right."

"That's beautiful," Faith said, her throat tightening. "I recently lost my mother, too. She'd been sick for a while, so it didn't come as a shock. But it's funny because even though she never wanted to celebrate the holidays, I can't help but wish she could have seen Juniper Falls all lit up like this."

She wanted to believe that her mother would have gotten caught up in the magic of the season. Just like she wanted to believe that her mother would be okay with her being here. With her getting to know her sisters, even if they weren't aware of it themselves.

Aiden looked at her suddenly. "Did you ever think of finding him? Your father?"

"All the time," Faith admitted. It was all she could think about for so many years, especially when the other girls at school talked about their weekend adventures with their fathers, or the annual father-daughter dance came along. "I didn't know his name until recently and by then it was too late. He passed away many years ago."

"I'm so sorry," Aiden said, looking at her gravely.

Faith brushed away his concern. "You can't grieve what you never had."

"But you can grieve for what you'd hoped to have," he said softly, then gave her a smile of understanding. "What do you say about a warm drink? I know that Star has been waiting all week for a peppermint hot chocolate."

Faith gave him a funny look. "Don't you make those at the coffee shop?"

"Apparently, the ones here are better."

Faith laughed, feeling better, and from the grin that crinkled the corners of Aiden's eyes, he did, too.

They pulled Star away from the woman selling the ornaments with the promise of a treat and joined the long line for hot beverages.

"Look! They're offering sleigh rides!" Star pointed across the snow-covered town square to where a horse was visible in the distance.

Faith immediately recognized the driver of the beautiful wooden sleigh as Toby, and she was just about to wave to him when she saw the woman talking to him.

"Hey, that's my—" She stopped herself, feeling her cheeks flush with heat. Aiden was so easy to talk to that she was getting swept up, but she had to be more careful not to let her guard down too much. He was still a local. And locals talked.

"You know them?" Aiden looked confused.

"That's my...innkeeper," Faith managed to explain, feeling unsteady on her feet suddenly. She hadn't thought of Nora as her sister or her family, but as a stranger, a woman she didn't know and might never know, especially now that Christmas was nearly here and soon the inn would be gone. Nora and Melody would go back to their lives in Manhattan and she...

Well, she didn't know what was next for her.

The plan stopped the day she arrived in Vermont.

"Sure enough! I haven't seen Nora Hart in years," Aiden said, giving a funny smile.

Faith looked at him sharply, doing the math, realizing that he was probably right around Nora's age. It hadn't crossed her mind that he might have known her, and now she was eager to get his opinion.

"Did you two...date?" she asked in a low enough voice that Star wouldn't hear. But the little girl was already running over to pet the horse, so she didn't need to worry.

Aiden laughed. "No, nothing like that. Not that I didn't like her. I liked both of the Hart sisters. They were a nice family."

Faith swallowed hard as they moved up in the line. "So you knew them all, then?"

Aiden nodded casually. "Not well, but living in a town this small, you get to know everyone. Gloria Hart was the best. The entire town loved her. She bragged about those granddaughters of hers constantly, even when they all stopped coming to visit." He shook his head sadly at this.

"I'm halfway in between Nora's and Melody's ages," he continued, and Faith leaned in, eager for more details. "Melody was always a hoot. Full of energy. Sometimes Toby and I would hang out at the pond near the inn in the summer, and Melody was always doing jumps off the side, always splashing Nora, long after she'd found it funny." Aiden was close enough that she could feel the heat of his breath on her neck, sending a shiver straight down her spine. "Between us, I think that Toby always had a thing for Nora Hart."

"Really?" Faith looked over at the sleigh where the two were talking to Star with newfound interest. There was no denying that Toby was handsome in a rugged sort of way, and Nora was—well, beautiful.

Faith had spent a lot of time scrutinizing both of her sisters' features, trying to figure out what parts of her were from her mother and which were from her—their—father.

She'd tried to find any similarities she might share with either of her sisters, grasping at something to confirm it was true, that they were related, but there was no denying that they looked more like each other than she did them. A reminder that they had a bond that she'd never shared and maybe never would.

"They seem to spend a lot of time together," she said, thinking of how she often saw Toby and Nora together at the inn, sometimes hanging decorations, other times deep in what appeared to be tense discussions.

"Toby went through a rough patch a few years ago when his grandmother passed away. She was his only family, well, other than Nana Hart. If it hadn't been for that inn, I'm not sure what would have happened to the guy. That place is special, if you ask me. It has a way of giving people a home when they need one the most."

Meaning that losing the inn would come as a blow to him. Did Toby know about it yet? He must. And maybe that's what he and Nora were talking about right now. Maybe, if Melody couldn't find a way to stop the sale, then Toby could.

Aiden was right—that inn was a refuge, and more and

more, it was starting to feel like a home. The one she'd always dreamed of, bustling and warm, and full of family.

Her family. The one she'd never known she'd had.

"We can take a sleigh ride," Aiden suddenly suggested, and then, maybe seeing the surprise in her face, he shifted on his feet and said, "I mean, for Star's sake."

"Do you know what I think?" Faith asked with a knowing smile as they finally made it to the front of the line. "I think you like this whole Christmas experience a little more than you're letting on. And...I think I'd like a sleigh ride. Very much."

❄

Star fell asleep five minutes into the sleigh ride, the excitement from the day finally catching up with her. Toby took a turn at the edge of the green, leading them out into snow-covered fields lit only by the moon.

"This is so peaceful," Faith said, taking in the surroundings as she snuggled deeper under the plaid wool blanket. "It's just like I imagined it would be."

"Juniper Falls?" Aiden looked surprised. "I'm surprised that anyone outside of New England has ever heard of it."

"I meant Vermont, I guess," Faith said, even though it was only partly true. She hadn't known where her father lived, much less where her grandmother did. It wouldn't have mattered if it had been Montana or Tennessee, wherever they were was where she needed to be, to see for herself, to learn all she could.

To find more than she'd expected.

"You've never visited your family here before?" he asked.

"No," Faith said, her voice catching. "This was my first time meeting them. With my mother gone, it seemed like the right time to come see this...beautiful place."

"And has it lived up to your expectations?" Aiden asked.

Faith didn't hesitate now. "It's exceeded them. I never knew a place like this could exist. It seems so happy. So...perfect, really."

Just like Melody and Nora's childhood. The one she would single-handedly ruin if she told them who she was.

She pulled in a breath as Toby took another turn, leading the horse and sleigh onto a quiet street lined with white wooden homes decorated with garland and twinkling lights. Inside the front window of each house, Faith could see a Christmas tree, some front and center, others nestled deeper into one of the back rooms. They were all different, some with colored lights, others all white, but each of them gave the promise of a happy family who had gathered around it, pulling out old ornaments, and decorating it with cherished memories.

She felt a lump rise up in her throat and she turned to see Star snuggling deeper into the crook of her father's arm. She wondered if her father had taken Melody and Nora on this sleigh ride when they were Star's age.

She wondered if he ever wished that she'd been here with him, too. His three daughters.

"It doesn't need to end," Aiden said softly, forcing her attention back to him. "I mean...the town. Do you need to rush back home?"

Home was no longer the cramped apartment she'd shared with her mother in South Carolina, and it hadn't been in some time.

"I don't have anyone waiting for me," she said, and then, realizing how that had probably come across, she blushed in the moonlight, happy that he wouldn't be able to notice. "My mother is gone, and I recently quit my job."

"So anything is possible," Aiden said with a small smile.

She nestled a little closer to him as Toby took another turn, and instead of scooting back to her side of the sleigh, she stayed right where she was.

Because she liked where she was for the first time in a long time. Here with Aiden. In this town.

And in the inn, with her sisters.

In a place that was starting to feel like home.

Or at least the way home could have been.

Chapter Seventeen
Nora

Christmas Eve was only two days away and the planner in Nora would have told her that the idea of throwing a party on this timeline was not just crazy but downright desperate. Did she really think the right buyer would show up on such short notice? And what if one didn't? That was the part that she was really worried about—the thought of being faced with having to sell the property to the wrong buyer, one who wouldn't just fail to cherish Nana's memories, but one who would take a bulldozer out and destroy them all without a second thought.

She pulled in a breath and told herself to take one step at a time. It was how she'd gotten through life ever since her father's death. If she could break down the big problems into smaller ones, they would become more manageable. She'd get through one day, and then move on to the next. No more looking too far into the future—for the bad...or the good.

And right now, she was saddled with a task far bigger than her to-do list.

"This is going to be so much fun!" Melody sang out as she came through the doors of the lounge.

Fun was not the word that Nora would assign to any of this experience, including planning this party.

"Well, it's a lot of work," she said. She'd barely slept, instead using the time to put together a plan of action while listening to Melody snore. Mr. Higgins would need to prepare a menu and order food. It would be heavy appetizers and punch, with trays of cookies for dessert like always. After their talk yesterday, he'd promised her it would be no problem, that he could cater this party in his sleep, and Nora could see the gleam in his eye as he started sketching on paper.

Toby had been more skeptical about their ability to pull this off with such short notice, but Melody's optimism was exactly what Nora needed right now, especially when she had doubted this undertaking nearly as soon as she announced it.

"The house is already decorated, and Mr. Higgins will have no problems creating tasty food," Melody assured her. "Other than opening up the lounge doors to the library for better flow and moving the dining room tables to the barn for space to dance, what's left?"

Nora was often amazed by Melody's ability to believe that life could be so easy.

"We don't have a band," Nora said. Nana always liked to use the same band each year, but Mr. Higgins told her that they'd all retired years ago, shortly after the annual party had stopped.

Melody just shrugged. "We'll use speakers and a playlist. I'm sure that Toby has some equipment at his house."

He did. And he'd already offered it. Secretly, Nora had been hoping for the band, though, not for tradition's sake, but because it would take the entire event to another level.

"And the biggest issue is guests. We have to spread the

word." She refrained from expressing exactly how far they'd have to spread it, but she knew that the real estate agent had promised to tell her colleagues in neighboring towns in case they had any potential buyers who might want to see the Hart Inn in all its glory.

"We can hand out flyers!" Again, Melody didn't seem stressed by the task. "Trust me, people won't want to miss this."

"You really think that people will give up their Christmas Eve plans to come to this party?" Nora wasn't so sure. It had been years since they'd all been invited. They'd made new traditions.

"People can come and go as they please. Some might only drop in, and some might stay all night. It's like an open house," Melody said.

Yes, Nora thought, looking back down at her list because she couldn't face her sister and the joy in her eyes at the moment. It was exactly like an open house because that's just what it was. The ultimate chance for buyers to see the house, and experience what they could have—and hopefully wanted.

"You're forgetting something on your list, though," Melody told her.

Nora frowned, scanning the long sheet once more. She couldn't think of anything she'd forgotten, not when she'd been so careful to think of everything.

"We need dresses. And shoes." Melody perked up at the mere mention of dressing up, and Nora was reminded of how excited she'd been as a little girl to show off her Christmas dress to the guests each year.

Once again, Melody was right. Neither of them had packed anything other than warm sweaters, and something a little more formal was required for the party. Nora wouldn't call the process of buying a dress she didn't need fun. She called it functional.

"I have so many dresses in my closet back at home," Nora said with a sigh, thinking of the various ones she bought with her store discount for the company's annual holiday party each year.

"And now you'll have one more!" Melody said happily.

Nora couldn't help but smile. That was her sister—always positive, always looking at the bright side of life.

She sometimes wished she could do the same.

❄

Downtown Juniper Falls wasn't exactly a fashion mecca, but there was a small boutique with some promising dresses in the window that would be a good place to start.

"Should we get a coffee first?" Melody suggested, pointing to the coffee house across the street.

Nora had planned to cross this errand off her list, not drag it out, but the hopeful look her sister gave her made her reconsider.

"Why not?" They had some invitations to hand out while they were in town, and maybe the coffee house had a bulletin board where they could spread the word about the event.

They waited until a car with a Christmas tree tied to its roof had passed before sprinting across the street and into the warm coffee shop that hadn't been there when they were younger. Immediately, the smell of freshly brewed coffee and baked goods made Nora relax. She could spare a few minutes before she hurried back to the inn.

"Isn't that Faith?" Melody whispered as they moved through the crowded tables toward the display case.

Nora looked and sure enough, there was Faith, sipping from a mug and laughing at something the man behind the counter was saying.

A handsome man, Nora was quick to note.

Melody must have come to the same conclusion because she gave Nora a waggle of her eyebrows.

Nora was more curious. Faith was a young woman alone at a country inn for Christmas. Was this the reason she'd come to town? Did she know this man somehow?

But wait—Nora did a double take. *She* knew this man. It was Aiden Barnes, all grown up. The last time she'd seen him he'd been a lanky teenager with a lopsided smile and kind brown eyes who loved nothing more than taking an afternoon dip in the pond on a hot summer day.

"Aiden?" Nora laughed as she approached the counter.

"Oh my goodness!" Melody exclaimed as she put the pieces together. "I didn't even recognize you!"

"Well, it's been a long time." Aiden gave them a good-natured grin and came around the counter to greet them each with a hug.

"Too long," Melody said, and Nora, taking in the experience of seeing an old friend, half a lifetime later, silently agreed.

It had been too long. And now it felt like too late.

This wasn't an overdue visit. This was…goodbye. Only this time without the hope of ever returning.

Quickly, Nora blinked and cleared her throat, then took in the space, all decked out for Christmas, right down to the menu. It was a cozy room, in warm wood tones, with just the right amount of chatter in the background to make it feel cheerful. The display case of pastries didn't look half bad, either.

"You work here now?" Melody asked.

"I own the place," Aiden said proudly, but, Nora noted, humbly. She felt a wave of nostalgia over how little had changed but yet, so much, too.

"*We* own the place," a little girl corrected from the end of the counter.

Nora stared at the child, who wore two braids in her hair and a sweater with a gold star on it.

"This is my daughter, Star," Aiden said proudly again, no humbleness this time. It was clear by the way his smile filled his face that she was the joy of his life.

Another wave of emotion hit Nora now, another hit of nostalgia, one that she'd managed to repress. Her father, coming home from work, beaming just like Aiden was now as she and Nora ran to greet him at the door.

"The best part of my day," he'd always said.

How had she forgotten that, any more than the light he'd always had in his eyes?

Aware that everyone was now staring at her, Nora shook the memories away and said, "Sorry. I just can't get over how much she looks like you. And that you're a father! Is your wife here, too?"

Immediately, Aiden's expression fell, and he glanced at his daughter, who had resumed her coloring.

"It's just me," he said, and the sadness Nora saw shadow his face told her everything else she needed to know.

That was the thing about loss. Once you experienced it yourself, you could recognize it in others. The change in their tone. The smile that didn't quite meet their eyes. The quietness that spoke more than words ever could.

"Well, this looks like a wonderful place," Melody finally said. "I'm glad I twisted my sister's arm into stopping in."

Nora and Melody exchanged a rueful smile.

"We're handing out flyers for our Christmas Eve Gala," Nora said. "It's short notice, but this would be a great place to help spread the word." One glance around proved that there weren't any empty tables, and she could only assume the place was popular with locals and tourists alike.

"The Christmas Eve Gala?" Aiden's voice was full of wonder. "I haven't thought of that party in years!"

"Well, there hasn't been a party in years," Melody said, giving Nora a pointed look.

"What's the Christmas Eve Gala?" Faith looked up from her chair, her eyes darting from Aiden to Nora to Melody.

Melody was the first to jump in with a response. "It's this big party that Nana used to host every year. The entire town was invited, and the house would be filled with music, food, and laughter. It was so much fun, and by the time it was over, we would just fall into bed, exhausted. It was almost better than Christmas. Almost, but not quite." She gave a little smile.

"Better than Christmas?" Star looked up from her coloring book again. "Can we go, Daddy?"

Faith knew that Christmas Eve was a difficult reminder for Aiden, but she also knew that he would do anything to keep his daughter happy.

He looked at Nora for approval. "I don't see why not. So long as the entire town is invited."

"Of course! And you have to come!" Melody smiled at the little girl and then turned to Faith. "And you, of course."

The light shone in Faith's eyes for one second before dimming. "Oh. But I don't have anything to wear. I didn't exactly pack properly for this trip."

"There's a dress shop across the street," Melody pointed out. "We're heading over there after this if you want to join us. A little girls' shopping trip?"

Faith seemed almost put out at this invitation, and Nora was about to cover for her sister's overenthusiasm when Faith nodded and a slow smile curved her lips.

"I'd...love that, actually," she said softly.

Nora met her sister's gaze, her gut twisting when she saw the happiness that shone in her dark eyes. They already had three guests, and if everyone else was as eager, they'd have no problem filling the house for the long overdue party.

And the last of its kind.

❄

The boutique was nicer than Nora expected, full of dresses and sparkly sweaters perfect for the holiday season. Nora admired the way the owner had set up the seasonal tables and festive decorations, and the inviting window display that easily topped the ones she created each Christmas.

She studied it for a moment, trying to draw inspiration for next year, only she was struggling to imagine herself back at Castle's next Christmas and that had nothing to do with nearly losing her job. It was hard to imagine being anywhere but Juniper Falls at Christmastime, even though that was how it would have to be.

She'd go back to her life in New York. Eventually, she'd get used to it again.

And eventually, all of this would be forgotten again.

But is that what she wanted? The ache in her chest told her that it wasn't.

Not what she wanted. Maybe not even possible.

It had taken everything in her to shut this place out of her heart the first time. She wasn't sure she could do it twice.

"Do you remember how when we were little, Nana would take us into town to go Christmas shopping?" Melody mused as she wandered the store.

Nora hadn't remembered—until now. She smiled as the memory came back, along with the feeling of excitement that accompanied it. How it felt to have a whole twenty dollars in her pocket, to have the autonomy to walk through a store, looking at every item, carefully selecting the one that would make the best gift for the special people in her life.

The budget was only five dollars per person—Melody, her parents, and Nana—but somehow the shop owners always managed to guide them, and they always walked out of the store feeling proud of what they'd bought and eager to wrap it in the privacy of their bedroom as soon as they got back to the inn.

"It was an annual tradition!" Nora said, her heart pulling tight now, somewhere between joy and sadness. She glanced at Faith, who was polite enough to look interested in their personal stories. "Nana would always take the two of us into town, leaving our parents behind to deal with the guests. We'd get lunch at Birdie's and then stop in all the shops, looking for gifts."

"We usually bought a book for Nana," Melody said.

"She always said they passed the time during the long winters," Nora recalled. "We didn't spend much money, but we always managed something nice. A Christmas pin for our mother's coat, or—" She started laughing when she looked at Melody. "Do you remember the year that you bought Dad handkerchiefs?"

Melody buried her face in her hand for a moment. "How can I forget?"

Faith looked at Melody with curiosity. "What's so bad about handkerchiefs?"

"Well, for starters, I wasn't exactly sure that's what they were. I just knew that they were white, and they had the initial of his first name embroidered on them. It seemed like the perfect gift until I started to wrap it and I wondered what I'd actually bought. I was too young to read and—"

"And she thought she'd bought our father underwear!" Nora sputtered. She laughed so hard that tears sprang to her eyes and several other people in the boutique stopped to stare.

Faith looked mesmerized. "Did you?"

"No, it was a box of handkerchiefs," Melody assured her. "But let's just say that I was on pins and needles Christmas morning waiting for him to open his gift." She flashed a look at Nora. "Of course, you were old enough to read and could have put me out of my misery."

"And ruin the fun?" Nora laughed again, then set a hand on Melody's wrist by way of apology. "Besides, the packaging was ambiguous. And *handkerchief* was a really big word for a six-year-old. I was honestly a little worried, too."

"It ended up being our dad's favorite gift of all time," Melody said as her smile turned wistful.

Nora saw the glistening of her eyes and squeezed her hand. "He kept one tucked in his pocket at all times," she said gently.

They locked eyes for a moment, sharing the heartache of loss until Nora cleared her throat and turned away. Really! They had a guest with them! And their father had died more than fifteen years ago!

It was this town. And all this...Christmas! It was making her sentimental. And where did that ever get her in life?

Heartbroken and disappointed, that's where.

"We'd better get shopping if we hope to find a dress today!" Nora said, steering the conversation back to safer ground.

Melody wasted no time hitting the dress racks, while Faith tentatively flipped through a rack of sweaters. Nora took her time walking around the shop, which was bigger than it had appeared at first glance. It seemed established, like it had been a part of this town for most of the years of their absence.

She eyed the woman who was standing behind the wooden checkout table, going over paperwork, wondering if she knew Nana or—worse—Nora's plans for the inn. Word hadn't spread around town yet or surely Aiden would have said something, but by the gala, everyone would know. And what would they say? Would they judge her, possibly more than some probably already did?

She forced herself to get back to the task at hand, but Melody was already on it, heading toward her with a triumphant expression and a dress in her hand the color of spruce.

"This one would be perfect for you!" she told Nora. Then, glancing at Faith, she said, "Don't you agree?"

Faith stepped forward and looked longingly at the dress before nodding her consent. "It's lovely. I love that shade of green."

As did Nora, and Melody knew it. She held the dress up to Nora's chest and said, "It brings out the color in your eyes." She smiled with satisfaction, but her forehead pinched when she caught Faith's gaze. "That's funny."

"What is?" Faith looked suddenly alarmed.

"Your eyes," Melody said. "I never noticed it until you were standing right next to Nora, but they're nearly the same shade of green."

"Are they?" Nora had always been told her eyes were unique, a shade that wasn't commonly found, even if she used to envy Melody's rich brown color as a child. She studied Faith, whose cheeks had flushed from the attention. "Sure enough! How odd! The only other person I've ever known to have this color of eyes was my father."

Faith looked uneasy as she fingered the sleeve of the dress. "My mother's eyes were close in color to mine. That's where I always assumed mine came from." Her cheeks reddened further. "I mean, that's where I got them. Of course."

"Well, we'll just have to find you a green dress, too, then!" Melody said happily and shoved the one she was holding at Nora. "Now that your dress is handled, we need to move on to the fun part. Accessories!"

"Accessories!" Nora shook her head. This was supposed to be a quick errand.

"You can't exactly wear your snow boots to the party!" Melody laughed. "Or your black flats. And some gold jewelry would look stunning against that color."

"Melody." Nora started to protest but then stopped herself when she saw that it was no use. Melody was already moving across the room to the accessories table, and beside it was a wall of shoes, all sparkling, all beautiful.

And despite the long list of things waiting for her to do back at the inn, Nora decided to let herself enjoy this moment.

It wasn't often that she and her sister spent time together like this, and once they went back to New York, they'd fall into their usual daily routines.

She wouldn't worry too much about what this was costing, not today. She'd look at it like an investment, in the party, and in their future. If the event was a success and a good buyer made an offer on the property, then all her financial worries would be over.

But her other concerns—the anxieties that crept up at every turn—would still be there.

She looked at her sister across the room, admiring her zest for life nearly as much as she was bothered by it.

Melody might think that Nora wanted the money for the inn as a nest egg for herself, but what Melody didn't understand was that Nora was doing this for her.

Everything she'd ever done had been for her sister.

Chapter Eighteen
Faith

Aiden greeted Faith with a cheerful wave when she walked into the coffee shop the next day. Without asking for her order, he started to prepare it, and this time, when she pulled out her wallet, he raised a hand. "On the house."

"Oh," she protested, feeling flustered. "But I want to support you. I mean—your business. I want to support it."

"Okay, then, a trade. A vanilla latte for information."

Faith felt herself blanch. "Information?"

"I've been hearing some rumors around town, and I was hoping that you might be able to clear them up for me," he said.

Faith realized that she was trembling. She stared at the man she'd come to feel so comfortable with, wondering what he knew—what she could tell him. This was a small town. The kind where everyone knew everyone—for a long time, too. Had someone known about her existence? And if they did, would they tell?

Aiden leaned into the counter and lowered his voice. "Word around town is that the inn is up for sale. A pocket listing. For now."

Oh. So he wasn't aware of her true reason for coming to town. But then, how could he be? Even her sisters didn't know that their father had another child. Surely no one else did, either.

"I'm afraid it's true," Faith told him, her shoulders sagging with both relief and disappointment. "It's a shame. It's such a lovely house, so warm and cozy, like a real home, you know? I hate to think of someone coming in and changing everything when it's so perfect just as it is."

"I couldn't agree more," Aiden said with a shake of his head. "Nana Hart filled her house with people who needed a home away from home."

Or in Faith's case, just a home. A place to land. A place she'd once dreamed of and finally found, just when it was about to be taken away all over again.

"I hate to think of Mr. Higgins no longer being in that kitchen or Toby hauling in firewood," she added.

"The inn is important to you," Aiden observed, looking at her curiously.

Aiden had finished preparing her drink by now and he handed it to her as she settled onto a stool at the counter. She took a sip, gathering herself, careful not to reveal too much.

It was a small town, after all. If word had already gotten out about the inn being for sale, then family gossip would spread like wildfire.

Faith hesitated and then nodded. "There aren't many places like the Hart Inn, at least, not in my world."

"You didn't want to stay with your family instead?" He stared at her expectantly, and she knew she couldn't dodge the question, as much as she wished she could.

"Like I said the other night, I'm in town to meet them for the first time," Faith reminded him.

"Anyone I know?" Aiden asked.

Faith struggled to meet his eye. "They don't really live here anymore. They're just in town for the holidays too."

He let it go, to her relief. "Seems like a pretty big chance, coming up here to visit relatives you've never met, and for Christmas?"

"Well, when I looked up this town on the map it seemed like the best way to have a true Christmas." It was partly true, if only due to the timing. When she'd dug deep enough to learn the name of her father and grandmother, she'd scoured the website for the Hart Inn, looking at every page more than once, scrolling through the photo gallery, and zooming in, eager to glean as much information as possible. There were photos from all seasons, but the ones she liked best, the ones that really made her long to see the house, to be a part of that world, were the ones of the inn all decorated for Christmas.

It looked like something out of a dream. And she had found a way to make that dream come true.

"Don't they do Christmas back where you're from?" Aiden joked. "I'm just saying, it's a long drive up the east coast."

"And I had the time. After leaving my job and with my mother gone...I felt the need to get away and get a change of scenery."

Aiden nodded, seeming satisfied by her answer, which was true, but not the whole story.

"Well, you always have a job offer here," he told her. "I'm short-staffed at the moment, and putting Star to work sadly isn't an option. Yet."

"Where is Star?" Faith took a sweeping look over the crowded room.

"At the Christmas Market with friends. She can't get enough of that place, and so long as I don't have to go twice..." Aiden shook his head. "I take that back. I had a really nice time the other night."

He stared at her until Faith felt her cheeks heat and she needed to look away. "It was nice." Wonderful, really. She looked over her shoulder through the window and onto the town square across the street, which was just as busy as it had been since the market opened. "Star will be sad when they take it all down."

"I won't," Aiden replied. Then, seeing the disapproving raise of her eyebrows, he said, "But not for the reason you might think. My usual part-time worker took the day off to enjoy the Christmas Market. Remind me again why I can't wait for the holiday to be over?"

Faith gave him a rueful look, but an idea started to form. "I could help you today," she offered. Then, trying to be more casual about it, she added, "I mean, I could spare a few hours. And I did work as a barista all through college."

"Seriously?" Aiden asked, looking at her in surprise. "I'll pay you, of course."

"You don't have to pay me," Faith told him, standing up. "But...I might call in a favor."

Aiden gave her a teasing smile as she came around the counter. "What kind of favor?"

She threw him a look. "Nothing crazy, if that's what you're thinking. But...if I need one, I'll know who to ask. Just like you knew to ask me. That's what friends are for."

He stared at her for a moment, and she wondered if she'd

misspoke. If they weren't friends yet—or, if they were becoming more than friends.

"You know, if the Hart sisters get a buyer for the inn soon, I suppose the town will lose more than just the inn," Aiden said as he went back to filling an order.

"Oh?" Faith took another sip of her drink and stared at him. "What? Or...who?"

"You," he said simply.

"Oh." She felt a blush creep up her cheeks. "Well, I'm still here for now. And I, for one, am looking very forward to the Christmas Eve Gala."

"You're really getting into the whole Christmas spirit," Aiden remarked.

It was true, she was. Maybe for the first time in her life.

Aiden stopped talking to greet a customer who placed an order for a muffin and a hot chocolate. Faith quickly plated the baked goods while Aiden heated the milk. Once the woman had her drink in hand, Aiden turned back to Faith.

"That party used to be the highlight of the year. Everyone dresses up, and there's music and food, and it's like the entire town is one big family in that house."

"Now look who's getting caught up in the spirit of Christmas," Faith teased.

Aiden was quiet for a moment. "It's a shame that Star's never been."

"Well, she'll be there this year," Faith reminded him.

But this year only, she could tell they were both thinking.

"You know," she said, "it's nice of you to offer to bring her. First the Christmas Market, and now this gala."

"There's nowhere else I'd rather be," Aiden said without a hint of jest.

She raised an eyebrow. "At a Christmas party?"

"With you," he said, giving her a bashful smile.

Faith avoided his gaze and then extended her hand. "An apron, please."

He handed her a fresh folded one and then pointed out a few of the basics, leaving Faith to wonder about something she hadn't thought of until now.

"You never told me how long you've owned this place," she said as she went about her first task, refilling baskets with assorted muffins.

"It was my wife's business, actually," Aiden said as he assembled sandwiches for the lunch crowd. "I worked in pharmaceutical sales, and I traveled a lot. When I lost my wife, being on the road so much was no longer an option, so I took over this place, and who knows, maybe one day I'll pass it down to Star."

"I bet she'd like that," Faith said with a little smile. Then, hoping she wasn't crossing a line, she said, "I bet your wife would, too."

Aiden nodded but he was quiet for a moment. "I didn't just take over this place because it was convenient. I felt like I owed it to my wife. We had a bad argument—before she died. I guess you could say I've never forgiven myself for it. But I'm not sure I've forgiven her, either."

Faith knew better than to ask for details as she continued consolidating the bakery baskets. But Aiden seemed to stare pensively at her for a moment, as if debating how much he wanted to tell.

Or maybe how much he wanted to remember.

"My wife was sick for months before she ever told me," he said. "Once I found out...things were pretty far along. I was blindsided. Angry. At her. At the circumstances. At the hopelessness of it all. For a long time, I kept thinking that if she'd told me sooner, things might have ended up differently, but I know that's probably not true."

He shook his head again as if arguing with himself.

"She must have had a good reason," Faith said delicately, realizing that it was a phrase she told herself, and often, about her mother. She must have had a good reason to never tell Faith about her father.

"She wanted to live a normal life for as long as she could," Aiden replied simply. "I get it, I do, but..."

Faith raised an eyebrow. "But?"

"But if you care about someone, you let them in. You share the journey."

"Oh, but I'm sure she cared about you—"

Aiden nodded once. "I know she did. I'll never agree with her actions, and I have no choice but to accept them. And learn from them."

"What do you mean?" Faith asked.

"I mean that honesty is important. And with love comes trust. My wife made me feel like she didn't trust me enough to share her secret. She carried the burden on her own, and it breaks my heart to think of that to this day. I can't ever go through that again. When you care about someone, you don't keep secrets, big or small."

Faith's mouth felt dry as she stared at him, and all she could do was nod, because to say anything else would be dishonest.

And she already had the uneasy feeling that she was being just that with Aiden, even if her reasons were good, too.

❄

They worked through the afternoon companionably, Faith mostly taking orders and serving pastries, keeping one eye on the handsome man beside her and the other out the window, where the activity at the Christmas Market seemed to grow by the hour.

She had just finished placing a dozen freshly baked cookies in a basket when the door opened and with a burst of cold, wintery air, in walked Melody. As she approached the counter, Melody gave her an equally quizzical look.

"Did you get a job here?" she asked in confusion.

Faith shook her head even though she wouldn't mind working here more often. It beat the boring office job with its great benefits package any day. And the ambience topped any gray cubicle.

"I'm just helping Aiden out for the day."

"I see." Melody gave a subtle lift of her eyebrow, and Faith shifted her back slightly to Aiden so he wouldn't see the blush on her cheeks.

"What are you up to today?" Faith asked, genuinely curious to know every detail of her sister's life.

"Christmas shopping," Melody said proudly. It was clear from the way she said it that it was an activity she took seriously, and with great joy.

Christmas shopping. Faith hadn't even considered buying any gifts this year, if only because she had no one to give them to now that her mother was gone. In the past, there had been Secret Santa gifts at her office holiday party, but those, too, were a thing of the past.

She suddenly longed to spend a few hours strolling the market, browsing shops, looking for the perfect gifts for the new people in her life.

Only she couldn't. It wouldn't make sense to give gifts to a few strangers she had just met, women who presented themselves as owners of the inn, and nothing more. There would be no thinking of what Melody or Nora might like, wrapping it carefully and presenting it to them on Christmas morning. That was something that one did for sisters—real sisters. Sisters who knew one another existed.

And she still couldn't bring herself to tell them the truth. Not when they were wrestling with the decision to sell the inn. Not when Melody was already so upset about losing it.

Not when there was a gleam in her eyes, like there was now, full of happiness and fulfillment for the festivities of the season.

Telling them would be taking all that away. And more. Taking away not just this Christmas but all the magical ones before it.

They'd never view their father the same way again. And who was she to take him from them when she'd never had him at all?

"What can I get you?" Faith asked, assuming her role for the day, her place for the week. She was friendly, but she was a stranger. Nora and Melody were kind to her, inclusive even, but it didn't stop with her.

Melody and James were chummy—maybe even more than that, not that Faith would dare to ask.

"I'll have a large cappuccino," Melody said. "With two sweeteners and a shot of vanilla."

Faith committed this to memory, so she'd always remember how her sister took her coffee.

"Are you going shopping at the market?" Faith asked as she started the order. Aiden tended to the next guest in line.

"I can't miss it," Melody said. Then, leaning on the counter, she said, "Can you make that a double? I'm going to need the extra caffeine to get through the day."

"Lots of gifts to buy?" Faith asked.

"More like one picky recipient." A shadow suddenly came over Melody's face. "When it comes to Nora, it's nearly impossible to please her."

Was this true? Nora was kind, and she doted on Melody, even if she did take on the big sister role well into adulthood.

But Melody was eager to please her, that much was clear. Maybe, Faith thought, in an attempt to butter her up and convince her not to sell the inn.

Wouldn't that be nice?

"I find that jewelry is always a nice gift," Faith said, thinking of the collection her mother had made over the years. "It doesn't have to be expensive, but it can still be pretty. And it's sentimental, too. Each time she wears it, she'll think of you. Of this Christmas."

"That's a great idea!" Melody said, her big smile returning. "Thanks, Faith!"

"Anytime," Faith replied, wishing that it were true, that this bonding moment, the opportunity to give her sister advice, could be more than just a one-time thing.

"You know, it's too bad you're helping out here today," Melody said. "It would have been fun to go to the market together!"

Faith felt herself stiffen and she glanced at Aiden and then at the long line that was forming, nearly all the way to the door. She knew if she asked, Aiden would tell her to hand over the apron and leave, but she couldn't let him down.

Besides, there was someone else who might enjoy going to the market with Melody today.

"Why don't you ask James?" she said casually.

Melody looked wide-eyed as she took her drink from Faith's hand. "Oh...I don't know. He's probably busy. He's a successful guy."

"But it's two days before Christmas, and it's the last day of the market," Faith said. Then, with a little smile, she added, "And I think he'd like to go."

Melody bit her lower lip, considering it. "He does love Christmas. Not as much as I do, but then, few can top that." She laughed, and Faith felt something tug in her heart.

Melody did love Christmas. And how could Faith ruin it for her, especially if it was the last one at the inn?

"James seems to like all the Christmas activities," Faith said, thinking of the way he happily participated in helping to decorate the inn, even hauling a tree up from the town square. "But I think what he really likes is getting to do them with you."

Melody lowered her eyes and then took a big slurp from her cup. "Oh, I don't know..."

"It doesn't hurt to ask," Faith said lightly, sensing that she was correct about the budding romance between her sister and the handsome guest at the inn. "What's the worst he could say?"

But even as she said it, she knew she couldn't take her own advice. Sometimes saying what was in your heart did hurt. And she'd been through a hundred worst-case scenarios of what Melody and Nora might say if she did.

"If you asked my sister, she'd say that he could say no," Melody said. "And that...well, that would take a little magic out of the holiday."

"Ah, so there's a little magic, is there?" Faith leaned into the counter and so did Melody.

"Well, he is really cute. And so nice. And he loves Christmas. And the inn. And..." Melody suddenly stood up, shaking her head. "That doesn't mean he would ever love me, though."

"Why not?" Faith asked, surprised by Melody's sudden bout of doubt. "Who couldn't love you?" she said, feeling a lump form in her throat that she struggled to push back.

"Did I tell you that you give great advice?" Melody said, tipping her head.

"You did," Faith assured her, feeling flattered. Touched, really. "But I'm sure Nora does, too."

"If I asked Nora about this, I'd get the same response I always do." Melody shook her head sadly. "Nora is a firm believer that if you never take chances, you never get hurt. She'd rather be all alone than dare to tell someone how she feels about them."

Faith fell silent for a moment, realizing that she was doing just that, following in her older sister's footsteps. And was that how she wanted to spend this Christmas? This life?

"You know, I think I will take your advice. Again." The sparkle had returned to Melody's eyes as she backed away from the counter to let the next person move up. "Wish me luck!"

"Good luck!" Faith called after her.

Because something told her that they were both going to need it.

Chapter Nineteen
Melody

❋

Melody stood in the upstairs hallway, in her coat and hat, her gloves in one hand, and her other hovering mid-knock over James's door.

Melody the innkeeper knew that she shouldn't disturb a guest unless she wanted to offer fresh towels, but Melody Hart wasn't an innkeeper, she was an actress, albeit an out-of-work one, and the only thing keeping her from knocking on this man's bedroom door was the fear of rejection.

She would have thought that she'd have outgrown it by now, or at least found a way to cope with the sting. But each time she was turned down for a part—or in this case, an invitation—she couldn't help but hear the words of doubt and relive every skeptical glance she'd ever received. And each time it happened, it became more difficult to dust herself off and lift her chin, but she did it anyway because there was no alternative.

To give in to fear would be to give up on herself and everything she wanted most out of life.

And today that was to enjoy the last few hours of the

Christmas market—with a person who would appreciate it just as much as she would.

There. She knocked. Holding her breath, she listened for any sounds coming from inside the room, hoping that she hadn't woken James from a nap, and wishing that she'd thought to mention this outing when she'd briefly seen him at breakfast that morning, but Nora had distracted her with more discussion about the Christmas Eve Gala that was now only a little more than twenty-four hours away, meaning that Christmas was nearly upon them and she hadn't bought any gifts.

Nora had no doubt purchased and wrapped everything by the first of December, and there was no way that Melody could show up Christmas morning empty-handed. That would be just what Nora expected of her, and Melody was determined to prove her wrong.

In more than one way, if possible.

The door opened to reveal James's smiling face, immediately putting Melody at ease.

"I was just about to look for you," he said.

"You were?" She tried to tamp down her excitement. After all, the man might have simply been in search of towels.

"I was about to leave for the Christmas Market, and I was hoping that you might be able to sneak away."

Melody could have finally earned an Academy Award for her performance. She chewed the inside of her lip, shifting her eyes to the side, looking doubtful even though inside she was doing a full-blown happy dance.

"Nora isn't my gatekeeper," she said. "And it is the last day of the market. And I do still have to buy gifts."

"So...it's a yes?" James's grin broadened as he stared at her. "I'll even buy you a mulled wine."

"What can I say? You had me at wine." Really, he had her with that first smile, not that she'd been letting on. Whether her sister believed it or not, she was sometimes able to restrain her excitement, even when it felt like it might burst out of her.

And James, as wonderful as he was, made her feel the need to tread lightly. He didn't live in her world. Even though here, at the Hart Inn, it felt like he did just that.

"What were you stopping by to ask me?" James asked, closing the door behind him.

Melody was grateful that she was already ahead of him, slowly taking the stairs to the lobby.

"Oh…I was just going to ask if you needed any towels," she said with a secret smile.

※

The market didn't disappoint, not that Melody thought it ever could. They stopped at every stall to admire the items and chat with the creators. A few times, Melody had to glance over at James to make sure he wasn't growing bored, but he seemed just as content as she was to take his time and enjoy the day.

"How many people do you have to buy for?" James asked when they stopped to get the promised mulled wine. It was warm in her hands, and when she took a sip, she felt the heat spread through her body.

The same way it did every time she locked eyes with James.

"I thought I'd get something small for Mr. Higgins and Toby," she said. "And my sister, of course."

"Of course," James replied.

"I was a little worried about what to buy her, but Faith gave me a great idea. I'm going to get her a piece of jewelry. Everything here is homemade. I think that will make it special."

"Definitely," he said, nodding. "But why worry? Wouldn't she like anything you got her?"

Melody thought about how to best explain her sister as they began walking again. "Nora doesn't especially love Christmas, and there's very little in general that excites her. Don't get me wrong, she'd be thankful for anything I bought her, but liking it—well, it's hard to find anything that Nora likes most days, other than her to-do lists."

"Seems to me that she might like Toby," James said with a suggestive lift of his eyebrows.

"More like Toby likes her." Sensing the need to explain, she said, "We've known Toby all of our lives. He was always like a brother to me, but he and Nora always had a different sort of bond. I saw it again when we returned. That spark, you could say."

"Do you think anything will come of it?" James asked.

Melody didn't need to ponder her response this time. "No. But I wish it would, and not just because if Nora fell in love with Toby, she might be more willing to find some way to keep the inn. Nora hardened her heart years ago. To Christmas. To love. To a lot of things," she said with a sigh. "Everything changed after our father died, and not just because we adored him. After he was gone, the entire family sort of fell apart, and Nora made it her mission to try to hold it all together. It made her strong, but it also made her pragmatic. If there was a problem, she was going to fix it. I think she just always started looking for problems, or at least anticipating them. She put up walls, and I'm afraid that it's all my fault."

James stopped walking to turn and face her. "Your fault? But how?"

Melody shrugged and looked down at the snow, shuffling her boots. "Nora felt the need to take care of me. To protect me."

"Ever think that she was also taking care of herself?" James asked. Then, seeing the confusion on her face, he said, "She was hurt. Heartbroken. Her entire world had been turned upside down. Trying to control her life was one way to try to protect herself, not just you."

Melody had to admit that was a good point, and it saddened her to think of Nora shielding herself from love and life to try to limit more pain.

"How did you get so wise?" she asked as they continued walking.

"Experience," James said grimly. "I told you that I came to the inn with my grandfather that one year, but I didn't tell you the story behind it. My parents had just died. I was an only child. My grandfather was a widower, and he took me in since he was the only family I had. He was older, and he didn't know what to do with a kid, especially one who had just been through what I had. It was a rough few months, and I think he didn't know what to do about the holidays, so he booked us at this inn."

"Oh." Melody tried to picture James as a lost young man instead of the confident one she saw standing before her now. "I'm so sorry."

James brushed away her concern. "That Christmas could have been the worst one of my life, but your grandmother made sure that it was the best one we'd ever have. The most memorable, at least. She and my grandfather hit it off, too. After I'd go up to bed at night, he'd stay downstairs, having a drink with her, talking until the early hours of the morning. It was the happiest I'd seen him in months. The happiest I'd been in months, too. And after we came home, things changed. We had a good memory to replace the bad one. New energy, you could say, and even...hope. It was a reminder that sometimes when you least expect it, things can turn around. And it just takes one special person to make that happen."

Melody wiped away a tear at the image of her grandmother creating a special Christmas for James and his grandfather. "I wish I'd been there, too."

James gave her a slow smile. "I wish that, too."

Melody inhaled a sharp breath and then started walking again. "Why didn't you come back then? Until now?"

James's jaw tightened as they stopped at a stall to briefly admire some handmade stockings that had nothing on Nana's.

"Life. We got busy. For a while we talked about it, always saying we'd go back, especially every time we hung the ornament Nana had bought us on the tree. Later, when my grandfather got sick, it was me who kept telling him we'd go back this Christmas. I wanted to give him something to live for. I wanted to give him hope." James paused. "He died over the summer. Coming back here was my way of keeping that promise to him. I want to believe that somehow, he might still be here with me."

"I want to believe that about my grandmother, too," Melody said softly. "And sometimes, I really do." She took a sip of her drink and then looked at him sidelong. "Can I admit something to you?"

"Anything," he said quickly.

Melody couldn't help but smile at how he made her feel so free to be herself. "Even though Nora is determined to sell the inn, there's some part of me that just...believes that it will all work out. That Nana will find a way to make it happen. That we didn't come back here to sell the house but for another reason. A better one." She stopped talking, realizing that James was staring at her now, thoughtfully. "Or maybe I'm just in denial."

"It's good to hope," he told her. "What is life without hope?"

Melody tried to imagine that, and it made her think of Nora. Did Nora ever dare to dream or reach for anything anymore? Would she ever again?

"You know," Melody said after they'd found the perfect necklace for her sister, a butterfly pendant on a silver chain that the vendor wrapped in a small box and tied with a red ribbon. "You should have brought the ornament with you. To hang on the tree."

James's face fell. "We lost it, years ago, when my grandfather moved into an assisted living facility. I searched everywhere for it after he died; it became an obsession, almost, a need to have something tangible to remind me of that special trip we took. Maybe I needed to hold it to know that it was all real. Or maybe, I thought that if I found it, it would be like having a piece of him with me again this Christmas, and each one after that."

"What did it look like?" she asked, if only to give him something else to focus on or to hold on to it once more, at least in his mind.

"It was a small glass bulb," he said, giving a wistful smile. "It was a hand-painted scene of the town. When you hung it near the lights, it was like all of Juniper Falls just lit up."

"It sounds perfect," Melody said, picturing it clearly and understanding why her grandmother had chosen it for them.

"It was," he said. Then, giving her a shy smile, he said, "You know, I didn't think anything could top that Christmas, but this one is pretty close. For the second time, being here has turned my life around for the better."

"The Hart Inn has a way of doing that," Melody agreed, only when she saw the way that James was looking at her, she dared to wonder if he was referring to more than just the town and that house.

If maybe he was talking about her.

Chapter Twenty
Nora

Nora stood in front of the full-length mirror of the room she shared with Melody, nervously smoothing the skirt of her dress. She'd gone with a dark green one, because it brought out the color of her eyes, while Melody had opted for Christmas red—of course.

Melody, who had been putting the finishing touches on her makeup in the bathroom, tutted as she crossed the room, the satin dress billowing at the waist as she walked.

"If you keep smoothing out that skirt, you're going to leave handprints on it," she said, coming to stand beside Nora. "And the only hands you should have on that dress tonight are Toby's."

"Melody!" Nora gasped at Melody's wicked smile in their reflection in the mirror, but she couldn't help but laugh. Melody had that effect on her, even when, like now, she was being exasperating. "Stop. You're going to make me mess up my hair." She underscored this by patting the back of her head, to make sure that the bun was still in place.

Melody's eyes gleamed. "And the only reason that your hair should get mussed—"

"Stop." Nora turned from the mirror and gave her sister a pointed look. "Nothing is going on between me and Toby."

"Not yet, perhaps, but there could be," Melody said pertly.

"No, there cannot," Nora said, even though saying those words out loud hurt her. She pushed her lips together and shook her head, rallying herself, the way she'd always done. Then, like she always did, she turned to a task to distract herself. This time it was adjusting her necklace in the mirror. "I'm going back to New York in a week and Toby...well, Toby will never be a city boy."

He'd made that clear enough when he'd told her about how miserable he'd been at his job, how much happier he was here in Juniper Falls.

"And are you really a city girl?" Melody countered. "Face it, Nora, you complain about Manhattan all the time."

"That's just because the traffic bothers me so much. And the subway is unreliable. And the snow always gets so dirty." Nora huffed as she crossed the small room to where her shoes sat at the edge of the bed.

"And you never complain about Juniper Falls," Melody said. Then, with a little sniff, she said, "Just sayin'."

Nora slid the shoes onto her feet, unable to look her sister— or herself—in the eye.

"Toby and I have only ever been friends," she said, hoping this excuse would get her sister off her back. And it was true, wasn't it? There was that kiss that had never happened, and maybe that had been for the best. She'd hurt so badly after they stopped visiting, but at least she hadn't known what his touch felt like, because that would have only made her long for it all the more.

"If you say so," Melody said lightly.

"What's that supposed to mean?" Nora looked at her sister, who was adjusting her earrings. They were big and sparkling, with rhinestones to match the ones along the neckline of her dress.

"Only that I've seen the way Toby looks at you," Melody said. She turned away from the mirror. "The way he's always looked at you."

"Please," Nora scoffed, but her heart had started to pound. Toby had looked at her in the way that Melody was describing—but that had been a long time ago. People grew, moved on, and changed.

Only that wasn't always true, was it? Toby was still warm and kind, content to live his life here in Juniper Falls, with his found family, the ones who welcomed him with open arms, and the ones whom he stuck by. He hadn't changed from the boy who would help Nana deliver her Christmas cookies to neighbors, or the one who was grateful to have known this house and the people inside of it.

But had his heart changed? And had it ever belonged to her?

She shook away that thought immediately. She'd already listed every reason why she and Toby couldn't be together, except for the big one. When she went ahead and sold this inn, Toby would never forgive her, especially if the buyer didn't cherish the property like he did.

Like they all did. Even her.

Especially her.

Nora swallowed hard, pushing back her emotions as she

stood, eager to get out of this room, even if it meant going downstairs and facing not just Toby but half the town. People who had been kind to her, people who had been friends of Nana. People who had no clue that this party would be the last of its kind.

"Toby has been good to us," she said. "To both of us. He's a good friend."

"He's more than a friend," Melody said pointedly.

"Okay, then, he's like...a brother."

Melody pursed her lips. She wasn't buying it. "To me, maybe. But he always treated you a little differently, and he still does." Melody sighed as she sat down on her bed. "Haven't you ever thought of him that way?"

Nora's hand stilled on her hips. She'd been smoothing her dress again and Melody hadn't bothered to stop her. Meaning she was fixated on something bigger. And there was no easy way of shutting this topic down.

"It doesn't matter what I ever thought of Toby," Nora said. "We stopped coming to the inn, and we lost touch after that. And next week I'll be leaving again. Life isn't a fairy tale, Melody," she said firmly.

"Says the girl who kept telling me that it could be," Melody said softly. She reached out and took Nora's hand. "Don't you remember, all those lonely nights after Dad died and Mom was out all the time, or home, but not really there? I was scared and sad, and you were the one who tried to keep things going. You were the one who would decorate the apartment for Christmas. You were the one who still read me the stories about the North Pole. You were the one who still made me believe that somehow, despite everything, no matter how bad things get, there is still hope."

Nora's heart beat loudly, and she struggled to swallow. "Yes, well, it didn't make sense for two of us to be sad."

"You did that for me," Melody said, "because you loved me. And you wanted what was best for me. But it's okay to do what's best for you, too, Nora."

Was it? For a moment Nora dared to imagine how that would be. Love. Laughter. A family. Reliving all the carefree moments that had meant so much to her as a child.

But opening her heart to that kind of possibility meant giving in to the potential of heartbreak, too. And she couldn't go through that again.

Even if, as she counted down the days in this house, it felt like she was doing just that.

"And what about you?" Nora asked, turning the topic to her sister. "You seem to be getting very cozy with a certain guest."

Melody dragged out a sigh. "I know, I know. I need to be more careful. Or better yet, keep my distance. He's a guest. And he's too good to be true."

Nora frowned at her sister. Was this what she thought of her? That she wouldn't encourage her to find love with the right man?

She realized that it was exactly what Melody thought of her. She thought that Nora hadn't just hidden herself from the possibility of love, but that she wanted her to do the same.

"That's not what I was going to say," Nora said, all too aware that the thought had crossed her mind several times, but only because she didn't want to see her sister get hurt.

How many times did Melody fall headfirst for a guy, putting her heart on the line just like she did with every other part of her life? Someone had to heed the risks. Someone had to warn her.

"Look, I wasn't a fan of your ex," Nora explained. Then, because she couldn't resist: "Rightfully so."

Melody looked fittingly chagrined. "He was a jerk. Still is."

"Always was. That's why I discouraged you from him, Melody," Nora explained.

"And the one before that," Melody said.

And they both knew the one before him, too.

"I haven't said anything against James," Nora pointed out. "I'm just here to look out for you." That's all she'd ever done.

Melody shook her head. "It's fine, Nora. I get it. He's this handsome, successful guy. And I'm an out-of-work actress."

"That has nothing to do with it," Nora said, stricken.

Melody just shrugged. "I know I'm an out-of-work actress, Nora. You don't need to remind me every chance you get."

"I don't..." Nora stopped herself, feeling breathless that this was the opinion her sister had formed of her.

The one she'd shaped and molded. Created.

"James is very handsome," she started. "I can see why you'd be drawn to him."

"Handsome." Melody nodded. "He's also nice, friendly, helpful, and a fellow New Yorker. And he's successful. He works on Wall Street. I'm pretty sure that he has a kitchen in Manhattan with full-size appliances and in-unit laundry. Meanwhile, I wash my clothes in the bathtub half the time."

Nora laughed, hoping to lighten the mood. "You do not."

But one glance at Melody told her otherwise.

"But there's a laundromat three blocks from your apartment!" she cried, more amused than shocked. This was Melody, after all. And she loved her for it.

"Do you want to schlep a bag full of clothes three blocks in the snow?" Melody countered. She let out a long breath. "James is great. But he's also too good to be true."

"Hey," Nora said firmly. "Maybe you're the one too good to be true!"

"Me?" Melody looked down at her dress and shook her head. "I'm a screwup, Nora. And you know it more than anyone."

Was that what Melody thought? The impression that Nora had given? With shame, she thought back on her words and actions, her lack of patience, her unsolicited advice. Her handouts.

"Any guy would be lucky to have you," Nora said, holding Melody's gaze until she was sure that her sister was hearing her.

Melody said nothing, just shrugging as she turned back to the mirror.

"Melody, you are bright and creative and funny and spunky." Nora swallowed hard as she stared at her sister in the mirror. How she sparkled in her new Christmas dress. How she sparkled all the time. "Sometimes, I wish I could be all those things. Even just for a little while."

"Who's stopping you?" Melody countered, pivoting to face her.

The correct answer was herself, Nora knew. But it wasn't the full answer, not the complete truth. And she couldn't be honest with her sister. Couldn't tell her that one of them had to be responsible. And that it fell on her.

"You know what I think?" Melody asked. "I think that there's no time like the present. And is there a better time to relax a little, have a few drinks, take a little twirl on the dance floor with a special someone—" Melody waggled her eyebrows.

So they were back to that. Toby. Who was probably downstairs at this very moment.

Why did her stomach suddenly roll over at the thought?

"Come on," Nora said, grabbing the shimmery evening bag that Melody had insisted would complete the outfit. She hadn't been wrong. Melody, she had to admit, was often right. But not in the case of the inn. Not when it came to the need to sell it. "We should get downstairs. We're the hosts."

Melody stood and put an arm around Nora, pulling her in for one last look in the mirror. "I think Nana would be proud of us tonight," she said.

Nora stared at the reflection of her and Melody, thinking of a time so many years ago when they'd shared this very room, dressed in matching tartan dresses with puffy underskirts and patent leather shoes, with red bows in their hair.

It felt like yesterday. Even though it felt like a time in her life that had almost never existed—or maybe she'd just willed it that way.

Would Nana be proud of them? Of her? Of the woman she'd become? Of the choices she'd had to make? Would she understand?

Would she think that Nora was being her best self? Because that's all that Nana ever wanted her to be.

"I hope so," she whispered.

But she wasn't so sure.

❄

It felt like the entire town had turned out for the Christmas Eve Gala. Every common room of the inn was filled with guests, and the long buffet table in the dining room was covered with trays and towers of delicious-looking appetizers and desserts. A punch bowl was set up on the entrance table in the lobby, and the sound of laughter and conversation nearly drowned out the holiday music that played on Nana's antique radio.

Nora had spent the first half hour of the party greeting guests, helping Mr. Higgins transfer trays of food, and trying not to look Toby's way too many times.

In a dark suit with a red plaid tie, he looked...different. Not better, not worse, but so different from the boy who used to dunk her in the pond each summer that she suddenly felt at a loss for words.

She frantically looked across the room to her sister, but Melody was in deep conversation with James. One glance in Mr. Higgins's direction proved that he was laughing with Edith. Even Faith was sipping a glass of wine in the corner and talking with Aiden.

There was no avoiding Toby now. No distraction or item to check off her to-do list. All that was left to do was relax and enjoy herself.

Just like Melody had suggested.

Nora was relieved to see that Toby was smiling as he approached her, holding two glasses of eggnog.

"I figured you could use this," he said, handing it to her carefully.

"Is it that obvious?" Nora said with a grateful smile.

"You worked hard to make this party happen," Toby said. "It's everything that Nana would have done."

"I wish she was still here," Nora admitted for the first time, and not just out loud. She missed her grandmother; she'd missed her for years, until the missing became too painful, and it was better just not to think of her at all, much like she'd done with her father, and then her mother. With this house.

"Oh, I think she's here," Toby said wistfully. "She never liked to miss a party. Or a chance to be with everyone she loved. Knowing that you came back here and did this...it would have meant a lot to her, Nora."

Nora felt a lump rise in her throat and even a sip of the punch did little to push it down.

"It means a lot to me," Toby told her, eyes searching her face. "To everyone. Heck, half the town has shown up, and the night has just started."

It was true, the house was buzzing, alive with music and laughter and hugs and all the Christmas cheer that Nora remembered as a girl. It was the best kind of energy, she remembered thinking, because it was just one night a year, a reminder of what the holiday was all about: people, coming together. Under this roof.

Her eyes instinctively went to the door as another group of people came in, some she didn't know. Prospective buyers?

"Can I ask you a question?" she said, turning to Toby. She needed to be strong. Practical. And more than anything, she needed to be sure of what she was doing, even if she didn't feel she had a choice in the matter. "Will you be okay when the inn is sold? Mr. Higgins would have kept on going here forever but he admitted to me that he would be fine retiring now, too. But you... What will you do?"

Toby pulled in a breath and then, to Nora's disappointment, shrugged. "I wish I knew. I don't really have a plan yet. But I've learned that sometimes good things come along when you least expect them."

Nora shifted on her feet, unnerved by the way he was

looking at her, starting to wonder if her sister was right—again. If Toby still harbored feelings beyond friendship. If she was blowing a second chance with him.

"Take my time here for example," he said. "It wasn't easy finding out that my grandmother was sick. I quit my job at the law firm, but it was never a sacrifice. It turned out to be a gift, one that my grandmother gave me without even knowing it. I'm not sure I would have ever realized how miserable I was on that career path until I moved back to Juniper Falls. Now I can't imagine being anywhere else."

"So, you plan to stay here, in town?" Nora asked.

"That's where the plan ends, but yes." Toby took a sip of his drink. "Maybe I'll go back to law."

"But you just said that you were miserable!" Nora said.

"I was on the wrong path," Toby agreed. "Coming back here set me right again, though. This place has a way of doing that."

Nora fell quiet. Truer words were never spoken.

Toby took a sip of his eggnog. "I've had some time to think lately, though, and maybe setting up my own practice here in this community wouldn't be so bad. Maybe it would be pretty great. Maybe I'd get back to something I loved...and lost...after all."

Nora's heart began to pound so loudly that she was sure that he could hear it, even over the buzz of conversation in the room that nearly drowned out the holiday music.

"I bet you didn't expect to ever say that," she said, feeling breathless by the way he was staring at her.

"I didn't expect a lot of things," he said, his voice low and deep as he inched toward her to let a group of people pass.

She stared up at him, feeling like she was sixteen all over

again, willing Melody not to interrupt them this time nearly as much as she hoped her sister would come along and save her from making a huge mistake. Because kissing Toby would be just that. A huge mistake.

Off plan.

Unexpected.

And probably wonderful. Wonderful and oh so wrong.

Toby kept staring at her until something in his gaze shifted, and he closed his eyes briefly, pulling in a breath.

"Nora, there's something I need to tell you. Something I wasn't sure about... Something I'm still not sure about."

Nora's heart fell and swooped, and she took a step back before he could say anything more. Anything that would lead to a decision and a choice that she didn't want to have to make.

"I—I should get back to the guests," she said. "It's...hard to talk. All the noise. We can...talk later, okay?"

And she turned, but not before she caught the confusion that crinkled his brow, and not before her heart felt like it wouldn't just explode, but something much, much worse.

Break.

She hurried toward the stairs, eager to get away from all the people—the strangers, the familiar faces, but more than anything from the friends and family that she seemed to only let down at every turn, even tonight, and tonight was supposed to be the best night of the year, at least according to Nana.

"Nora," a deep voice said, and she looked up to see James standing at the bottom of the steps, looking up at her. "Do you have a moment?"

She frowned at him, wondering what this could be about. Had Melody sent him to convince her to change her mind? She'd already told the staff and the other guests. Nora supposed she should have known it was just a matter of time before she tried James.

Nora sighed as she walked back down the few steps she'd climbed.

"Is this about the inn?"

James nodded. "Melody told me about your intention to sell."

Of course she had. Half the people in this room probably knew by now. Nora looked around, hoping that the party wasn't going to turn into some sort of intervention.

"It was a very difficult decision to make," Nora said. "Trust me, if there was a way to keep it in the family, I would, but I'm trying my best to find a buyer who will cherish it as much as my grandmother did."

"And you've succeeded." James smiled. "I'd like to buy the property."

Nora stared at him as a chill swept over her that had nothing to do with the opening and closing of the front door. She didn't trust herself to move for fear of breaking this moment.

"You...want to buy the property?" she managed to clarify.

James nodded. "I think we can reach a fair agreement." He started detailing the terms of his offer, which were brief. When he was done, he looked down at the scuffed floors and then back at her, smiling from ear to ear. "I wouldn't want to change a thing."

"Flaws and all," Nora said, feeling her heart lift.

"Oh, I wouldn't call them flaws," James said, tipping his head. "I'd call them character. Some things are perfect, just as they are."

Nora stared at this man, thinking that Melody was right

about him—he was kind and helpful. And he did deserve her. They deserved each other.

But Melody was also right about Christmas. It wasn't just the busiest time of the year. It was, Nora dared to feel again, the most magical time of the year, too.

Chapter Twenty-One
Melody

After James had excused himself for a moment, Melody sighed with contentment and then turned her attention to the rest of the party. She'd already made the rounds at the start of the night, hugging and greeting all the familiar faces that had once shared this special evening with her. There was Jean Garvey, who ran the town library and always used to help Melody find the books on theater that she loved so much, and Marge from Birdie's, who had closed the restaurant especially to be here tonight. Mr. Higgins was technically on duty, but Melody was happy to see that he was taking a break to enjoy a glass of wine with Edith, who must have done a little shopping, too, this week from the looks of it. In her long, slim-fitting burgundy dress, she was hard to miss, and she seemed to sparkle while she talked with the old cook.

Melody walked through the library that was connected to the lounge through French doors, left open for tonight so guests could freely move around, and helped herself to another one of Mr. Higgins's delicious bite-size crab cakes, before moving back to the lobby to refill her punch, deciding to get

James another while she was at it. But she stopped when she spotted James standing at the base of the stairs talking to Nora. Their serious expressions hinted that they weren't exchanging typical party pleasantries, and Melody watched with growing curiosity as Nora looked around and then motioned for James to follow her to the front door.

Melody worked her way through the crowd toward the lobby just in time to see her sister and James slip out the front door, Nora in her coat, James only in his suit. Was the conversation expected to be so brief? But why did it need to take place somewhere so private?

Somewhere out of earshot. Away from the guests.

Maybe away from her.

Wasting no time, Melody snatched her coat from the rack, draped it over her shoulders, and then cracked the front door just enough to lean her ear toward the porch. Nora's and James's voices were hushed, making it impossible to hear everything they were saying, but enough words jumped out at her that it didn't take long to get the gist.

Offer. House. First of the year.

There was no other way to interpret what they were saying.

An offer had been made on the house. By James.

"You made an offer on the house?" Melody cried as she pushed out onto the porch, startling her sister and James. She stared at this man whom she thought she'd come to know—to trust—realizing with a sinking feeling that she'd been wrong. That he wasn't interested in her at all—he'd been interested in the house!

She'd been touched when James told her how much the inn meant to him—but she'd never thought it would be enough to buy the place out from under her.

Bells seemed to ring in her ears, and all the warnings that Nora had given her over the years came rushing to the surface.

You couldn't trust anyone. Only yourself. And family.

But now, looking at her sister, realizing that all of this had been worked out without her knowledge, she didn't even know if she could trust Nora again.

"You didn't think I had the right to know?" she accused them both, her voice rising with anger. They stared at her blankly, and she turned her focus on Nora, the one person in this world who should have loyalty to her. "You're going to accept an offer without telling me?"

"It just happened, Melody," Nora said patiently. "We came outside to discuss the details."

"And you." Melody stared at James, who had the decency to look distressed. "You must have been planning this all week. Maybe even before that! Is that why you came to the inn? Were you trying to swoop in before the place could hit the market? Was that why you—"

But her eyes burned with tears, and she couldn't finish that question, even as she asked it to herself over and over. Was that why he had been so nice to her? So invested in making the inn look its very best?

James looked stricken. "What? No. I told you why I came here."

Melody was momentarily silenced, remembering what James had shared with her, knowing what this house meant to him. She'd thought that was why he was so eager to help with the decorations—that he shared her love for the inn. And her concern.

"I told you why I came here," James said again.

Melody looked into his eyes, wanting to believe him, but

the facts were the facts, and whatever the past few days had meant, they ended here. With an offer on the one thing in the world that mattered the most to her.

The loss hit her square in the chest, a weight that seemed to press down, making it hard to breathe, even on a clear winter night. It was a loss that she hadn't felt in so long, not since her father died so unexpectedly when she was still so young.

And so naive.

When she'd still believed in something wonderful. When she'd dared to think that life, like Christmas morning, was full of endless possibilities.

Once again, all that magic was just pulled out from under her, with no warning. Only heartbreak.

And this time, Nora wouldn't be the one to lift her spirits or make things right.

"I told you what this inn meant to me," she said to James, fighting back tears. "I thought...I thought...we shared that. Our love for the inn."

"We did," James said, stepping closer to her, but she took a larger step back. "We do. That's why I made the offer! I thought you'd be happy!"

"So what, you were just going to swoop in and buy it and think that would make everything okay? Problems solved for us? Nice guy buys our family home, we don't have to worry about it getting torn down?"

Only she wasn't sure he was so nice. *Opportunistic* seemed more fitting.

"Melody—" James started, but she'd heard enough.

The house was officially being sold. And she'd been the one to bring the buyer to the table. The irony of that wasn't lost on her. She couldn't even blame Nora for this outcome. All the same, tears blinded her vision as she turned her attention to her sister.

"Were you even going to tell me that you were accepting an offer? Or did you think you didn't have to? That you still make all the decisions, that you know best?" She didn't wait for an answer before saying, "You forget that I'm not that heartbroken little girl anymore."

Even though that's exactly what she felt like right now.

"We've been over this, Melody," Nora pressed as James lowered his head, leaving the matter to the family, where it belonged. Just like this house.

"I know," Melody said, lowering her voice, along with her spirit. It suddenly felt all too real, instead of a dark possibility that she'd dared to hope might never happen. A small part of her had thought that Toby might find a way to buy the property, and she'd been okay with that, because it was Toby, and he was family. But James... She'd thought she knew him, but she was wrong about that. Wrong about many things, it would seem. He was a stranger. A stranger who happened to love the inn. But not like her. Or Toby. Or Mr. Higgins. Or Nana.

She gave Nora a pleading look even though she knew she had lost the argument. "It's our house. Our legacy. Our decorations and our memories. Our party! Nana left this to us. Us! Doesn't that mean anything to you? Don't you care?"

"Of course I care!" Nora's eyes flashed and she spoke with such emotion that Melody was momentarily silenced.

She stood, shivering in the cold, listening to the sounds of the party from the inside. People were laughing, talking over one another, and the music played in the background, all coming together as one simple sound: joy.

That's what Christmas at the inn had always been. Pure joy. And now it would be gone forever.

"Did you ever stop to consider that I loved this house as much as you did? That it broke my heart to leave it behind just as much as it did yours?" Nora blinked quickly. "I did what I had to do, Melody. I closed it out of my mind and out of my heart because any other way would have been too difficult. And I'm doing what I have to do now. Unless you come up with a miracle between now and New Year's Day, I'm selling the house to James. I'm happy with the offer he's made, and I think when you hear him out, you will be, too."

"Wait." A deep voice caused them both to turn toward the door, where Toby stood staring at them.

"Toby, please don't make this more difficult than it already is," Nora pleaded.

Melody stared at her sister, realizing for the first time how tired she looked, how weary—and sad.

Toby took a step toward them. "I tried to talk to you earlier, Nora. Your grandmother had asked me to help her with her will when I first moved back to town. I pulled it out again this week, to see if I was missing anything."

"Missing anything?" Melody looked sharply at Nora. Like money? She didn't dare say it out loud. Instead, more diplomatically, she bit her lip and then said, "Like a way to keep the inn in the family?"

Toby sighed and looked down at his shoes for a moment before lifting his head again. When he did, there was a hesitation in his eyes that she'd never seen before. He looked like he was about to deliver bad news—if more could even be possible.

He looked, Melody thought, like he'd seen a ghost.

"Your grandmother stipulated in her will that the estate would be left to her granddaughters," Toby said carefully.

"We know this," Nora replied, seeming exasperated.

"By granddaughters she meant plural. Meaning it's not just your decision, Nora."

"Ha!" Melody said, but the satisfaction she felt was short-lived. She couldn't afford to keep this place going any more than Nora could. Together they couldn't even manage. She knew it, in her head, but her heart just couldn't accept it.

Gone. Sold to the highest bidder. To the man she'd dared to think was her friend.

She felt James's gaze on hers, and she glanced in his direction, seeing the pain in his face before she looked away again.

Maybe what he'd said was true. And maybe he really did love the inn. And maybe he'd meant it when he said he thought she'd be happy.

But how could she ever be happy about losing the first and last home she'd ever known?

"Actually, it's not just yours, either, Melody." Toby's jaw was set as he stared at her.

"What's that supposed to mean?" Melody asked, feeling suddenly as tired as Nora looked. So they'd never agree, but in the end, did it matter? They couldn't afford to keep the house.

Toby looked from Melody to Nora and then let out a heavy breath. "I didn't want to have to be the one to tell you. Not like this. It's not my place. But you have to know. You have to know the whole truth."

"Know what?" Nora asked, darting her gaze to Melody. "What's going on?"

"What do we have to know, Toby?" Melody asked, her tone unnaturally calm as her heart began to pound with panic. She'd known Toby for so many years that she could almost say that she knew him by heart because that's how she had to know him for so long, how she had to know everything about this place. It all existed in her memory, and in that part deep inside her reserved for the Hart Inn and all the people who lived here. He was always there, stuck as a teenage boy with kind eyes and a warm smile. She'd never seen him this distressed, this visibly upset by something he seemed unwilling to share. But wanted to.

Needed to. For all of their sakes.

He raised his gaze to hers and then stared intensely at Nora. "You need to talk to Faith. You both need to talk to Faith."

Chapter Twenty-Two
Faith

Faith and Aiden had been tucked into a corner in the library for the better part of an hour, while Star ran amuck with the other children who were wound up with Christmas anticipation, too much punch, and definitely too many cookies.

"She's going to sleep well tonight," Faith said with a laugh every time they spotted the little girl happily running past them in her glittery gold dress.

"She's going to have a sugar crash," Aiden said knowingly. "But I'm glad she's having fun. She'll be disappointed that we can't do this again next year."

Star wouldn't be the only one. This night—this party—was everything Christmas should be—warm, cheerful, full of laughter and music and good food and a warm fire blazing in the hearth.

"Maybe they won't find a buyer," Faith suggested, though she wasn't sure what would happen in that case. Nora had made it clear the night they'd all had dinner in town that keeping the property wasn't an option.

"It's a big place with a lot of land," Aiden said. "I'd buy it myself if I could afford it, but a property like this won't be cheap."

"No, and I would think the field would be narrowed down further by the age of it." Faith looked around the room, at the treasures that her grandmother had collected over the years, filling the house bit by bit with not just objects that she'd chosen, but people, too.

She'd made this house a haven. A true home.

And everyone, even Faith, felt welcome in it.

Even in her absence.

She caught Toby's eye as he entered the lounge, and he beelined toward her. She smiled, but her heart began to race when she saw the set of his jaw.

"Hey there, Aiden," Toby said, giving his friend a quick handshake. "I'm glad you could make it tonight."

"Well, there was no way I was going to miss this," Aiden replied, giving Faith a sidelong glance and a secret smile that made her heart race with excitement instead of anxiety.

Faith watched Toby carefully, sensing that he was forcing a bit of cheer while he chatted to Aiden, rushing through the pleasantries. That he hadn't come over to them to talk to Aiden at all.

Her suspicion was confirmed when he turned to her.

"Faith." Toby kept his tone light, but his expression was serious. "Can I talk to you for a minute?"

Faith glanced at Aiden to show her confusion, but she felt her cheeks grow hot when she shrugged and said, "Sure."

On shaking legs, she followed Toby through the groups of people that took up every inch of the lounge and into the lobby, where Melody and Nora were both standing, for some reason in their coats.

"Is everything okay?" she asked, even though she could tell from the somber expressions they wore that things were far from okay, and she had a bad feeling that she was a part of the reason.

"We've had an offer on the inn," Melody said, shooting Nora a pained look.

"Oh." Faith released a pent-up breath. She wondered for a moment why they had felt the need to tell her this, but then she realized that she'd never given an end date for her stay. "Do you need me to leave the inn, then?"

The thought of it saddened her more deeply than she'd expected. Even though she'd always known she couldn't stay forever, somehow, being here this past week had almost made her believe she could. She'd been lulled into a state of comfort, enough to make her almost forget the reality of her circumstances, the fate of this inn, and even the secret that she hadn't yet shared, and still wasn't sure if she ever would.

Nora looked at Toby, who was still staring at Faith. "Faith, I don't know how to say this, and maybe I'm off base, but I need to know. I need to ask..." He hesitated, and she saw him assessing her, not just her but her features, her eyes—the color of Nora's—her smile, wide like Melody's. Her nose, her forehead, her chin, her hair. Were any of them from Gloria Hart herself? But how could Toby know the truth when Melody and Nora didn't seem to have any idea?

"Are you...who I think you are?" he finally asked, his jaw twitching.

She stared at him, realizing two things all at once: that he was still protecting Nora, for as long as he could, at least, and that the time had come to tell the truth.

"Yes," she said, closing her eyes.

She heard him pull in a sharp breath, and then Nora exclaimed, "But what do you mean? Who is she? How do you know her? What is going on here?"

Faith opened her eyes to see Toby looking at her not with the anger she feared, but with something gentler, more understanding. More kind.

She swallowed hard. She'd spent every night here thinking about this moment, planning it out as she'd lain in bed, staring at the ceiling, thinking of the best way to phrase everything, and imagining her sisters' reactions. But now the moment had arrived, and she felt at a complete loss for words.

She looked at Toby, hoping he might just explain, but he was waiting for her, just like they all were.

She let out a breath. "My name is Faith Barnes. Does that name mean anything to you?"

Melody and Nora glanced at each other for confirmation and then shook their heads.

"Should it?" Melody asked.

Faith closed her eyes again, dreading what she was about to say next, knowing that it would hurt two people she had come to care about very much. And maybe even love.

She glanced at Toby, trying to convey to him that maybe this was a bad idea, but he gave her a nod of encouragement and said to Nora, "In your grandmother's will, she stated that the property was being left to her granddaughters."

"We know this! You just said that. We get it. We don't agree about the sale and maybe we never will, but that doesn't change the reality of the situation." Nora sighed with exasperation. "Melody, I'm sorry, but we have to take the offer."

Melody looked down at the floor. "I know. I don't like it, but...I know."

"There's more to what your grandmother wrote in her will," Toby said, then paused. "She didn't list names. She left the house to her *granddaughters*. And she..." He stopped to look at Faith this time, and she gave him a nod of approval as her stomach clenched in a hard knot. "She had another granddaughter."

The room around Faith blurred as all the sounds of the party seemed to fade. She could see only the two women in front of her now, their confusion as clear as a summer sky.

"But...our father was an only child," Nora said, shaking her head. "How is that even possible?"

"Did he—" Melody clasped a hand to her mouth. "Did he marry someone before he met Mom? Or did he father a child before they got married?"

"But he would have told us, or Nana would have!" Nora shook her head. She obviously didn't believe a word of it. "Where did you hear this, Toby?"

"From your grandmother," he replied evenly.

Now it was Faith who tried not to react. All this time, all these years, the woman everyone called Nana had known about her, and she'd never reached out. Tears prickled the backs of Faith's eyes as the reality of that fact set in, and at once she felt like a fool for coming here.

She looked around the inn, at all the people who felt so at home here. Who were so welcome.

And she hadn't been. Not then. Maybe not now.

She turned to Toby, panicking, trying to make him stop before more damage was done and more people were hurt, but he wouldn't meet her eye. His attention was fixed on Nora, and hers on him. And even though no words were being spoken, the pained look on both their faces told Faith that they had an understanding, a connection that only two people with a long-shared history could have.

"Who could be her other granddaughter?" Melody wondered out loud.

"Me," Faith said before she could overthink it or chicken out and run out the door, into the cold winter night, without a coat, or a plan. Or a single person outside of this town who cared about her or made her feel like the people in this room did. "I'm the other granddaughter. I'm...your sister."

Now the entire inn seemed to go still, and Faith was too scared to turn and look to see if the entire party had stopped at this news because it felt like the world had.

"You're..." Melody peered at her and then shook her head. "But that doesn't make any sense!"

"Oh my God," Nora said, putting a hand to her mouth. Her face had gone ghostly pale and her eyes darkened when she looked at Toby. "What I told you...about that night...what my grandmother and mother were arguing about..." She looked back at Faith as she dropped her hand. "It was you. Faith. They were arguing about you."

Faith could only stare in silence as the story became clearer. Nora and Melody's mother had known, too. And like their father and grandmother, she'd never said a word.

"I'm going to leave you all to talk," Toby said. He set one hand on Nora's shoulder and then another on Faith's, squeezing them before he walked back into the party, which hadn't come to a full stop, but instead kept on going as if Faith hadn't just single-handedly shattered her sisters' world.

The three women stayed quiet for a moment until Melody finally spoke. "Does that mean our father had an affair?"

"It wasn't an affair," Faith felt the need to assure them. "It was one night. My mother didn't know he was married. And... he regretted it immediately. She never expected to hear from him again. That's all she ever told me."

"It was more than one night," Nora said, looking outraged. "He had another child. One our mother knew about! And Nana! Meaning that he knew about you too!"

Faith nodded. "I didn't know until last month. My mother never told me his name no matter how many times I asked over the years. When she died, well, I found out everything. Except you. I didn't know about the two of you."

She wondered if her mother knew about Nora and Melody, or if she'd chosen to keep their existence a secret like their mother had made Faith one.

Her sisters stared at her, scrutinizing her in a new way, much like Toby had, this time no doubt searching for some resemblance to the man they'd idolized and adored.

"When I found out his name, I looked him up, and I learned then that he had died. The obituary was brief, it didn't list many personal details, but it said he had grown up here, in Juniper Falls. When I searched this town, the inn came up, and your—our—grandmother. I knew she had died, but I still wanted to come here. To get to know her and my—our—father somehow."

"But you knew who we were the entire time that you've been here," Melody said, looking so betrayed that Faith felt instantly guilty. "Were you ever going to tell us?"

"I don't know," Faith admitted softly.

"How old are you?" Nora suddenly asked, her expression unreadable, her tone demanding, as if she had to piece together this information, had to make sense of it.

Only Faith knew that they might never be able to do that.

She sighed, knowing that Nora was trying to pinpoint the moment when the life she'd thought she had known became a lie.

"I'm twenty-eight."

"Two years younger than Melody, then." Nora closed her eyes and shook her head.

"And in all that time, you never met him." Melody looked so sad that Faith thought she might cry right then and there. "And now you never will."

"No," Faith said, forcing herself to stick to the facts.

She paused, wondering if she should mention the letters, but decided from the wave of emotions that seemed to change with each passing second that now wasn't the time. Maybe there never would be.

She'd rocked the world of these two women. Permanently changed the memory they had of the father they had known and loved.

And for what?

If she was hoping for some whoops of joy over finding a long-lost sister, that wasn't going to happen. There was no tearful group hug. This wasn't a reunion.

It was...an intrusion, she decided. She'd intruded on their holiday, in their home, and now she'd tainted their memories, all the wonderful, idyllic moments that they'd shared with her.

She waited to see if they would say more, if they needed to hear something from her, but all she was met with was silence.

"I'll go," Faith said. "In the morning. And I'm sorry. I'm so sorry. The last thing I wanted to do was upset either one of you."

Or ruin Christmas.

But it seemed that she had managed to do both.

And when she turned to go up the stairs and her eyes locked with Aiden, she knew that she had ruined something else, too. Even with good reason.

"Aiden—" she started to explain, but there was a flatness in his eyes where normally there was so much warmth.

"I'm just waiting for Star. We're going home," he replied brusquely.

"Aiden, I—"

But he held up a hand. "I thought you and I had a bond, Faith."

"We did," she insisted. "We do!"

He stared at her for a moment and then shook his head. "Was anything you told me true?"

She blinked at him. "All of it! Everything that I told you was true!"

"Except for your reasons for being here," Aiden replied drily. His gaze cut to the right, where Star was running over, holding her coat. "You had plenty of chances to be honest, and you weren't."

"But..." But it didn't matter. She saw it in his eyes when he bothered to glance at her. She'd let him down.

And she'd let herself down, too. What was stopping her from being honest with him? From seeking his advice?

Fear, that's what. She'd let it hold her back, afraid of losing what she'd just found.

And she'd lost it all, anyway.

"I have to go. Goodbye, Faith."

"Merry Christmas, Faith!" Star said happily, throwing her arms around Faith's waist.

Faith looked up over Star's head. "Aiden, please. I wanted to tell you, but I couldn't. Not without telling Nora and Melody. Surely you can understand?"

"I can understand, but that doesn't mean I like it. And it doesn't make it right." Aiden took Star's hand, giving Faith a fleeting glance. "You know what I told you," he said in a low voice so that Star wouldn't hear.

"And you have to know that I cared about you. I still do. And I wanted to tell you, so badly," she insisted.

"But you didn't," he said.

"No," she admitted.

"So how am I supposed to trust you?" he said in a voice barely above a whisper. "How do you build something on that?"

"I guess, if you care about someone, you find a way to understand. And forgive," she added pointedly.

Now Aiden just shook his head and looked away. And this time, as he headed to the door, he didn't bother to say goodbye.

Chapter Twenty-Three
Nora

Nora didn't even remember how the party ended but somehow, she'd gotten through all the goodbyes and hugs, the well-wishes for a very merry Christmas. Then there was the cleanup, a task that she embraced because it kept her busy, kept them all busy: her, Melody, Toby, and Mr. Higgins, the one member of the bunch who didn't seem to know about their family secret, or at least had chosen not to say anything about it.

Nora couldn't bring herself to even look at Toby, so she'd focused on carrying trays of uneaten food to the kitchen instead, while Melody and Toby had worked to move the dining room furniture back in place so it would be ready for their guests by morning.

Guests. Would they be down to two by morning? Or one?

Faith had fled the room, and Nora was too shaken to chase after her. Besides, what would she even say to a woman who had hidden her identity from them for days? Instead, she'd stayed in the lobby, her loyalty to her sister.

Only Melody wasn't her only sister, as it turned out. And Nora still didn't know how to handle that.

Not when she still didn't even know what she would say to Toby.

Flinging off the covers, Nora sat up in bed. A few feet away, she saw Melody's form huddled under her duvet. She hadn't even heard her sister come into the room. It seemed that Melody was avoiding her, too.

She was mad, of course, about selling the inn. About James's offer.

But did Toby have a point? Could they still sell the property now that Faith had a voice in the decision? Did Faith have the money to buy it? It was possible. Nora knew next to nothing about the woman.

Other than the fact that they'd shared a father.

That they hadn't known each other existed until this week.

That people they cared about—people Nora thought had cared about her—had kept the secret from them all these years.

She changed and readied herself for the day quietly, but by the time she emerged from the bathroom, Melody was awake, looking as miserable as she had been last night.

"Merry Christmas," Nora tried because she hated seeing her sister like this when for so long, this was the happiest morning of the year.

But they weren't little girls anymore, tucked into their beds, waiting for dawn. They were grown adults, and their lives had just been changed forever.

"I kept thinking that it was all a nightmare," Melody said, sitting up against the pillows. "But it's all true, isn't it? Last night really happened."

Nora nodded and then walked over to sit at the bottom of

Melody's bed. "I don't think I would believe it if you weren't here to remind me."

"Dad fathered another child," Melody said, her tone one of complete disbelief. "Everyone knew and no one told us."

"They made a collective decision not to tell us, I guess."

"But it doesn't seem like Dad to have done that. And worse, to not care about his own child. Especially when..."

"When he cared so much about us?" Nora nodded, still struggling to understand that part herself. "There's a lot we don't know. Maybe Faith's mother didn't want him to have contact."

"Or maybe Mom didn't want him to." Melody gave her a pointed look.

"Maybe they planned to tell us when we were older," Nora said.

"Or maybe they just decided to leave it be, once Dad was gone." Melody sighed deeply. "Whatever the reason, Nana chose not to tell us, either. For nearly all my life, Faith has existed. And we never knew. A sister!"

Nora pulled in a breath. It didn't seem possible that another sister had been out there all this time. Long lost, and only found now because Nana had died—and left them this house.

A house that they'd all come back to, for one last Christmas.

"Nana always used to say that this house had a way of bringing people together," Nora said wistfully, thinking of the woman with gray hair and kind eyes, always eager to welcome a stranger through her doors, to give them a comfortable room and a delicious meal.

But something more, too. Something that kept them coming back, or at least wanting to stay.

Something that they couldn't find anywhere else.

And maybe something Nora never would again.

"Do you think Faith is still here?" Melody asked. "Maybe we should have run after her last night, but I didn't know what to say."

"Neither did I," Nora said, burning with shame now that the shock was starting to wear off. She suddenly had a hundred questions she wanted to ask Faith. A deep need to fill in all the gaps, to hear all of Faith's memories, since up until now they'd been the ones to share theirs.

But more than anything, she wanted to apologize. For last night. For selling the inn. For everything.

"I feel like I let her down," Nora said, shaking her head. "Sometimes, I feel like that's all I do."

"You?" Melody was incredulous. "But you're the one who always held the family together!"

Nora wished she could believe that, and one look at her sister almost had her convinced. But then she thought of this past week, of Toby, Mr. Higgins, and Nana.

"This inn means so much to so many, and I'm the one who insisted we sell it," she said.

"I shouldn't have been so hard on you," Melody said, leaning forward to give her a long, hard look. "I guess I just turned to you to solve the problem because that's what I've always done. And you always found a way to make things right."

"Well, I didn't do that this time," Nora grumbled.

"You did, in a way." Melody gave her a small smile. "I've had some time to calm down. Selling to James is probably the best option. He loves this inn, and he'll preserve its honor."

"But he's not family," Nora pointed out.

"No," Melody agreed. "But he knew Nana. She gave him

one very special Christmas, one he never forgot. One that brought him back here, this year of all years. I'd like to think that there was a reason for that."

"Maybe there was," Nora said, working up to telling Melody the details of the offer. "He seemed pretty disappointed last night when he realized he had upset you."

Melody shook her head as she smoothed her hands over the quilt. "No, you've been right all along, Nora. When it comes to love, and letting people in, you have to be…careful."

"Is that what I said?" Nora asked. Her chest ached with guilt when she considered how her words may have injured her sister.

"It's how you live," Melody told her with a knowing look.

Nora was quiet for a moment. It *was* how she lived, and it certainly didn't make her happy. The truth was that she couldn't remember the last time she'd been truly happy.

Until now.

"I think I was wrong," Nora said bluntly.

"About selling the inn to James?" Melody asked with wide eyes.

This time Nora didn't try to stomp out the hope she saw in her sister's gaze. "About a lot of things. You've been right, though. More and more, what you say is how things turn out, or how they should be. I should listen to you more, Melody."

Now Melody laughed. "Listen to me? But—"

"Not buts," Nora said. "You've always trusted your gut, lived by your heart, and I've always been worried what would happen if you did. Worried about what would happen if you fell. So I was always careful to be sure I could catch you."

"But who was going to catch you when you fell?" Melody

asked, because they both knew it wasn't her, and not because she wasn't willing, or capable.

"I made sure to never be in a position to fall," Nora said simply.

Not even to fall in love.

"But you can try," Melody said. "To go for something. To take a risk. And I'll always be here. I always have been."

Nora felt her eyes fill with tears, even though she'd made a point to never cry. Couldn't cry.

Now, she let the first tear fall. To fall, slowly down her cheek, free.

"I'm sorry," she told her sister. "For not believing in you more."

"Oh, Nora, don't you see? Because of you, I could do anything! You're my rock."

Nora reached out and clasped Melody's hand. "And you're mine. You're...all I have. You and me...and this inn. It's like you said, Mel. It's the last piece of our family."

And all Nora had seen it as was one more problem that she had to solve.

Melody smiled. "Not anymore."

Nora pulled in a shaky breath. Melody was right. They had more than just each other and a bunch of memories now. They may not have this house, but by coming back here, maybe they'd found more. What Nana had wanted for them all along.

A sister. Somewhere waiting to be welcomed with open arms.

If Nora could find it in her heart.

"I'm going to find Faith," Melody announced, flinging the covers off her legs.

Nora scrambled out of bed. "I'll join you. First...I need to talk to someone else."

Melody gave her a little smile. "Toby?"

This time, Nora didn't roll her eyes at her sister's suggestion. She did need to find Toby. It was time to be honest with herself and him. And hope that he could do the same in return.

※

Nora found Toby stacking firewood behind the kitchen. It was a cloudy morning with a strong wind, but even with just an open coat, Nora was too fired up to feel cold. Or maybe she'd finally warmed to the idea of embracing her past.

All the parts of it.

He stopped his task when he saw her approach, his gaze searching her face until she was standing in front of him.

"Merry Christmas," he said with a hint of a cautious smile.

"It doesn't feel very merry, I'm afraid," Nora replied, feeling worried about how this conversation would go. About finding Faith. About what tomorrow would bring.

She stopped herself right there. She had trained herself to close her heart once. Now, it was time to work on opening it.

She didn't want to live being worried all the time. She wanted to enjoy every moment before it was gone forever. She wanted to see the good in each new day and person.

She wanted to enjoy Christmas again.

Starting with this Christmas.

"I don't suppose it could." Toby looked at her for a long moment. "I'm sorry, Nora. For last night. Maybe I shouldn't have said anything—"

"No," she stopped him, stepping forward, her boots

crunching on the frozen ground. "You needed to tell me. Someone should have told us a long time ago. There's a lot that I don't understand, and maybe I never will."

"I think your grandmother always hoped that you would learn the truth," he told her gently. "After she died, I didn't see the point in drudging it up. It didn't feel like my place. But then..."

"Then you had no choice," Nora said with a nod. She understood that part; his need to speak up when she'd found a buyer, and when he'd found Faith. But there was a bigger, more pressing question that she needed to have explained. "If Faith hadn't come here this week, would you have kept Nana's secret forever?"

Toby let out a low whistle and rubbed the back of his neck. When he looked up at her, his face was resigned.

"It wasn't my story to tell," Toby said simply. "And I think Nana knew it wasn't her place, either. She respected your mother's wishes, even if it drove them apart."

"That's what they were arguing about. When I told you the story—"

"I was trying to figure out what you knew. And...why you never came back."

Silence hung between them for a moment, filling their hearts with more sadness than any words ever could.

"Did my grandmother ever tell you why our parents kept Faith from us?" she asked. There was an ache in her chest, a need to know.

"Not exactly," Toby said, his tone one of regret. "But—"

But. There it was. A funny feeling, in her chest. A bloom of something new and bright, even on such a cold winter day.

Hope.

Something she'd thought she'd lost so long ago, only to find again, here, with Toby. And Faith.

"But there was no malice in it," Toby said. "It was complicated. They were always just waiting for the right time..."

Until time ran out. Nora nodded softly.

Toby set a heavy hand on her arm and left it there. "None of us can change the past, Nora, but we can change today. And tomorrow. We can live the lives we want to live."

Nora thought about that for a moment. Toby had done that, giving up his life in Boston, the law firm, and the security that came with a big salary. He'd come back here instead, to the place where he was most happy. He'd made it work. Until she'd come along and tried to snatch it all away from him.

"Why didn't my grandmother ever reach out to Faith?" she asked him.

"I only learned about the other granddaughter when I moved back to town. Nana felt bad about never knowing her, but without a last name, she said she'd done all she could to try to find the girl. She didn't want to tell you and Melody about her if she couldn't be found. She never even told me her first name, and I never pressed her for it, but when you told me about the argument your mom and Nana had, and then when Melody told me about a guest who had paid with cash, well, I became suspicious. Here was this guest, the right age, with your eyes, all alone, at Christmas? And her name was Faith?"

Some might call it a coincidence. Others might call it Christmas magic.

"I had a feeling one day she would show up," Toby replied. "That was Nana's Christmas wish. For all three of her girls to be here under this roof."

Nora felt a sharp pain in her chest as she looked back at the big house, towering behind them. "She got her wish. I just wish that she could be here to see it." When she turned back to Toby, there was a lump in her throat.

Toby looked up at the sky as snowflakes started to fall all around them. "Oh, she's here. She's always here."

The snowflakes dropped on Nora's cheeks, mixing with her tears, until she didn't know where the heartache from her past ended and the hope for her future started. She felt a smile lift her spirits, one that started deep inside her, straight from the heart.

"You're right," Nora told Toby, the happiness feeling like it could burst from her chest. "She is here. She's never left. And neither will I."

Toby looked at her sharply. "What do you mean?"

Nora laughed, with joy that had been pent up for so long. "I mean, I'm keeping the house!"

Toby stared at her, disbelieving, until slowly the light filled his eyes and his lips lifted into that smile that first stole her heart and never let it go.

"I never got a chance to finish telling Melody the details that James and I were working out on the porch last night. He's buying the property, but he's going to be a silent investor," Nora explained. "He has a career and a life in New York."

"But don't you, too?" Toby replied, growing cautious again.

"A job, maybe. But not one I love. And definitely not a life I love." No. Everything and everyone she loved was right here, at this house. For the best Christmas ever. "Melody is the one who loves New York City. She loves the drama and the thrill of it, the bustle of people, and the energy. Me...I've always preferred the simple things."

Toby was smiling down at her. "You tried to hide it, tried to even deny it at times, but I knew deep down that your heart was always with this place."

"And with the people in it," she said, giving him a slow smile. "Should we go inside and find Melody? See if James has shared the big news yet?"

"That can wait a little longer. But this..." Toby wrapped his arms around her waist and pulled her close against his chest. "This has waited long enough."

He brushed a lock of hair from her face and brought his mouth close to hers, kissing her once, twice, and then deeper, his warmth flooding her until she didn't know where her body ended and his began. Once, she had dreamed of this moment, imagined how it would feel, wondered if it would ever happen, and then, when it almost did, how it might have been.

She'd given up. On him. On herself. On love and all its sweet possibilities.

But this...oh, this was worth the wait.

And the risk.

Chapter Twenty-Four
Melody

The lobby was quiet when Melody came downstairs, disappointed that Faith hadn't responded to her knock on the door. She checked the dining room, following the smells of warm spices that could be found only in Mr. Higgins's decadent eggnog French toast, but the only person she saw sitting at a table was Edith.

"Merry Christmas!" she greeted the older woman, though not with her usual cheer.

Edith seemed to match her strain as she set down her teacup. "Merry Christmas, my dear."

"Are you the first one down?" Melody asked her, eager for information about Faith.

And James, if she was being honest with herself. Once she'd calmed down, thought with her head, instead of just her heart, she knew that she'd been too hard on him.

The inn had to be sold. And he was the best buyer for it.

Maybe the perfect buyer.

Edith took a sip of tea and glanced back at the kitchen door.

"It's been a quiet Christmas morning. Just me and Mr. Higgins."

From the little smile she couldn't hide, Melody suspected that she preferred it that way.

"You like him," Melody observed.

Edith's cheeks flushed but she didn't deny it. Instead, she sighed and nodded. "Maybe even more than that. I've spent ten Christmases with that man, and now it's the last one."

Melody looked at the woman sadly. "So then, you know the inn is being sold after the holidays."

Edith looked as sad as Melody felt. "I had hoped that was just a nasty rumor. Or that someone would come along and save the day."

Was that what James was trying to do? Melody wanted to believe it nearly as much as she knew that she couldn't. James's decision to buy the inn had nothing to do with her. And despite what Nora had said, the rare encouragement she'd given, for once it was Melody who was holding back. Guarding her heart.

Because for the first time in a very long time, she'd experienced the pain of losing something—and someone—she'd come to love…or could love.

First Nana. Then all the people at this inn. Then James. And Faith.

"Have you told Mr. Higgins how you feel?" Melody asked, suspecting that the woman had not.

Sure enough, Edith shook her head. "I'm from another generation. Maybe I'm just old-fashioned. Or maybe I just want the fairy-tale ending. Or maybe…I just never wanted any of this to end."

But end it now would.

"Christmas won't be the same without this inn to visit," Edith said, staring into the fire that roared in the hearth.

"Why do you only ever come at Christmas?" Melody asked. "If you like Mr. Higgins so much, or maybe even love him..."

They shared a smile.

Edith took a sip of her tea and set it back on the saucer. "Christmas is the most magical time of the year. And if you can't fall in love at Christmas, then when would you?"

Melody thought about that, her mind drifting again to James, who was probably upstairs in his room right now, or maybe already gone, on his way back to his apartment in Manhattan.

Disappointment pulled at her chest at that thought. James had come here to celebrate Christmas. To relive a special memory.

They'd shared that. They'd shared a lot of things.

Maybe too many, Melody thought as her sadness once again turned to anger.

She'd thought he was different than all the other guys she'd dated. She'd thought he was...special.

And a part of her still felt that way, even though she knew that she couldn't.

Straightening her shoulders, she turned her focus back to Edith.

"If this is our last Christmas at the inn, and since it is a magical time, then maybe this is the day that you finally tell Mr. Higgins how you feel. You have nothing to lose," Melody added.

"Oh, but I do." Edith looked deep into her eyes. "Hope. Sometimes, just that is enough to keep us going."

Melody felt a lump rise up in her throat, knowing just how true this was. And how empty it felt when hope was truly gone.

It was that emptiness that had changed her sister all those years ago. Made Nora harden her heart to the joys of the season—to the magic of love. To the possibility of feeling whole again.

But it was hope that had kept Melody going, after losing her parents, being turned down for roles, and even this past week, when losing the inn felt more impossible than keeping it. Hope had kept her going, and maybe it still could.

Maybe even Nora didn't think it was so silly anymore.

She looked out the window, where snowflakes fell steadily and softly, and she couldn't help but think of Nana, sending her a message, to never give up.

Even when she wanted to.

"Well, the day is still young," Melody said, daring to think of all the possibilities that it brought. "Maybe you'll get your Christmas wish."

"I hope so, dear. I hope we both do." Edith reached out and squeezed Melody's hand before collecting her teacup and leaving the room.

Melody watched her disappear into the lobby and then turned her attention back to the hearth and the mismatched stockings all lined up in a row. There was hers, and Nora's, Mr. Higgins's, and Edith's tucked firmly beside it. Toby's. Nana's, because she was still here, even if only in spirit. James's. And... Faith's.

Her sister.

She closed her eyes, trying to remember what her Christmas wish was for this year. A month ago, she would have said it was a part in the show she'd auditioned for in the fall. A week ago, she would have said it would be to keep this inn.

But right now, being here in this room, in a house that was filled with memories, all she wanted was to have another wonderful Christmas in this house, one that she could hold on to when the inn belonged to someone else.

She opened her eyes at the sound of a shuffling in the doorway, and when she turned, she saw James staring at her with a sheepish look, his hands pushed into the pockets of his jeans, wearing another soft-looking cashmere sweater over a plaid button-down shirt.

Only this morning he didn't look as polished as usual. His ashy hair was a little tousled, or maybe it always had been. Maybe she'd been so busy thinking of him as slightly untouchable that she hadn't stopped to realize he was just a regular guy. And one who had liked her.

And maybe still could.

"Merry Christmas," he said, giving her a small smile.

Melody stepped forward. "James, about last night—"

But he held up a hand. "You walked into the middle of a conversation. It must have come as a shock to hear that I'd made an offer. I should have told you first. I guess I just wanted it to be a surprise."

A Christmas surprise. And she'd gone and blown it.

Melody shook her head. "I have a way of letting my emotions take over sometimes."

"I know." James gave a shy smile. "That's what I like about you."

"Oh?" Melody felt her cheeks flush. "Go on," she said coyly, and they both laughed.

"You don't hold back," James told her. "You live life to the fullest, you bring energy to the room. You put a smile on my face, and between you and me, I haven't smiled in a long time."

Now they shared a different expression. Understanding.

"When I came back to the inn for Christmas, I didn't know what to expect," James said. "I worried I would feel worse by being here, but instead, it felt like the only place I wanted to be. And then I met you. And then I learned the inn was for sale. I knew I could do something about it, something to ensure that it didn't fall into the wrong hands. There was no grand scheme. No ulterior motive. Just...two people who had good memories in this house."

"Including a few this week," Melody said. She blew out a breath and then stepped a little closer to him. It was time to say goodbye to this house, to the little treasures that Nana had collected over a lifetime, to the framed photos of days gone by that she and Nora would carry with them back to the city. It was time to face reality, but also to believe that Nana's kindness had brought James back to Juniper Falls for a reason, and that his kindness in return would make this all okay in the end.

But it wasn't easy.

"From the day I met you, all you did was help me bring this house back to life. You care about this inn, James, and I can't think of a better person to buy it than you."

There. That wasn't so hard. And if she really let her imagination go wild, she might even say she could sense Nana giving her a nod of approval.

Or maybe it wasn't her imagination at all.

"You mean that?" James asked warily.

She nodded. Firmly. "I do."

"Then I guess this is a Merry Christmas," he said, coming a little closer to her. This time, she didn't take a step back. "But on Christmas, there are always gifts."

Melody looked at the small stack she had brought down and

set under the tree. For Nora. For Toby. Mr. Higgins. And one for James. She reached for it now and handed it to him.

"For me?" He looked at her in surprise as he took the small box, but wasted no time ripping at the paper because Christmas had a way of bringing out the kid in people—and the best in them, too.

His expression sobered when he opened the box and pulled out the ornament painted with a scene of Juniper Falls. "It's just like the one I couldn't find."

"I know," she told him. "I found it in a box of ornaments we missed. Nana must have kept one for herself, too. It's like it came back to you somehow. Like it was finally found."

"I don't know what to say," he said, turning it carefully in his hand.

"Well, hang it on the tree!" Melody said. "It's your house now."

And somehow, saying this didn't hurt nearly as much as she thought it would.

But instead of hanging the ornament on the tree, James carefully returned it to its box and set it on the coffee table.

"Have you checked your stocking?" he asked like Nana always did. "Sometimes, when you hang your stocking in this inn, you find a surprise on Christmas morning."

She always said that, too.

Melody knew that Nora had already placed her gift under the tree, just as Melody had done for her and the staff at the inn; she'd seen it when she'd set out her gifts. Still, she turned to her stocking, and even though it didn't look filled, her chest bloomed with that same childish sense of wonder she'd always felt on Christmas morning here at this house.

Feeling silly, she crossed the room and slowly sank her hand into the soft yarn, surprised when her fingertips brushed something small and metal.

"It's a key," she said, pulling it out.

If James was going to say some cheesy line about how this was a key to his heart, he may as well get on the next bus back to New York.

Well, not really. Because James had already said the worst thing he could have, and she'd found it in her heart to forgive him. To understand. And even to be pleased for him.

But James said nothing, forcing her to look back at the object for the answers to the questions that filled her mind.

"It's...a key to the inn!" She'd recognized the old-fashioned key anywhere, even though the door was never locked, but always open, a haven for those who needed a home. For a night. A weekend.

Or a lifetime.

She looked at James, searching his face, which now wore a smile that crinkled the corners of his eyes.

"It's yours, Melody. Yours and Nora's. And...Faith's," he said delicately. "This is your family home. It's meant to be yours."

"But..." She couldn't make sense of what he was saying. "But Nora..."

"You only heard part of the conversation last night. I'm not buying the inn to live in or run, but I am going to help invest in it. And maybe play more than a completely silent role in it, if you're still willing to give me a place in your life."

"My life..." Melody couldn't even believe this turn of events, and tears filled her eyes as she tried to make sense of it all. Her life was in New York. But her heart was in this room.

Standing in this room.

"Nora's going to run the inn," James said as if he knew what she was thinking. "I think it's what she wanted all along, but she just didn't know how to make it happen."

Melody nodded slowly, thinking of all the ways that Nora had once brought this house to life, every Christmas in the past, and now, every Christmas going forward. "Yes. Yes, Nora should be the one to run this inn. I just didn't think she still cared to—I guess I lost faith in her somewhere along the way."

Faith. Her breath caught when she thought of Faith—her sister—an heir to this property just as rightful as she was.

Where was she now? And what was she thinking? She'd come here alone, on Christmas, but she wouldn't leave that way.

Maybe she wouldn't want to leave at all. And, like all of them, she wouldn't have to.

"Nora knows that you'll want to get back to New York," James said. "I'll be going back, too, tomorrow, unfortunately. And I thought...maybe, once we're there, you might do me the honor of joining me for dinner one night."

Melody felt her heart swoop, and instead of tamping it down, she listened to it. It wasn't always right, and sometimes, she was mighty disappointed. But she had to keep trying.

She had to keep believing.

"Oh, I don't know about that," she said, giving him a sly grin. "Why wait for the things that bring us happiness? And you do make me happy, James. You make me very happy."

"I seem to recall seeing a sprig of mistletoe in this room somewhere," James said as he wrapped his arms around her waist.

"It's right above you," Melody said, lifting her chin until

her lips finally met his for what she knew would end up being the memory that would always mark this Christmas.

※

"Nora!" Melody broke away from James only when she saw her sister coming into the lobby. She hurried out of the lounge, grabbing her sister by the arm. "Have you found Faith?"

"No," Nora said. "But her car is still here."

Melody felt her shoulders relax, wondering why she hadn't thought to check such a simple thing. But then she thought of James. The gift. The kiss.

"Why didn't you tell me that James is investing in the inn and that you're going to be running it?" she asked her sister.

"So he told you." Nora looked pleased by this. "I was hoping you'd give him the chance to explain. And...you don't mind that I want to run the inn?"

"Mind?" Melody hooted. "How could I mind? You know that if one of us should run this place, it should be you."

"Yes, but this inn means so much to you," Nora said.

"It means so much to both of us," Melody corrected. Then, seeing Mr. Higgins come through the kitchen door and join Edith at the dining room table, she corrected herself. "To all of us. Everyone who came here this Christmas had a reason. We were all searching for something. We're connected, all of us."

"You know you can stay on, too. Help out..." Nora trailed off when she saw Melody's expression.

"Help? Since when do you need my help?" Melody joked.

"Since always," Nora said, reaching out to squeeze Melody's hand. "Taking care of you helped me in more ways than you'll ever know."

Only Melody did know. Or she was starting to understand.

"I don't think that being an innkeeper was ever the right role for me," Melody admitted. "But nothing could keep me from coming back. For Christmas. And summer. And maybe a few weekends in between. But my life is in New York," Melody said. "And there's this guy…"

Nora's smile shone in her eyes. "James is a good guy."

"So is Toby," Melody said pointedly.

"I know," Nora said simply, but the flush that spread up her cheeks gave her away.

"You do know!" Melody gave her a playful punch on the arm. "After all these years, you finally admitted it!"

"Oh, I think I always knew," Nora said. She gave a little sigh. "But wanting something and going after it are two very different things. You do that."

"And so did Faith," Melody said, thinking of the woman who had shown up here that first night, all on her own, not sure of what she would find but needing to discover it all the same.

To see it through to the end. Only this wasn't the end. It couldn't be.

Christmas was always just the beginning.

"You and Toby are going to run the inn together?" Melody asked Nora.

Nora hesitated and then said, "Maybe. I don't know. I think he might go back to law. But he'll always be here—"

"Yes," Melody said firmly. "He will. You can trust him, Nora."

"I'm trying to," Nora said, giving Melody a pleading look. "I want to."

Melody hadn't ever seen this look in her sister's eyes, and she realized that right now the tables were turned. That it was

Nora's turn to look to her for guidance. Her turn to repay her sister for all the times that Nora had supported her, in so many ways.

"I know you were hurt when Dad died. We both were," Melody said softly. "Our lives changed because his life ended, but love... Love lasts forever. So take it when it finds you. Hold on to it, Nora. Don't let it go."

"I want to believe that," Nora said. "But now, all I can think is how maybe it wasn't all what we thought. We had a happy family, and when we lost that, everything changed for the worse. But maybe we never had it at all. Maybe Dad wasn't who we thought he was."

Melody shook her head firmly, not because she didn't want to hear it but because she didn't believe it. "Dad was always Dad. The man who pulled us back to the house on a sled. Who danced with us at the Christmas Eve Gala. Who would kiss Mom right under the mistletoe. He was the love of her life. And he was the best dad a girl could ever have. Those memories are real, and they're all we have. And we can't question them any more than we can deny them."

"I'm still trying to understand how Dad could cheat on Mom," Nora said, shaking her head.

"But Mom knew," Melody pointed out. They would never know the full story; anyone who could fill in the gaps was now gone. But they had lived part of it, experienced the ups and downs and joys and sorrows, the moments that mattered. "Mom knew and she stayed with him. And they seemed happy, Nora. And I have to believe that they were."

Believe. It was a big word. One that didn't always come with certainty, and certainly not a guarantee.

After a pause, Nora nodded. "I can see that. I can maybe

even accept it. But what I can't accept is that Mom knew about Faith. And she never told us. Not even when we were adults."

"I think it's for the same reason that Faith's mom didn't tell her the name of our father," Melody said. "I think that they were both just trying to protect their children. They were trying to shield us from hurt. Just like you always did for me."

"I did," Nora said, her eyes filling with tears. "I never wanted you to be heartbroken again. Or disappointed. You have to believe me, Melody. That all this time, when you wanted to keep this house, I wanted to make it happen. And if I thought I could have, I would have—I just didn't want you to wish for something you could never have."

"But that's what life is," Melody said. "Wishing. Hoping. And yes, even getting hurt along the way. But you pick yourself up and you keep going. Just like you did, all those years ago when Dad died. And just like I do every time I don't get a callback from an audition."

Nora let out a breath. "I haven't given you enough credit, Melody. You're so optimistic that sometimes it worries me."

"Everything worries you, Nora," Melody said frankly, and this time, they both laughed. Even Nora. And oh, it felt so good to hear her sister laugh like that.

"I know," Nora said. "Don't you see? You're the strong one, not me. You're the one who managed to keep moving forward without losing your spirit."

"It's not too late to find it," Melody told her. And then, thinking of what Edith had said, she added, "Christmas is the time for magic. If you can't find your spirit today, then when would you?"

"There's something bigger we need to find today," Nora told her decisively. "We need to find Faith."

Chapter Twenty-Five
Faith

Faith finished her quick shower, dressed, and had just pulled the zipper on her last suitcase when there was a knock on her door. She froze, imagining who it could be, assuming that it was Nora or Melody—or both.

Or maybe Aiden.

Her heart pounded as she walked to the door, knowing that there was no sense in pretending that she wasn't in her room. She'd have to face someone eventually, if only to make her exit from this home. And the mess she had created here.

With a steadying breath, she slowly turned the knob and opened the door just wide enough to see Toby standing in the hallway, looking more than a little chagrined.

"Oh," she said in surprise.

"I take it you were expecting someone else?" he asked.

It was only then that she realized she had been more than expecting someone else—she'd been hoping for it. It wasn't her place to reach out to Nora or Melody again. Or even Aiden. She'd hurt them all, despite how much she'd come to care for each of them.

"Can I come in for a moment?" Toby asked.

Faith nodded and opened the door wider, letting him inside the room that had started to feel like her own in just a small number of days. Now, all signs of her were gone. Each belonging was carefully accounted for and packed away.

It was like she'd never been here. And maybe that would have been for the best.

Noticing the suitcases near the window, Toby said, "You're leaving?"

Faith hesitated. "I think it would be the right thing to do."

"For whom?" Toby asked, raising an eyebrow.

"I think everyone could benefit from some time to process this...news," she said.

"I hope you're not upset with me," Toby said, his face shadowing with distress.

She shook her head and looked into his kind eyes, knowing he had never been full of anything but good intentions—for all of them. He took care of this place. Before that, he took care of Nana.

And her secrets.

"You gave me the courage to admit who I was. I was afraid. Afraid of how Melody and Nora would react. Afraid of ruining their Christmas. And all the ones that came before it." She gave him a little smile. "But you care about Nora. And I know you wouldn't do anything to hurt her. So, if you thought it was best that she find out, then I trusted you."

"It was for the best." Toby nodded, and his conviction nearly cast away Faith's lingering doubt.

Still, she didn't see how she could stay now, not when she knew this was more than an inn. It was Nora and Melody's home, at least for today, and she hadn't been invited to stay.

"Coming here was the best," Faith whispered. It wasn't how she'd planned, or even what she'd dreamed, but somehow, it was better. "This house. These people. I can see why you love it so much here. I'm just sorry to see the house go." Now, when she'd finally found it.

"Then you haven't heard?" Toby lit up.

She looked at him warily. "Heard?" How could she have heard anything when she'd been in her room since last night's revelation? She'd even skipped Christmas breakfast, and Edith had gone on and on about how wonderful it was all week.

"The inn is staying in the family," Toby said happily.

"What?" Faith stared at him, grinning against the heartache that still lingered in her chest. So a happy ending had been found, after all—at least, for some of them. "That's wonderful. I'm so happy for you, Toby. For all of you."

"It's your family, too," Toby said. "Your house, too."

Faith shook her head, but Toby held up a hand.

"You had a voice in this. It's why I had to tell them who you were. But as it turned out, Nora and James had already reached a deal. James will help finance the inn and Nora will run it. Of course, all of that will change if you have a better idea."

She shook her head. She didn't. In fact, she couldn't have thought of a better one herself.

Faith smiled at the thought of her oldest sister taking over the inn with Toby at her side. But just as quickly, that warm feeling faded.

"This was all about keeping the house?" Faith asked, feeling stung at the thought of being used for an end. "That's why it was important for my sisters to know the truth?"

"No," Toby said softly. "No, Faith. This was about making things right with this family at long last. Nora and Melody lost a lot over the years. Their father, their mother, their grandmother. This house. Christmas."

And Faith couldn't help but feel that she'd stolen that from them.

"They needed to be here this year. To remember the joy of the holiday. To reconnect with the memories they'd made here. To reclaim the family they once had. And you're a part of that, Faith. To some degree, you always were. None of you knew it, though."

"But how did you know?" Faith asked.

Toby sighed as he dropped onto the small bench at the foot of her bed. Silently, she joined him, waiting to fill in the holes of a story that they all shared but no one fully knew.

"When I came to work for Nana, she told me about you. She said that her son had another child, another daughter, one that hadn't been a part of his life and one that she wanted to be a part of hers. Part of Nora and Melody's, too. I encouraged her to find you. But she'd said she'd tried for years and she only had a first name to go on. Her only hope was that you'd come looking for her." He shook his head. "There was a reason that she didn't list her granddaughters by name in her obituary, and the same for your father. They both expressed that wish because it wouldn't have felt honest, or fair, or complete."

"I wondered about that," Faith said. One question was answered. There were so many more to be explained.

"Every time a young woman called for a reservation, she dared to think it might be you. That was all she could do, you see. Wait. Your father hadn't ever told her your last name. I'm not sure why."

"He must not have wanted her to try to find me, or to interfere," Faith said, trying to process the thought. She glanced sidelong at him, wondering how much more he could know, and deciding probably not much. "But...he tried to find me. Or connect with me."

Toby looked at her in shock. "He did?"

Faith nodded and then stood. She crossed the room and rummaged through one of her packed bags until she found the small stack of letters that she now brought with her everywhere.

"I found these letters after my mother died. That's when I learned his name. That's what led me here."

"May I?" Toby held out a hand, looking at the letters. One was dated not long after her birth, and another, on her first birthday, and every birthday after that. Until they just stopped.

"He died," Faith said.

"He did," Toby said heavily. "I wonder if you're mother even knew."

"I'll never know," Faith said, taking the letters back. She ran a hand over them, feeling the smooth paper under her skin, and then walked back to her bag where she tucked them away for safekeeping.

"You can't change the past," Toby said gently. "None of us can. But we can change the future. And this house is the future of this family. It's the one thing connecting you all and Nana knew that. So don't go. Not now. And definitely not today. It's Christmas."

Faith wanted to trust him, to believe that staying would be the right thing to do, but she couldn't bring herself to agree. She'd barged into this house as an uninvited guest, only able to do so because it was an inn, open to the public. But if she stayed, she'd need to be invited by the two women who called this house home.

A word she yearned to use herself.

"Promise at least that you won't leave without saying goodbye?" Toby stood and inched toward the door, stopping and waiting for an answer before he opened it.

Faith nodded. It wouldn't be easy, saying goodbye to a person she'd come to respect and admire, but she owed him that. She owed him a lot.

He opened the door and then stopped, turning to give her a slow grin. "I think your departure might be delayed. There's someone else who wants to see you."

He opened the door to Nora and Melody. Nora frowned at Toby with surprise but then smiled, and the look between them was one of more than understanding. Any passing observer could see that it was a look of love.

"I was so worried that you'd left!" Melody said, lunging forward, pulling Faith into such a long, hard hug that she nearly lost her footing.

"I almost did," Faith admitted, holding her sister tight, never wanting to let her go. She blinked back tears, overcome by the emotion that she was finally able to release.

"But is that what you want?" Nora asked when Melody dropped her arms. Her face was lined with concern, and Faith realized that, unlike last night, Nora was turning to her for acceptance. "Finding us must have come as every bit as big of a shock as it was for us to find you."

Faith blew out a shaky breath and wiped the tears from her eyes. "It was a surprise. I thought I was alone in the world. No other family. Now I know I have not just one sister but two." She bit her lip, hoping she hadn't said too much or been presumptuous. Nora and Melody were true sisters. She was just...blood.

"I wasn't being deceitful," she hurried to say. "Not by

coming here and not by keeping the secret, even once I knew we were related. I came here just to see the house, to get a sense of where my father grew up, and instead, I found you. It came as a shock. I guess I was processing all of it. And when you talked about your father, I just wanted to hear more. To know as much as I could. And I never, ever wanted to ruin your happy memories of him. Not when you were so wonderful. Everything about this place is just wonderful."

"I just wish you could have experienced it sooner," Melody said, reaching out to squeeze her hand. "I wish we had known."

Faith tried to be pragmatic, knowing that wishful thinking often came with a price. "There's no way of knowing what might have happened if we had known, I suppose. You had a life with your parents. I had one with my mother. We had our families, even if we didn't know the other part of that family was out there somewhere."

"And your mother never told you anything?" Nora wondered aloud.

"Not even his name," Faith said with a shake of her head. "She told me from a very young age that I didn't have a father, and that was that."

"And Mom never told us about you," Melody said. "But she knew. She knew!"

"I don't know if my mother knew about you girls," Faith said, even though she suspected that she did, that it might have been the reason for her hurt, for the need to keep Faith all to herself. "But she must have known something about my father. That he was married. That he had a family. Enough to stay away. Or...keep him away."

"I think our mothers were just trying to protect us," Nora

said slowly. "It doesn't make what they did right, but it does help me to understand why they kept us apart. Until now."

"But that still leaves Dad," Melody said sadly. She shook her head and searched Nora's face and then Faith's. "How could he have not cared? You were his daughter too!"

Faith took a steadying breath. She'd been unsure about revealing this part to them, but now she knew with certainty that it was the right thing to do.

"He did care," she said. "He wrote letters. I didn't find them until after my mother died and I was packing up her things," Faith went on. "When I saw he only wrote for ten years, I thought he'd given up trying to find me. I went from feeling angry at my mother to angry at my father. But then I started looking online and I saw that he'd passed away. And I saw my grandmother's name listed as a living relative and I searched for her. But by then..."

She'd been so close. A matter of weeks away from knowing the woman who was so loved by everyone who'd graced these four walls.

"I didn't find her. But I found you." Before she could compose herself, her eyes filled with tears.

Nora was the first to put her arms around her and hold her tight, but Melody wasted no time joining in, laughing through her tears, and despite all the years that they'd lost and all the uncertainty that Faith had felt, for the first time in a long time she felt excited again. About the future. And about not having to face it alone.

"Obviously, you will be unpacking those bags," Melody said when she pulled away. She gave a dramatic look at the suitcases. "Like we were ever going to let you slip away when we just found you."

"I wouldn't have done that," Faith said, even if she'd been tempted.

"It will be nice not being the youngest anymore," Melody said with a lingering look at Nora.

Nora swatted Melody playfully. "Just remember I'm still the oldest."

"Still the boss," Melody said with a sigh. "At least of this inn."

"I'm so glad that you found a way to keep it," Faith said.

"It belongs in the family," Nora said firmly. Then, with a little smile, she said, "And that includes you. I know you're between jobs right now, and it won't pay much but—"

"Yes!" Faith exclaimed before she had even heard the full offer. Details could wait. They didn't even matter, not when she already had everything she needed.

"Let's not waste another minute, then. It's Christmas," Nora said. "And I intend to make it a good one."

They walked downstairs, Melody chattering about how they needed to turn up the music and scour the kitchen for breakfast leftovers since the entire house, other than Edith, had missed the breakfast feast.

Faith felt like she might have as a little girl, had she come here for her holiday, walking down the stairs with her sisters on Christmas morning, barely able to contain her excitement as she anticipated all the wonderful events of the day ahead, the joy that was waiting for her at the base of the steps.

And she wasn't wrong, because there, standing in the doorway, was the one person other than Nora and Melody who could make this Christmas everything she could have ever hoped it could be.

"Aiden."

He gave her a funny smile as Nora and Melody muttered their excuses about checking on Mr. Higgins, leaving Faith alone in the lobby.

"I...didn't expect to see you again," she said. She wondered briefly if they'd left something behind at the party. If Star had forgotten her favorite scarf. If he wasn't here for her at all.

But his smile broadened a little and he stepped forward. "I was afraid that you wouldn't let me see you again. I've been up all night, Faith. I shouldn't have said what I did."

Faith shook her head, knowing that he had a right to react as he did. "What you said was true."

"And what you said was true, too." He raised his eyebrows. "When you care about someone, you find it in your heart to forgive them. I hadn't done that yet for my wife. But when I heard those words last night, it hit home. It hit me right here." He put a fist on his chest. "I needed to get to that point. To let go of the hurt and the anger and to move forward, holding on to the good times."

Faith gave a small smile. She had needed to get to that point, too. Only with her mother. She may never understand why her mother kept so much from her, but she had her reasons; she cared about Faith and loved her more than anyone had or ever would, and for that, Faith knew she could forgive her.

"But I've come to care about you, too," Aiden said. "I didn't expect that—to find...someone again. And I don't want to push you away. I don't want you to leave."

Now Faith couldn't hide her smile. "I just found my family. This town. And you. I have no reason to go anywhere."

"You mean you're staying in Juniper Falls?" Aiden's face lit up.

Faith nodded eagerly. "I'm going to run the inn. With Nora."

"With Nora? But—"

"But there's so much I want to tell you." She stopped, slowing herself. "If you want to hear it."

"I do," he said, taking her hand in his. It was warm and solid, and he showed no signs of letting go anytime soon. Or maybe ever. "I want to hear everything."

"You'll stay for Christmas, then?" she asked. "I mean...I know it's not your favorite holiday, but Mr. Higgins is going to make a big brunch, and there's going to be music, and—"

"You," Aiden said, stepping closer to clasp both of her hands in his. His gaze never left its hold on her eyes. "You're all I need. And Star, of course."

"Where is Star?" Faith asked, glancing into the lounge.

"She's in the kitchen helping Mr. Higgins. And his new lady friend," Aiden said with a little smile.

Faith frowned and then said, "Edith! Of course! Oh, how sweet is that? A Christmas romance."

"A Christmas romance," Aiden repeated. "I sort of like the sound of that."

Faith felt a heat creep up her cheeks. "I do, too."

Her heart drummed in her chest along to the beat of the music that Melody must have turned on, and she squeezed Aiden's hands a little tighter. There was only one thing that could have made this moment more perfect, but they were interrupted by the sounds of noise coming from behind them. The croons of Melody's singing, James happily joining in beside Mr. Higgins, with his rich baritone, and Edith, who shyly added to the harmony, her eyes as bright as the Christmas tree itself.

Nora came through the dining room, sharing a secret smile

with Toby when Melody hit a particularly high note, and then took his hand, before being nearly toppled over by Star, sprinting at full speed in her red dress.

"Presents!" she squealed, running over to the tree. She stopped and frowned down at the small pile. "Did Santa skip your house this year?"

Everyone laughed as they gathered in the room, and it was Melody who said, "Quite the opposite. Santa looked after all of us this year." She reached for James's hand as she looked up into his eyes.

"And so did Nana," Nora said, linking Toby's arm, and setting her other hand on it.

"Well, open them then!" Star exclaimed, handing out the gifts and watching expectantly.

There was a necklace for Nora from Melody that she wasted no time in putting on—with Toby's help—and promising never to take off again. Melody caught Faith's eye across the room and slipped her a little smile, one that felt not much different than the night they'd all decorated the Christmas tree, and Faith felt a connection that time hadn't created, but somehow, another bond had. For Melody, Nora had purchased a beautiful wool scarf—one that wasn't full of holes, even though Faith secretly loved the hand-knitted one.

"What about Faith?" Star asked, looking at her with round eyes that threatened to burst into tears. "Where is Faith's gift?"

"Oh..." Faith pulled the girl into a hug and stroked her hair to reassure her, but Toby just gave a knowing look.

"Well, Faith hasn't checked her stocking yet," he said.

Faith frowned at him. Had he slipped something in there? It would be just like him to be so thoughtful.

She pinched her lips, feeling a little embarrassed as much as she was completely touched, and walked over to her stocking, sensing every eye in the room on her when she pushed her hand down to the bottom.

"It's just a piece of paper!" Star cried when Faith revealed the contents.

Everyone laughed again, but Faith was too busy opening the small blank envelope.

Her breath caught in her chest as she unfolded the piece of paper inside, filled from top to bottom with words. So many words. So much to say.

"It's a letter. To me. From...Nana." She was the only person in this room who hadn't referred to her grandmother by her beloved nickname, and the word felt both strange and comforting all at once. As if she, too, belonged. That she wasn't an outsider anymore.

But a letter. From a woman who had never known where to find her. Who was no longer here. Faith stared at them all in disbelief. "But how?"

Melody and Nora exchanged uncertain looks, and Mr. Higgins shook his head. But Toby gave her the subtlest of winks, one that only she might have caught.

"Christmas really is the time for magic," he said.

"And wishes meant to come true," Melody added, resting her head on James's shoulder.

A wish come true. That's what this was. Not just the letter. But this house. These people.

And her sisters.

She'd found everything she'd been searching for, even though she hadn't known it was out there, waiting to welcome her with warm, open arms.

She tucked the letter back into her stocking where she knew

it would be safely kept until later when she'd read it alone. But somehow, just knowing it was there, that all this time, her grandmother had hoped, maybe even wished for this Christmas Day to happen, filled her heart with something she'd lost somewhere along the way.

Joy. And belief. That anything was possible.

About the Author

Olivia Miles is a *USA Today* bestselling author of heartwarming women's fiction and small town romance. After growing up in New England, she now lives on the North Shore of Chicago with her family and an adorable pair of dogs.

Visit www.OliviaMilesBooks.com for more.